9.9.2017

00401118974

SECRET WORLD

SECRET WORLD

M. J. Trow

Severn House Large Print
London & New York

This first large print edition published 2016
in Great Britain and the USA by
Crème de la Crime, an imprint of
SEVERN HOUSE PUBLISHERS LTD of
19 Cedar Road, Sutton, Surrey, England, SM2 5DA.
First world regular print edition published 2015 by
Severn House Publishers Ltd., London and New York.

British Library Cataloguing in Publication Data
A CIP catalogue record for this title is available from the British Library.

ISBN-13: 9780727894199

Severn House Publishers support the Forest Stewardship Council™
[FSC™], the leading international forest certification organisation. All
our titles that are printed on FSC certified paper carry the FSC logo.

One

The first rays of the sun gilded the towers of St Angelo across the narrow entrance to the harbour. The sea looked different this morning as the mist rolled back. Jack Barnet could make out their sails on the horizon, the crescents curling on the canvas, the black flags snapping at the mastheads.

No one had slept. Most of the men on the ramparts with him that morning had gone to the chapel to confess their sins, even Harry Bellot. *Especially* Harry Bellot. Jack had not been among them. Like everybody else in that charnel house, he wore a crucifix around his neck, but he was not a Papist. This wasn't his faith and this wasn't his war. What the Hell was he doing here, in this place and on this morning?

He had heard the mournful dirge of the Mass, the chanting of the priests and the solemn Latin rumble through the open doors of the chapel, its walls scarred and pockmarked with heathen iron and lead. Now he heard the single toll of the bell ring out for the Order and the followers of Christ. Two days ago, they had all gone through the ritual of the Knights of St John, for it had been the feast of Corpus Christi and there were

1

traditions to be observed. Traditions? The bloody idiots had carried on as if 40,000 Turks weren't closing in on them for the kill, intent on silencing that bell for ever and to consign to ashes all the Christian feasts, the Christian saints and the Christian God.

That maniac de la Valette, the Grand Master, in his white robes with the cross of the Order emblazoned in blood on his chest, had led a procession through the streets, the crosses held high and the incense swinging. But that was across the harbour in Birgu, not on the isolated headland that was St Elmo. And what had the fool said? 'St Elmo is the key to Malta.' And he expected them all to die for the place, to buy him precious time to build his fortifications with the bodies of the valiant.

'Master Barnet?' He turned at the sound of his name. A little, black-robed priest stood smiling at him, a leather canteen of water in his hand.

'Father,' Barnet replied and nodded.

The old man looked at the soldier. He didn't wonder what he was doing here; he *knew*. Barnet looked exhausted, his face as grey as the stones he was called upon to defend. There was brick dust in his hair and on his cheeks and he had long ago lost the buttons on his leather jacket and the ties of his shirt.

'I didn't see you at Mass last night,' the priest said softly. 'Nor at Confession.' It was not a scold. He was concerned for the man's eternal soul.

Barnet licked his lips. 'I am not of the faith, Father,' he said. 'Not of your faith, at least.'

The priest frowned. 'But you are a Christian, my son?' The old man felt the ground shifting under him. He would believe anything about this place and about these men who were about to die.

'Oh, yes.' Barnet still had the sangfroid to chuckle. 'Yes.' He looked out to sea again, at the Turkish galleys growing ever larger on the horizon, a line of black creeping forward in a deadly silence. 'I am a Christian.'

'Ah,' the priest said and smiled. 'Of course. A Protestant. With all the races here, I had forgotten you are with the English contingent.'

'I have not forgotten God, Father,' Barnet said, suddenly, chillingly, afraid.

The priest smiled. 'And He has not forgotten you, my son,' he said. 'Here.' He passed him his canteen.

Barnet frowned. For days now the priests had walked the walls among the defenders of St Elmo, making the sign of the cross in the air over them and sprinkling the water from their canteens.

'Isn't this holy water?' the soldier asked.

The priest nodded. 'And about now,' he said, 'I can't think of a better use for it. Drink it, my son, in remembrance of Him who died for us both.' He raised his hand, passing it to the north, the west, the east, the south. Then he was gone. Barnet was still watching the priest weaving his way along the ramparts when someone crashed down heavily alongside him.

'That was a lucky escape!'

Barnet turned to look at the new arrival. 'What was?'

3

'If I'd been a moment earlier, I'd have been blessed by a priest.'

'That wouldn't kill you, Joshua,' he said.

'No, but they might.' Joshua pointed to his right where, beyond the walls on the landward side, the army of Mustapha Pasha, Commander of the Faithful and descendant of the standard bearer of the prophet Mohammed, was on the march, rolling forward on the bare grey rock of Mount Sciberas as surely as Mustapha's navy was rolling in from the sea.

Barnet checked the apostles dangling around his neck, hoping the powder in those flasks was as dry as his mouth. He suddenly remembered the canteen and took a swig. Then he remembered the man on his left and passed it to him.

'No thanks,' Joshua said with a grin. 'But don't go too far away. I might need it later.'

'Well, if there's any spare.' Harry Bellot crouched on the other side of Barnet. The man had diced away the night, preferring the chance to a night of misery and worry. Except that he'd lost everything but his shirt and had even *more* reason to worry and be miserable. Why hadn't he run away to sea while he still had the chance and the inclination? Barnet passed the canteen to him.

'What did you mean?' He decided that small talk might make the time pass quicker this morning, might drown out that damned bell and the rumble of heavy cannon over rocky outcrops as the guns – and the end – got nearer. 'What did you mean about narrowly escaping being blessed by a priest?'

4

Joshua looked at him oddly and beyond to Harry Bellot. Then he laughed and turned away. 'Out there,' he said, waving vaguely with his right arm in the direction of the oncoming Turks, 'is one El Louck Ali Fartax.'

'The pirate.' Barnet had heard of him. 'Yes, I know.'

'Did you know he was once a Christian?' Joshua asked. 'More, he was a Dominican monk?'

Barnet's mouth dropped open. He didn't think it possible to be surprised any more, not after three weeks in this Hellhole. 'What are you saying?' he frowned. 'That the Father there is . . .'

Joshua shook his head. 'I am saying,' he said, 'that Ali Fartax is a Christian fighting for the Turks. There are Turks in this very fortress fighting for the Christians; but me? Well, I'm a Jew.'

Barnet blinked at him, feeling the sun creep higher on his neck. He looked at Bellot who just shrugged. He wasn't a man easily surprised.

Joshua leaned closer to Barnet. 'I'm still waiting for my Messiah,' he said. 'And for all his goodness, I doubt that the good Father could stomach that.'

'What are you doing here?' Barnet asked.

Joshua looked into the man's face and laughed. 'I could ask you the same question, Englishman. At least I'm from Venice, just around the corner, so to speak. The Turks are the enemies of my blood. But you, you're from the far side of the world, where headless women have their faces on their chests.'

'Ah, you've met my wife,' Bellot grunted. 'And

live and let live, I say. You can meet funny folk wherever you go, even before you leave your own garden, oftentimes.'

'And this is not our fight,' Barnet said. No amount of levity was going to change that.

'You got that right,' Joshua replied with a sigh, checking that he still had his dagger with him. He had been sleeping rough on the battlements all night and there were some light-fingered buggers among this lot, Knights of St John or no. He thought he was tired of the furnace and the lathe. Now his old life whispered a siren song to him, of safety and comfort. 'It's rather ironic, really; my namesake in the Book of the same name knocks down the walls of fortresses and it's my job to try to hold this one up.'

There was a noise like nothing else in the world as the fleet opened fire. Black plumes of smoke burst from the bow-chasers, the forward-pointing guns and the iron balls, invisible and deadly, screamed and snarled through the air to smash into the parapet to Joshua's left.

'Shit!' he hissed and scrabbled to his feet, dragging his matchlock with him. Bellot cursed as dust and pebbles sprayed all over him.

'Take cover!' they heard Sir Oliver Starkey call.

'Arsehole!' Barnet muttered. 'I've heard some redundant orders in my time.'

'Now, now, Jack.' Bellot was still picking grit from his teeth. 'That's no way to talk to your—'

But he never finished his sentence because a second salvo demolished the ramparts alongside him and he found himself somersaulting down

6

the steps to crash on to the carts below. Barnet had fallen with him and he had dropped his matchlock. He was lying, dazed, in a wagon they used to carry away the dead and wounded. The planks were stained and spattered with the dark brown of men's blood. Barnet struggled upright, coughing and spluttering in the stone dust. He saw Joshua briefly, running with the others along the wall walk, their matchlocks at the ready, fuses primed and boots clattering on the masonry.

He climbed out with the help of a priest and Harry Bellot and dashed across the courtyard, clambering up the next steps to join the rest.

'Where's your musket, man?' Starkey asked him as he reached the top. 'Where *do* you think you are?' Knight of the realm he may be. Knight of St John he certainly was, but Oliver Starkey was a pain in Jack Barnet's arse. Did the man have nothing better to do than pick on his inferiors? Now, it was a matter of waiting for dead man's weapons. If a soldier fell beside him, Barnet could grab the matchlock. Otherwise, at this range, he was defenceless. All he could do was to pass his powder to Bellot from the apostles still dangling across his chest. He glanced back over his shoulder. The Turkish galleys were almost lost in the battery smoke now, but they were veering off, two by two and rowing like things possessed to port and starboard. They had done their bit and now it was up to the men on the land.

All eyes looked to the south-west, to the rock of Sciberas, and to the black guns pointing to the heart of Jack Barnet. Above the rattle of running feet and the shouting of the troop commanders, the fort's battle horns brayed out. The thatched roofs in the compound were blazing now with the fleet's battery attack and the courtyard was full of monks scurrying backwards and forwards with buckets of water, holy or otherwise.

Jack Barnet saw it clearly through the smoke, as if some god of war had drawn his personal attention to it. 'Mother of God,' he heard Bellot mutter. The huge Turkish gun they called the Basilisk had been hauled round from its earlier position, oxen slipping and sliding in their heavy yokes as they dragged the monster into place. Now, in the still early morning, the Basilisk spoke, bringing death to those who looked on it. The great gun rocked backwards as its muzzle gave birth to iron and fire and the shot whistled down to crash and roar through the battlements, sweeping men aside, as chess pieces on a board might be swept away by a bad sportsman who has just lost a game. A drill sergeant ceased to exist as the ball went straight through him, black and unstoppable. Joshua was catapulted into the courtyard, a bloody sleeve dangling from a broken arm. For a second time, Barnet was nearly blown to kingdom come but he clung on to the parapet until his fingers bled and he withstood the blast.

Coughing and blinded, he shook himself free, spitting somebody else's blood out of his mouth and he looked towards the main gate. The Basilisk had spoken again and there was no gate now, just a gaping hole in the wall where the masonry crumbled and fell, crushing the defenders ranged below.

'Down!' Barnet heard Starkey yelling. 'Down to the yard. Form front. Form front!'

He clawed free his sword, half-stumbling over bodies in his path. He couldn't see a face he recognized anywhere. Through the blackened archway and above the heap of dead and dying, he could see the enemy coming on in perfect order. The janissaries with their long, padded coats and tall white turbans were first, marching like some unstoppable juggernaut, their murderous pikes coming to the level as they reached the gate. Behind them, wave after wave of the layalars, swinging their curved swords below their crescent flags, the horsetail banners swaying in the dust. He could not see the spahis, though he knew they were there. This was no action for cavalry, but they would be waiting behind the slaughter, ready to ride down any group of Christians who might try to break out from the stricken fortress.

The noise of battle filled his ears and he felt weak. His wrist was heavy and the blood was pounding in his head and chest. On each side of him, the matchlocks came up to the level, fuses smoking.

'Fire!' Oliver Starkey had not quite finished the word when the guns roared. Barnet couldn't hear anything now, his head singing with the impact.

'Reload!'

But there was no time to reload. The janissaries had crossed the space between the gate and the

Order's front line. Steel-tipped pikes were slicing through leather and skin and muscle, skewering the defenders as the sheer tide of men carried them backwards. Barnet almost lost his footing. Once, twice, he parried the probing pikeheads with his sword. Then he fell back, turning away from the line, running for the relative safety of the courtyard's rear. He could barely see now for the smoke and found himself stumbling blindly, swinging his blade and screaming.

Suddenly he stopped, staring at the most bizarre sight he had ever seen. De Guras, the Order's commander at St Elmo, was sitting in a chair in the centre of the yard, the white cross on its black field flapping in the wind behind him. He had a pike across his lap because he was too old and too ill to stand to fight. There was a serenity about him, a calm that shone from his grey old eyes. Come, he seemed to say, see how a Knight of St John dies. Then, with a sickening rip, a ball took off his head at the shoulders and it bounded across the yard, rolling among the bodies there.

Jack Barnet wasn't screaming now. He threw away his sword, ripped the apostles from his shoulder and he ran. He heard Oliver Starkey's voice roaring at him. 'Come back, you coward! Stand and fight like a man!'

How he got out of that death trap he never knew. He just ran and ran, his legs aching, his lungs pulling at every stride, until the smoke of battle left his nostrils and the din of battle became a dream, distant, remote, like a nightmare forgotten, never to recur.

But it did recur. And St Elmo would recur for

ever, in the darkness of his years. 'Come back, you coward!' And he saw, too, the faces of the men who had dared those ramparts with him; Joshua the Jew and Harry Bellot.

St George's Lane, Canterbury, England
Saturday 23 June 1565

He had listened to the tapping for . . . he didn't know how long. He had heard that sound all his life, the hammer on the nails in his father's workshop. He could hear a tune too, whistled by the tapper, by the big man with the huge hands who he'd been told to call 'Papa'. He rolled over in the little wooden crib and saw the crucifix looking down at him, the strange figure of that sad man with his arms outstretched and his eyes looking toward Heaven.

He didn't know who the man was or what Heaven was, but he had heard his mother talk about it. It was a beautiful place far away above the clouds, where the sun always shone and no one ever cried.

He knelt up on the straw mattress and hauled himself upright. His nightshirt had tangled itself around his legs again so he half fell on to the floor. He'd done that before, so he didn't cry. He tottered across the room, the half-light of the early morning drawing sharp, bright lines through the room's shutters. His sister Mary was still asleep in her cot, snoring softly. From somewhere he heard a great bell tolling, the solemn sounds of Sanctus Georgius that woke the city he lived in. But he wasn't interested in that. He

11

was making for something he hadn't seen before. It was lying on the table, at his eye level. It was large and shone in a dull, brown sort of way. He reached out. It felt hard and warm, all at once, as if what it was wrapped in had once been alive and real. He used both hands, because he sensed this thing, whatever it was, was going to be heavy.

But he wasn't exactly ready for the weight and its impact, as he lifted it off the table, carried him downwards and back, so that first his bum and then his head hit the floor. Now, he *did* cry, not because of the pain or the shock, but because the thing he had just dropped *was* alive. Its insides ruffled and fluttered like wings as it fell, and there were small black flies, fleas, bugs in the feathers that danced in front of him, flicking past his eyes like black smuts thrown out by a new-lit fire. Mary just turned over in her bed, the noise just part of her dream, her little brother's crying of no consequence.

His cry brought her running, as it always did, although the tapping went on, unbroken. He looked up through his tears at the blurred face that swam in his vision. It was his mother, the beautiful lady he called Mama. She was smiling at him, wiping his cheeks, rubbing his sore head in the dark curls. She had a baby, she had told him, in her belly, but there was no sign of it yet.

'Now, Kit,' she mock-scolded him. 'What *are* you doing with Master Tyndale's Bible, eh? It'll be a while before you need that. Come on, now.' She picked up her son and the book in one swift, practised movement and he cuddled his face into her neck. She kissed him quickly and laid him down in his bed again, tucking him in firmly.

'Would you like me to read to you, Kit?' she asked. 'See what the Book's all about, eh? Would you like that?'

Kit put the middle fingers of his left hand into his mouth, as he always did when he was tired and let his head sink into the pillow. His mama opened the book, cleared her throat and read. And as she read, he felt himself drifting through the early morning.

'In the begynnynge God created heaven and erth. The erth was voyde and emptie and darcknesse was upon the depe and the spirite of god moved upon the water. Than God sayd: let there be lyghte and there was lyghte.'

Katherine Marlowe leaned forward over the thin pages of the Bible and peered into the crib, to be met by the sleepy eyes of her son. She smiled and read on.

'And God sawe the lyghte that it was good: and devyded the lyghte from the darcknesse and called the lyghte daye and the darcknesse nyghte: and so of the evenynge and mornynge was made the fyrst daye. And God sayd: let there be a fyrmament betwene the waters and let it devyde the waters a sonder. Then God made the fyrmament and parted the waters which were under the fyrmament from the waters that were above the fyrmament: And it was so.'

Another peep, and this time the eyes, rich brown as molasses, were closed, the tear-clotted lashes drying on the boy's cheek. For good measure, she read one more line, dropping her voice as

13

she did so, so that the last syllables were as quiet as a breath. 'And God called the fyrmament heaven. And so of the evenynge and morninge was made the seconde daye . . .'

As she softly closed the door, the boy stirred, mumbling around his fingers, but still mostly asleep. The distant bell of St George's was still tolling and his papa still tapped the iron into leather in his workshop and his mama's voice, talking softly to someone out on the landing completed the comforting patchwork of sound in the little house on the corner of St George's Lane.

And he fell asleep.

And he dreamed.

Two

The river meandered along with almost unbelievable twists and turns, sometimes almost seeming
to form circles; circles in which a man may get
becalmed for a lifetime of twirling, twirling,
twirling round and round without cease. But just
before the left and right banks must surely touch,
mixing the waters of now and then, the current
would pick up speed and pull the little boat in
which he sat at his ease, back into the rapids and
he would be off again, twisting and spinning in
an eddy, then shooting off towards a duck-haunted
fen.

Dipping his head to avoid a dreaming willow,
fending off the trailing fronds with a lazy hand,
he missed the point at which the river widened
into a broad lake, dotted with small islands, only
a foot or two above the level of the still water,
moss green and luscious, ripe with possibilities.
The boat bumped against the edge of one and
he reached out to steady himself against the
little jetty, rotting and falling into the water
though it was. Although the lake looked still, it
was full of hidden currents and the boat rode
one now, bucking him whether he would go
there or no, towards the narrow channel that led
to the west. The entrance was only an inch or

two wider than the boat and he pulled in his hands, memories of pinched fingers and scraped knuckles of the past rising like the little fish that gaped and mouthed at the surface of the deep, green water. He had never heard fish speak before, and yet it didn't surprise him to hear these now.

'Kit! Kit! Kit, must I call all morning?' The voice was not angry, more exasperated and he could hear the love in it.

He focused his eyes on the here and now, dragging his gaze away from the crack in the ceiling that had been his own personal waterway of the imagination since he was a boy. It had developed a few extra tributaries over the last few years, but he still knew every meander. Looking up at it was proof, if proof were needed, that he was home again, in Canterbury, at the Bull Stake in the parish of St Andrew, under the roof of his father and mother. The big man on campus, the fêted playwright, back again in his old room, waiting to be served his breakfast by his mother and sisters, once his father was safely out of the house. *Nihil mutatur* – despite himself he felt the old need to show off his learning rise to the surface like scum. Nothing was more guaranteed to drive his father to foaming apoplexy, nothing more guaranteed to make his mother smile her fondest smile. And he knew he would be able to rely on his sister Dot to translate under her breath. Nothing changes.

'Kit!'

There it was. The final, single syllable that meant his breakfast would be in the dog's bowl

16

if he didn't reply now. Oh, indeed, nothing changes.

'Coming, madam, coming.' The playwright rolled out of bed and walked over to the window, heavy-footed so the woman below would know he had got up. This summer was as hot as Hell and he had slept with the shutters open, with his bed-hanging thrown back and he leaned on the sill and looked out into the garden, every bush strewn with bleaching linen. Leaning further out, he saw below him the top of his sister's head and, in the spirit of the years that had fallen away this June morning, he reached back into the room and scooped up a handful of water from the ewer on the press and then, leaning out again, dribbled it slowly on to the chestnut hair.

The scream was satisfying. But it sounded rather light to be his sister Dot. And his ear had not deceived him. The face that turned up to his was not Dot at all, but a stranger.

He opened his eyes wide and, gathering his wits, apologized profusely, as prettily as only a poet can.

'As thou bespatteréd by false dropped dew,
Look up with flaméd face and speakst thy mind,
Forgive me, I mistook another one for you, To whom I owest many a—'

'Kit!'

'Madam?'

'Don't you madam me!'

The door burst open and a furious girl stood on the threshold. No one could have mistaken her for anyone but the poet's sister. She had his sensitive mouth, his curling hair, his liquid eye.

17

A fierce intelligence burned in her stare and he read her mind as he had been able to do since she was in her hanging sleeves. With a rueful smile, he hung briefly out of the window. The other girl was still underneath, leaning on a besom, looking up in bemusement at his sill. 'Sorry,' he said, giving her his best dimpling smile. 'I am very sorry I tipped water on you. I thought you were my sister.' He turned back into the room and sketched a bow at the girl in his doorway.

'That's better,' she said. 'Now, will you please come down for your breakfast. Mother's fretting.'

Dorothy was at that awkward age – but what age is not awkward in a sister? She was sixteen, an old maid in some peoples' eyes. Her big sister Joan had married John Moore, a shoemaker, when she was twelve. And she had died in childbed a year later.

'Don't let her bully you, Kit.' Margaret was in a hurry. She swept past the stairs into the hall carrying a tray of bread with a pot of honey. She was Marlowe's little sister too, but there was barely a child-carrying between them and she always saw herself as his twin. But she had no time for her wayward brother today. She was promised to John Jordan the tailor; and the tailor was going up in the world. She was proud of Kit, of course, but London? The stage? All that was a world away from reality.

Dorothy was following Marlowe down the stairs, prodding him in the arse with her toe until he flung both arms back and lifted her off her feet so that he carried her pig-a-back for the last five stairs and swung her unceremoniously down to the rushes. She squealed and yelled at him, 'Rakebell!' and instantly clapped her hand to her mouth.

'I heard that, Dorothy Marley,' her mother's voice called from the kitchen, but she was not scolding. It was lovely to have her boy back again and to hear her children laughing. The sun was warming the herb garden beyond the back door, filling the air with the sharp smell of rosemary and the bitterness of rue. The new maid was mopping the flagstones, the cloth slapping and spraying water as she swayed from side to side.

'Tom!' Katherine Marlowe popped her head out of the door and her youngest child came running out of the jakes, blushing as he realized his hose were still untied and the maid was looking at him. As he got to the house, Anne fetched him a sharp one around the head. If there was ever a middle child, it was Anne Marley. She had inherited her father's looks and her father's disposition. Most of Canterbury hated her.

'Now then, Anne,' Marlowe wagged a finger at her. 'Pick on somebody your own size.'

She laughed and threw her arms around him. Her big brother, home at last. They had heard such things about him. How he had dared God out of Heaven with Tamburlaine. How grown men wept at the passing of Dido. People queued for hours in the rain and snow to watch his plays at the Rose and Ned Alleyn himself demanded to play the leads, no matter what the play.

19

'What's he like?' Anne flounced around the table and plonked herself down next to Marlowe.

'Who?' Kit smiled up at his mother as she poured the breakfast ale for him.

'Ned Alleyn.'

'Who?' Marlowe looked blank until Anne hit him with her napkin. She had been asleep last night when Kit arrived and had not seen his face for years. In that time, all his siblings had grown. Margaret had been a woman in all but name before he left for Cambridge, but since he'd seen any of them last, they had all grown up, even little Tom whose doublet didn't quite fit him any more.

'You wouldn't like him, Annie,' Marlowe said with a frown, shaking his head. 'He's ugly. And not much more than four feet tall.'

'You liar!' Anne shrieked and leapt in to tickle her brother, who fought her off manfully with the wooden trencher his mother had placed in front of him, waiting for his food.

'What's next, Kit?' Dorothy asked him, resting her chin on her hand and gazing into his eyes. Until little Tom had come along, he had been the only boy in the family. It gave him an air of safety and comfort that not even the Cambridge whips or the daggers of London's roaring boys could ever take away.

'Well,' he said, his face solemn. 'It's only the vaguest of ideas as yet, but the next play is going to be about a girl. She'll have to be played by a boy, of course, but that's the way of it. She's bossy and somebody's kid sister. There's another sister . . .' he said louder so that Margaret could

20

hear, 'and she's mooning over some local oaf who stitches for a living . . .'

'And the father?' a gruff voice asked. John Marley clattered his way over the cobbles in the kitchen beyond the open door.

Marlowe smiled, nodded but did not turn his head. 'Good morning, Father,' he said.

'Christopher,' the shoemaker said as he nodded back and sat down heavily at the head of the table, opposite his eldest son.

'Isn't it nice, John?' Katherine beamed. 'Kit coming to see us like this?'

'Lovely,' the man said, but he wasn't smiling. 'How are you, lad?' He looked across the table to where his wife stood, her hands tucked behind the bodice of her apron. 'Manchet?' He held up a hunk of bread. 'Since when did we have manchet bread for breakfast?' He looked at his son and snorted. 'Oh.'

'I am well, Father, thank you,' Marlowe said, ignoring the exchange. 'And you?'

'Well,' John said and shrugged as though he had last seen his son yesterday and not four years ago.

'What's this play called, Kit?' Anne asked, tucking in to her bread and butter, a smear of honey transferring itself to her cheek.

Dorothy looked at her as one might a pet lamb. 'It's not real, Annie,' she said, and Annie, eighteen though she was, stuck her tongue out at the girl. What was it about the proximity of John Marley that brought out the worst in people?

Little Tom was suddenly on his feet. 'That's Great Harry,' he said when he heard the bell toll.

21

He still had a mouthful of bread. 'Choir practice. I'll be late.'

'Choir practice?' Marlowe smiled. 'Tom, I didn't know you were a chorister. That takes me back. May I come along?' The playwright choirboy was on his feet already. His little brother looked at him. He had only been four when his big brother had gone away to Cambridge. He didn't know what that was or where or how far. But his mama had told him of other brothers and sisters – of Mary, of the little boy they had never named, of his namesake Thomas – they had all gone to Heaven; and for all he knew that was where Kit had gone too. But here he was, larger than life, with his flash velvet doublet and Venetians, his buckled buskins. Tom had not seen the dagger, with its elaborate curled hilt, because Marlowe had hidden it in his valise rather than alarm his mother and prompt too many questions. John Marley had carried a knife all his life, but that was a shoemaker's blade, short and single-edged, not the murderous weapon constantly at his son's back.

'All right,' the boy said, uncertainly. 'Do you remember the way?'

Kit Marlowe smiled. 'In my sleep,' he said.

And they were gone, after they'd both given their mother a kiss.

'Did you see that?' John grunted, breaking into a warm crust of bread. 'Didn't so much as get up when his father came into the room.' He tutted and shook his head.

Katherine Marley was barely listening, because

something else had disturbed her more. 'He didn't say Grace either,' she murmured.

Nicholas Faunt sat his chestnut mount under the spreading arms of the oak. He was hot and sticky in his velvet and brocade. Before him, the motte of Norwich castle rose steeply to the grey keep at the top, square and forbidding. The sun was high and the crowd was becoming impatient. Faunt appreciated the cool under the branches and would appreciate it more soon enough when those faggots were lit.

'We do God's work this day, Master Faunt.' The bishop smiled at his men's handiwork. In the ditch in front of them, dry and rubbish-filled in this hottest of summers, a stake had been driven into the iron-hard ground and faggots of brushwood had been thrown against its base. Edward Scambler was a stickler for how things should be done. When he'd been Bishop of Peterborough, he'd earned a reputation for it and here, at Norwich, he continued that.

Faunt looked at the man and nodded. For more years than he cared to remember Faunt had been watching the back of the man who watched the Queen. Faunt was Sir Francis Walsingham's left-hand man and he kept to the shadows. He had been watching Francis Kett too for months now and knew him to be a madman. But Kett was also a scholar, a Fellow of Corpus Christi College, Cambridge and he was an atheist, a blasphemer who denied the existence of God and the Trinity. And God alone knew how many young men he had corrupted in the University along the Cam with his rubbish.

23

Even so, Nicholas Faunt didn't like the glint in the bishop's eye. He didn't like fanatics of any persuasion, not Papists, not Puritans, not, for that matter, Bishops of Norwich. They were all equally dangerous in his eyes. The solemn bell from the cathedral rang out across the expectant city. All Norwich held its breath as the Devil's disciple was led past the Strangers' Hall and through the Maddermarket, spat at, kicked and punched all the way.

The crowd roared their delight as the grim little procession reached Castle Hill. One of Scambler's officials carried a huge crucifix at its head. Faunt found this a little Papist, but he realized that the Bishop was making a point. The clerics, in their black and white ambled alongside. In the centre, flanked by guards in the city's livery, their halberds flashing in the sun, came Francis Kett himself. He had aged years in the weeks since Faunt had seen him last. The blond beard was wild and streaked with grey, like brambles in hoar frost. His face was bruised and bloody and his hands were bound in front of him with rough hemp that cut and tore at his skin. His sackcloth robe was white with the spittle of the Godly and all kinds of offal and excrement covered his hair and shoulders.

In front of the Bishop, the procession halted and the drums beat a tattoo, sharp, loud, as if to bring an end to the journey and the life of Francis Kett. The man did his best to smile through broken teeth. 'Good morning, Master Scambler,' he croaked.

'You will address me as Lord Bishop,

blasphemer!' Scambler snapped as his horse shifted under his weight, lashing its tail and stamping a hoof on the cobbles.

'Lord Bishop,' Kett half-bowed, as far as his ropes would let him and Scambler raised a gloved hand.

'May the Lord in whom you do not believe have mercy upon you!' he shouted and two of Kett's guards suddenly dragged the beaten man sideways. He didn't struggle, but let them bind his hands behind his back, around the oak stake and tie his ankles at the base.

At another signal from the Bishop, they lit the torches that crackled and sparked in the sunshine. When they met the brushwood, the smoke billowed black and white, eclipsing for a moment the motte, the keep and Francis Kett himself. The crowd roared their delight, cheering wildly as each new brand caught fire and the sparks flew upward, sending sooty specks into the cloudless blue.

Suddenly, there was a shriek from the woman nearest the pyre. Kett's legs had all but gone but he was still alive and the fire had burned through the ropes around his wrists. His hands jerked upwards, raised, as if to Heaven and he yelled, time and time again, 'Praise be to God. Praise be to God,' and he was still screaming that, leaping and dancing in the flames, as the fire finally took him and he died.

The Bishop nodded, a grim smile on his face. 'He recanted,' he said and looked at Walsingham's man sitting his horse beside him. 'You heard him. He recanted.'

25

Faunt looked the Bishop in the face. 'I hope so, your Grace,' he said. 'I hope that was the sound of a guilty man finding his God again rather than the sound of an innocent one calling out what he really believed all along.' He touched his feathered cap and turned his horse's head. It was a long ride back to London and he needed to get the stench of this morning's work out of his nostrils.

The two brothers walked at a cracking pace through the alleys and bye-ways of cobbled Canterbury, along Mercery Lane and through the Christchurch Gate, leading to the side door of the cathedral as though pulled by strings. Marlowe's feet found every indentation of the cobbles awakening memories he had thought forgotten but which were just buried deep inside him and as they approached the weathered stone wall that cut them off from the sun, he was humming under his breath the tenor line of his last piece he had sung as a treble in the choir stalls there.

'If you love me,' Thomas came in on cue, 'keep my commandments.'

'You know it?' Marlowe was delighted. It had always been his favourite piece and Master Bull had allowed him to choose his own swansong. It was all William Byrd in London these days, but the elder Marley was a Thomas Tallis man through and through.

'Of course,' Thomas said with a nod, and gave the beat again. 'If you love me –' his young voice reverberated off the ancient stone of the cloisters,

26

making him his own counterpoint – 'keep my commandments, and I will . . .'

To Marlowe's amusement, the boy nodded him in at the right place. With a smile, he came in, 'And I will pray to the Father.'

The brothers beat time for a bar and heard in their heads the absent altos and basses. Then, with another nod, Thomas was back. 'And He shall . . .' Nod.

'And He shall give you another Comforter.'

So engrossed were they in the toils of Master Tallis that they arrived, still singing, at the choir stalls and almost walked into the back of Master Goodwin, the organist and choirmaster, who was studiously ignoring the interruption.

Coming down from the heights of harmony, Thomas scuttled, head down, into his place and Marlowe bowed to the choirmaster.

'My apologies,' he said. 'My brother and I got rather carried away.'

'Your brother? So *you* are Kit Marley.' The choirmaster's eyes were sparkling now with mischief. 'Come with me.' And he took the playwright's ornate sleeve and led him down the stalls, moving boys out of his way by means of his conductor's staff. Finally, he found the space he wanted and pointed. In the flickering candlelight from the choir's sconces, Marlowe could read, although he didn't need to, the words carved deep in the dark oak. He glanced up at the choirmaster.

'I understood that that was to be erased,' he said, sheepishly. He hoped his brother never sat in this stall; the graffiti was a little scurrilous.

'I'm keeping it,' the choirmaster said. 'I am hoping it will be worth money one day, if you get any more famous. Now, would you like to sit in? Gentlemen,' he raised his voice at the decani tenors, 'would you like to shuffle along a little. Master Marley –' he looked at the playwright – 'or is it strictly Marlowe these days?'

'If I may insist,' Marlowe said, modestly.

'Master Marlowe is joining us for practice. Tell me, Master Marlowe, have you kept in practice?'

'I only sing for my own pleasure these days, Master Goodwin,' he said.

'We sing for the pleasure of the Lord, of course,' the man said, piously. 'But no one says we can't enjoy it too. Take your place, Master Marlowe.' The choirmaster banged his staff on the floor. 'Since Master Marley and Master Marlowe are in good voice, perhaps they can lead us in *If you love me*. Master Marley, if you please . . . one, two, three, four, and . . .'

'If you love me,' the clear voice of Thomas Marley rose to the rafters in the service of the Lord.

Three

The brothers had barely turned the corner on their way to the cathedral and did not hear the scream ring out. But everybody at the Bull Stake did. Katherine raised her head like a deer at a watering hole who senses danger but her husband, the city constable for this year of his Lord 1589, carried on eating without a sign that he had heard anything. For all he had complained about the manchet bread for breakfast, he seemed to be enjoying it, especially when spread with new butter a finger thick.

Anne raised her head too. 'Mother?' she said. 'Was that a scream?' Anne was always ready to panic and run around making a bad situation worse, so her mother flapped her apron at her.

'Calm down, Annie,' she said, wondering as she did so how many times she had had to say that in her life. Too many, she would wager. 'I don't suppose it is anything that need bother us. Just Mistress Benchkyne finding another rat in the wash-house, I expect.'

But the scream went on, wavering in pitch and intensity, as the screamer drew the occasional snatched breath, but definitely intended to attract more attention than would be warranted by the finding of even the biggest rat.

Dorothy spoke to her father. She was always the one who stepped out of the line, who was

29

prepared to risk his wrath. 'Papa,' she said. 'Someone is screaming.'

He lifted his head briefly and nodded. 'So they are. Pass me that last piece of bread, will you, Dot? It is expensive enough, in all conscience. It needs eating up or it will go to waste.'

Katherine Marley, who had not yet breakfasted and was hoping to pick up everyone else's leavings, turned away with a sigh.

'But . . . Papa,' Dorothy persisted. 'People don't scream like that unless . . .'

This time she had her father's attention, to the extent of a quick slap around the head. The tears started into her eyes, but she didn't let them fall. The women of John Marley's house knew that tears only had one reward, something he called 'something to cry about'.

Before he could raise his hand again, there was a hammering at the door and voices raised in cacophonous yelling, suddenly cut short. Then, one voice came and John Marley could enjoy his breakfast no longer.

'Constable Marley! Come quick. There's terrible murder been done. Mistress Benchkyne is dead!'

Sighing, the shoemaker pushed his chair back from the table and rose to go. 'She'll have fainted at one of those rats,' he said. 'But I suppose I should see what's what.'

The little maid had finally wrestled with the bolts and had opened the door on to the street. The family could hear her asking who was wanting to see the master, but she was batted aside and a tousled-looking man strode into the room.

30

'Are you deaf, John Marley?' he said testily, nodding briefly to Katherine who was standing in the kitchen doorway, her girls around her. 'If you didn't hear the screaming, you could have heard me knocking.'

'Just breaking my fast, Master Grijs,' he said. 'What is so urgent?'

The man looked at the white, soft crumbs which littered the board. 'Manchet bread?' he said. 'Perhaps we pay our constables too much, Master Marley.'

Katherine leaned forward. 'Our Kit is home, Master Grijs,' she said. 'We thought we'd—'

'London ways!' John Marley spat. 'He'll be gone ere long, it is to be hoped. But what about the screaming? You say somebody's dead? Mistress Benchkyne? She's no age.'

'No, indeed. But being beaten around the head is no respecter of age, Master Constable,' Grijs thought it necessary to point out.

'Beaten . . .? No, she'll have fallen in a faint, like she always does when she sees vermin in the wash-house. Mad as a tree, that one.'

Grijs was not usually a patient man, but he was fond of Katherine Marley. In fact, back in Dover in the old days he had courted her until the cobbler had come along and for some reason, had swept her off her feet. Looking at him now, hose half-undone, unshaven and with butter and honey smearing his cheeks, it was hard to say why. But for Katherine, he kept his temper in check. 'If she fell, John –' he decided to take the more friendly approach to get this lazy man to do his duty – 'she got up again

31

and fell again, over and over until she was dead.'

John Marley stood like an ox in the furrow and slowly laced his hose and shrugged on his jerkin. 'I'll come and see her, Master Grijs,' he said, 'but by the time I get there, she'll be sitting up and rubbing her sore head, I'll be bound.'

Grijs hung back as Marley made for the door and spoke quietly to Katherine. 'If she is sitting up, then Hell will have opened here in Canterbury, for she is as dead as a nit, Kat . . . my pardon, Mistress Marley. Find some of the women and come to Mistress Benchkyne's house. It won't be pretty, I warn you; only come if your stomach is strong.' And with another nod, he turned on his heel and followed the cobbler.

Choir practice over, the Marley boys were making their way back home. To Kit, something didn't seem quite right. People were standing at street corners, muttering, whispering, looking in the direction of Water Lane.

'What's the trouble here?' he asked an old man he vaguely recognized.

'There's a woman done to death,' the man mumbled, 'cruelly violated in her bed.'

'Go home, Tom,' Marlowe said. 'I must see to this.'

'No fear,' Tom said. 'Papa's the constable. He'll be there already.'

They followed the drifting locals in their ones and twos, weaving past them and muttering their 'excuse mes'. The houses along Water Lane were the same as all the rest in the city, old and tired, their timbers dry, their plaster dusty and peeling. They almost leant against each other in the morning's heat. And the sun was high already.

There was quite a crowd at the gate that led into the Benchkynes' garden and Marlowe's heart sank. His mother had been a maid to old Katherine Benchkyne soon after her family moved from Dover and he remembered being dandled on the old lady's knee when he was still in his hanging sleeves. He remembered her too, sitting in the great cathedral as he sang the Agnus, with tears trickling down her face. The old lady had died four years ago, the last time Marlowe had come to Canterbury and he had signed her will and read it out to the interested parties because old Katherine Benchkyne would not have a lawyer across her threshold.

John Marley stood in the doorway, the cool dark of the passage behind him. He stopped his eldest son with a hand on his arm. 'Nothing to see here,' he growled.

'A woman is dead,' Marlowe said. 'Violated in her bed, I've just heard.'

Marley squinted into the sun. 'You heard wrong,' he snapped. 'She just fell and hit her head, that's all. I'll get her laid out and sent to the charnel house. Master Grijs,' he called to the man who had called on him. 'See if you can find a vicar, in this town that's full of 'em . . .'

'No vicar,' Marlowe said. 'Not yet,' and he pushed past his father into the darkness.

'I'm the constable here!' John Marley barked, spinning on his heel and striding after his son.

'Then act like one!' Marlowe flashed back,

turning at the end of the passage. 'Get those people out of there.' He looked across at the bed and the corpse lying on it. 'A woman has been murdered here.'

John Marley was furious. He half-raised his staff of office, scowling and grating his teeth, then he relented and stormed out into the garden, bellowing orders left and right and scattering the crowd.

Jane Benchkyne was lying on her back, her arms spread wide, her feet apart. Her mouth hung open and her sightless eyes were transfixed on the ceiling, as though she had found a cobweb and the sight appalled her. Marlowe felt her neck. She was cold. He lifted her right hand and it flopped back on to the mattress. No stiffness of death yet. She had been dead, he guessed, about six hours. That would make it perhaps four of the clock when someone had shattered her skull. The attack had come from the front, delivered quickly and savagely; three, perhaps four blows, it was difficult to tell under the mass of blood that was clotted and matted in her hair.

He heard a stifled sob and spun round, instantly regretting that his dagger was back home.

'Who's there?'

A frail girl emerged from the corner where the shadows had hidden her. She was perhaps sixteen, pale and with eyes wide with terror. 'It's only me, sir.' She tried to bob a curtsy but her balance was off and she gave up, lip quivering.

'Who are you?' he asked kindly, knowing the look of abject shock when he saw it.

'Please, sir, I'm Alice, Mistress Benchkyne's maid.'

'Did you find her?' Marlowe asked. If she was First Finder, she would have to appear in court and face the wrath of the magistrate. But the magistrate was Roger Manwood. Terror of the night prowler he may be, but he had daughters of his own, not much older than this girl. And he was a fool for a pretty face.

'Yes, sir.' He could barely hear her.

'You screamed.' It was a statement, not a question, but he remembered it as he and Tom were crossing Mercery Lane. Screams in London were ten-a-groat, where the smock alleys ran dark and the river rushed, taking all manner of dead and dying things into its cold embrace. But Canterbury was God's own city. This sort of thing didn't happen here.

'Did I?' Alice asked. She couldn't remember.

'Is this how you found her?' Marlowe asked.

She nodded.

'Do you live here, Alice?'

'No, sir. I live at home. In the parish of St Mildred.'

That was the far side of the city.

'And when did you get here this morning?'

'I don't rightly know, sir,' she said. 'I heard the bell calling . . . at the cathedral.'

That would be Great Harry, summoning the faithful – and Kit Marlowe – to choir practice. He looked around the room. There was blood, a great deal of blood, on the pillow under the dead woman's head and spatters of it on the bedhead and the post-curtains. A mat had been rucked up and chairs were overturned. Cupboard doors had been thrown open and pewter plates scattered over the floor, along with cups and flagons.

Marlowe reached out a hand, careful, slow, and took the girl's arm, leading her gently out of the room into the passage. John Marley was grumbling to some gentleman just outside but Marlowe couldn't see who it was. Tom was standing off to the left, trying to peer into the house itself, as ghoulish, when it came down to it, as the rest of Canterbury that John Marley had just scattered. Marlowe helped Alice into a chair and said gently, 'I want you to stay here, Alice; I shan't be long.' And he made for the stairs.

He knew this house well because its rear garden backed on to the Marley house around the corner. A high stone wall separated them, too high for even the Marley boys to climb, but little Kit had been in and out of the Benchkyne house all his life. He knew the cold damp of the scullery, the sound of the rats in the wainscoting, the chirrup of the baby swallows in their nests in the eaves. He knew the lavender in the knot garden, the rosemary and the rue, slips of which had taken root outside his own back door and flourished like the green bay tree. The Marleys had not always had a garden, because there had been times when life was hard and the family would move quickly, at dead of night, flitting from one temporary shelter to another. The tower of Great Harry had watched them go, as it watched over all of Canterbury, keeping a stern eye on its children.

But the house in Water Lane was a constant.

It never changed. It was old and solid and safe. Until today. Today it was a slaughterhouse. He ducked his head as he entered old Jane Benchkyne's room. It was empty. Not a bed, not a curtain, not a stick of furniture. The cupboards were empty. He tried the next room, the one with the chimney breast where the crucifix had been fastened before the world turned upside down and the Pope had become Bishop of Rome. The nail marks were still there on the mouldy plaster, but again there was no bed and no furniture. He tried the last room in the house and found it deserted. The spiders ruled here, defying Alice's broom and daring her to clear them out, once and for all. And every time she did, they built their sticky palaces again that floated in the breeze and glistened in the sun, specked with flies long dead and the dust of the dying house.

Alice barely heard his pattens on the stairs but suddenly he was alongside her, kneeling down, lifting up her chin. 'Did Mistress Benchkyne live in this one room?' he asked her.

'Yes, sir,' she replied with a sniff. 'It has been so always.'

'Always?' Marlowe frowned. His memory was longer than the girl's.

'For all the time I've been here,' she told him. 'Three years or more.'

Marlowe patted her hand and went back into her mistress's room. He had been in this position before, alone with the dead, and he felt the hair on the back of his neck crawl. It was as if Jane Benchkyne would sit up in a moment and scream at him, demand to know what he was doing in

37

her house, so near the bed. He hated himself for what he did next, but he had to. 'Cruelly violated' – that was the phrase the old man had used. Was that it? Was that why Jane Benchkyne had died? He lifted her shift, sprayed with her blood and looked at her nakedness. There was no blood here, no bruising. Jane Benchkyne had never been known to go with a man. There would be signs if she had gone with one now, viciously, against her will.

Then, something else caught his eye. Under the window, there was a linen chest, oak and deeply carved. Its lid had been forced upwards and its lock had been smashed. There were one or two blankets still inside, but pulled aside as though . . . He knelt down and tapped the chest's base on the inside. It sounded hollow. He tapped each corner, one by one, shifting the woollens aside. On the last corner, there was a loud click and the floor of the chest jerked upwards, as far as the weight of the few thin blankets would allow, to reveal a space beneath it. It wasn't large, perhaps three inches deep but it covered the whole length and width of the chest. There was nothing here nor any sign that anything had ever been here.

'Alice,' Marlowe called. 'Will you come here?'

Nothing.

'Please,' he added, sensing the girl's fear. 'There is nothing in here to frighten you. The dead are dead and don't bother the living. I just want to ask you something.'

She peered around the door, as if expecting to see her mistress sitting up in bed and waiting for her breakfast. Praying she would see that, perhaps.

But it was not to be, for all that hard-eyed constable had said when he arrived at the house. She couldn't see the dead woman's ghost either, so perhaps this gentleman was right. The dead couldn't hurt her.

'Did you know about this?' he asked her. 'This chest has a false bottom. Did you know about it?'

'No, sir,' said Alice, frowning.

'She kept her bed linen here?'

'Yes, sir. I washed and pressed them and put them in there. With a little crushed lavender.'

Marlowe could smell it. He got up and took the girl back out into the passage. 'Tell me, Alice, was the mistress expecting company last night? A visitor?'

'No, sir. A solitary one, was the mistress. I never knowed anybody come here.'

'All right, Alice,' he said. 'Thank you.'

'Please, sir, I won't get into trouble, will I?'

'No, of course not,' he assured her.

She looked up into the gentle, handsome face, the dark, kind eyes, still the molasses brown of his babyhood, but molasses laced with bitter experience now. 'Who are you, sir?'

'He's just passing through.' John Marley was suddenly standing there, blotting out the light in the passageway. 'On his way north.'

Marlowe ignored him and brushed past his father into the sunlight. 'Tom,' he called his little brother over. 'Can you ride?'

'Tolerably well,' the boy said, glad to be doing something at last. He had listened to his father making small talk to a stranger for the last ten

39

minutes; ten minutes he would never get back.

'Get over to Latimer's stables. Saddle my black and take yourself on a ride. Then go to Haw and give my compliments to Sir Roger. Tell him we have a murderer on the loose.'

The trout were leaping from the lake at Haw that evening, catching the gnats that teemed there. A copper sunset followed a golden day and the men of Kent had almost forgotten what rain felt like. Kit Marlowe was walking with Roger Manwood, the magistrate, the scourge of the night prowler, in the knot garden at Haw. He had to walk a little slower these days because the old man's gout was getting to him and his pace was not what it once was.

Marlowe owed a lot to this man. Crusty though his exterior undoubtedly was, Roger Manwood had a heart of gold. He had put Marlowe forward for the King's School when the lad had been a pot boy at the Star and the most he could hope to inherit was John Marley's workshop. Made a fine shoe did John Marley, but Manwood knew there was something entirely different about his son, something special that would be wasted at the awl. And the King's School had led on to Corpus Christi and Corpus Christi to . . . what?

'Plays, Christopher,' Manwood queried with a frown. 'Plays?'

Marlowe laughed. 'And you had me down for the Church, Sir Roger.'

Manwood laughed in turn. 'Oh, no,' he said. 'Never that. Will it catch on, d'you think, the theatre?' Travelling players came to Canterbury now and again but Roger Manwood didn't go. He was old enough to remember the Mystery Plays with their Angels and their Devils and their Mouths of Hell. He hadn't cared for them either.

'I think it might, yes,' Marlowe said. 'There's plenty of money to be made in London. Playgoers can't get enough of the things.'

'But is it literature, Christopher?' the old man wanted to know. 'Is it *art*?'

'It's clever,' Marlowe said. 'Well, some of it.'

'I really must get up to London more. It's been a while.'

'I hate to raise it again,' Marlowe said as they wove their way between Manwood's apple trees, 'but . . . Jane Benchkyne.'

'Yes,' Manwood acknowledged with a sigh. 'Tragic. Tragic.' It had been some hours since the younger Marley boy had galloped, lathered, into his courtyard. There had been a time when the old man would have got Nicholson to saddle his mare and he'd have galloped back with the boy, racing him along the Stour and placing a wager he would reach the bastions of the West Gate before him. But that was then. Today, Nicholson had rigged up his carriage and pair and while Cook looked after Tom Marley in the kitchen, Manwood had slung on his chain of office and found his staff from somewhere. Everything took so much longer these days.

He had met Christopher in Water Lane and had looked at the battered body on the bed. Tomorrow he would be back in the city again, empanelling the sixteen men and true who had been the dead

41

woman's friends and neighbours. Not that she had many of those.

'She was as mad as a tree, of course,' he said to Marlowe. 'You knew that?'

Marlowe stopped. 'No,' he said. 'No, I didn't.' He had not gone back home since meeting with Manwood as the magistrate had invited him back to Haw, so he'd had no chance to talk to his family about her.

'Yes. She was up before me last year. Witchcraft.'

'Witchcraft?'

'Don't look so horrified, dear boy. Kent is crawling with them. Oh, not as bad as Essex, of course, but then, nothing's as bad as Essex.'

Marlowe had read those reports too and had seen the engravings of Joan Prentice suckling her familiars Jack and Jill. They had hanged a number of women from the same beam to save time and to save the town the extra expense. 'I assume there were no grounds,' he said, 'in Jane Benchkyne's case.'

'Because I didn't hang her, you mean? Well, between you and me . . .' Manwood suddenly became confidential. This was, after all, Lord Burleigh's England – walls (and even trout lakes) had ears and anybody could be lurking behind the trunks of apple trees. 'There was *talk* of familiars. A cat that talked, that sort of thing.'

'A cat that talked?' Marlowe had stopped again.

'Don't look at me like that, Christopher. I had this from a particularly unreliable witness. Do you remember old Petty, kept the forge along St Dunstan's Street?'

Marlowe did.

42

'Well, he's dead now, of course, but he hadn't passed a sober hour for the last twenty years of his life. The talking cat came from him. Swore on holy writ that he'd seen it with his own eyes. Jane Benchkyne used to talk to the damned thing all the time.'

'I used to talk to the Corpus Christi cat,' Marlowe said. 'Old Tiberius.'

'Ah, but did he answer back?'

'No, indeed,' Marlowe chuckled. 'We had never been formally introduced and he was known as a bit of a stickler for etiquette.'

'No, I couldn't trust a word from old Petty.' Manwood was hobbling on, fighting his gout every step of the way. 'But I spoke at length with Jane. And Alice, her maidservant. Oh, just a chat, you understand. No thumbscrews or anything. Jane had gone rather peculiar – well, some women do, don't they, at a certain age? She'd never been exactly the life and soul of Canterbury, but she sold many of her movables and lived in one room. Alice cooked and cleaned for her and she never went out. Of course, it's the mother I blame.'

'Katherine?'

'Yes, well you knew her, Christopher. Lovable old besom but quite demanding, I would think. When did you see Jane last – alive, I mean?'

'That would be four years ago, when her mother died. I signed the old girl's will.'

'Yes, that's right. I remember. How did she seem to you then; Jane, I mean?'

'Upset, naturally. She had waited on her mother hand and foot.'

'Exactly. All her life. If I remember aright, the Benchkynes had no maidservant then. So Jane was doing it all. No time for nature's natural course, you see.' He leaned closer to Marlowe. 'No *man* in her life. It sends them funny in the end.'

'How, funny?' Marlowe wanted to know.

'Well, she denied the cat talked to her, but then I expected that. She laughed a lot, a sort of silly giggle about some secret joke I couldn't understand. She kept saying – and this *was* odd – she kept saying she had the whole world in her hand.'

'What did you take that to mean?' Marlowe asked. 'I know some people say witches can create storms and other disasters but . . . would she say such a thing if she was denying being a witch?'

'Hardly, I should have thought.' Manwood shrugged. 'So I'm damned if I know what that was all about. As I told you, mad as a tree.'

'Who brought the witchcraft charges?' the playwright asked.

'Gammer Wilson; lived over at the Greyfriars. She's met her Maker too, of course, since then and I hope He had a stern word with her, the murderous old hag. Unless of course, she's roasting slowly as the guest of the Dark One.'

The pair walked on towards the house, the purple clouds merging now to blot out the dying sun that gilded the timbers and gargoyles of Haw.

'You'll stay the night, Christopher?' the old man asked. 'I want to know more about this new life of yours, those London streets.'

Marlowe patted the old man's arm. 'They're not made of gold, Sir Roger,' he said, 'as we both know. Thank you, but I must be getting back. Mother frets.'

'Yes,' Manwood said with a sigh. 'Mothers will. I had one once, but all that was a long time ago.'

Half of Canterbury had turned out the next day, to the extent that most people expected the Archbishop himself to be there. Sir Roger Manwood, Magistrate of Her Majesty's County of Kent, sat in his scarlet robes of office with the roses and portcullises glittering around his shoulders. He wore his best starched ruff and his black cap of estate had been specially pressed for the occasion.

Earlier that morning, Marlowe had quizzed his family on what they knew of the late Jane Benchkyne and they essentially told the same story that Manwood had. A sad, lonely woman, who had been driven by demons, real or imagined, to hide from the world in her one little room.

John Marley was at the West Gate bright and early, in his capacity of Constable, staff of office in his fist and an ornate cudgel at his hip, the arms of the city bright on his cap. He stood, flanked by his two under-constables, as the great, the good and the just plain nosy of Canterbury wound their way through the little door in the tower of the West Gate. It was a Thursday and the axes and hammers of the workmen demolishing the old bridge rang out over the sun-kissed city, echoing and re-echoing around the cloisters, the closes and the ancient stones.

'Thirteen hundred and nine,' an old man had said to Marlowe as he reached the West Gate. 'That's when that bridge was put up. Wonder how long the new one will last, eh? Five minutes?'

Marlowe stood at the back, partly because there were no seats in the cramped solar and partly because he wanted to see who was there. The air was already thick with the smell of the gathered humanity, the stones of the tower having baked in the sun for weeks, drying the air and driving out any freshness there might once have been. Sweat was already trickling down many a forehead and those who had room to move their arms were fanning themselves with whatever came to hand.

Sir Roger Manwood called the crowd to order, swore in his jurymen and the inquest began. Whoever had smashed the skull of Jane Benchkyne had got in to her house, killed her, stolen whatever he could find and had gone without a trace being left behind. No one had heard the dead woman's screams. No one had seen a shadowy figure near the house. The killer was like a will o' the wisp and Canterbury had plenty of those, hovering over the riverbanks and fields to the south and mingling with the corpse lights in the churchyards.

Alice was there, as First Finder and she sat on the chair in the middle of the hall, looking small and afraid. Roger Manwood did his best to soothe her, talking quietly, nodding, smiling, trying to put the terrified girl at her ease. But she knew, as well as anyone there, that his gaze was the one that sent men to the gallows, as surely as the basilisk turned them to stone. Tearfully, wringing her hands in her apron and darting furtive glances at the jurymen, all of whom she knew by name, she told her story of how she had found her mistress's body early the day before and how the kind Master Marley, the son of the constable, had helped her. Master Marley senior, standing beside Manwood on the dais, was less than impressed.

When he had finished his questions, the magistrate leaned back in his carved chair and said, in a loud voice, '*Cui bono?*'

Marlowe knew what that meant. It had been the common cry of the great lawyer Cicero in the days of ancient Rome. But this was Canterbury now, and beyond the handful of lawyers and the churchmen, Latin was beginning to fade from the land.

'Who benefits?' Manwood translated for the benefit of the jury and the mob. 'Is there a will?'

'There is, my lord.' John Marley pulled a folded parchment from his tunic and handed it to the magistrate.

Marlowe couldn't believe it. There had been no such document in the dead woman's room in Water Lane when he got there; nor anywhere in the house, as far as he knew. His father must have found it and helped himself before he arrived. Manwood broke the wax seal from its ribbon and read the contents. Then he cleared his throat and read aloud, 'I, Jane Benchkyne, of the Parish of St Andrew in the city of Canterbury, being of sound mind . . .' Here he paused, and then continued, '. . . and body do hereby leave all my worldly goods including my house in Water Lane, and the movables thereof, with the whole world to Alice Snow, my maidservant.'

Murmurs ran like the ripples of a rising tide around the courtroom. John Marley slammed the butt of his staff to the floor to restore silence.

'This is most irregular,' a voice sailed clear and true over the heads of the court and all eyes turned to the speaker.

'What is irregular, Master Marley?' John Marley asked, scowling at his upstart son.

'The reading of private correspondence in a public place such as this,' he said, unperturbed.

'Enough, sir!' Manwood roared. '*I* will decide what is regular and irregular in my own court-room. Constable –' he half-turned to Marley senior – 'take this woman and place her under lock and key here in the West Gate. She is to have no visitors until such time as I can examine her further.'

The under-constable lifted Alice bodily out of her chair. The look on her face said it all. She didn't know what was happening to her and looked around for help. There was none.

'Gentlemen,' Manwood said as he turned to the jury. 'The appearance of this document changes everything. There is clear implication here of the potential guilt of this woman. We'll sort out the Deodand later. In the meantime, Master Foreman, I invite you to deliver your verdict.'

The foreman looked as nonplussed as Alice who had vanished with the under-constable through a side door. He struggled to his feet, looking backwards and forwards between the magistrate and his fellow jurors. 'Er . . . we, the jury, find that Jane Benchkyne of the parish of St Andrew in the city of Canterbury . . . met her death through the malice aforethought of Alice Snow, of the same parish.'

'Nonsense!' Marlowe shouted and moved forward as though to address the court.

'Got all that?' Manwood ignored him, muttering to the clerk, scribbling furiously away at his elbow. The man nodded, crossing t's and dotting i's with a scratchy pen and his tongue tucked firmly into the corner of his mouth to help him concentrate.

'The court is adjourned, Master Constable,' the magistrate said and Marley bellowed out the announcement, slamming his staff to the ground again.

In their ones and twos, they left the West Gate, muttering and whispering, eager to carry the news to their friends and neighbours who had not been there. It was definite. That Alice Snow, who was probably no better than she should be, had murdered her mistress for the inheritance. She would be put to the torture, no doubt, and then they'd hang her from the walls of the West Gate. Well, well, well . . . and her always so meek and mild. A witch, like her mistress, as likely as not.

'Master Constable.' Kit Marlowe blocked the man's path at the side door. 'A word in your ear, Father.'

John Marley frowned at him. 'I've nothing to say to you,' he said, 'shouting at Sir Roger like that. You owe that man . . .' But before he could finish the sentence, he felt himself forced backwards, his head banging on the West Gate's stonework and his son's dagger glinting at his throat. For too many years, Kit Marlowe had thought about this moment; how, one day, the surly bastard who was his father would push him too far. And now, that day had come. And he had been right in all his daydreaming; it felt good.

'Why didn't you tell me about the will?' he hissed, staring the man in the face. 'When I asked you last night whether you had found anything, you denied it.'

'Because it was none of your damned business!' Marley growled and pushed himself free. Instinctively, Marlowe jerked his blade back. If he hadn't, he would have cut his father's throat. 'Stay out of my house,' the constable yelled. 'When I get off duty today, I expect you to have gone.' And he stormed off to the cells.

For one moment, both terrible and tantalizing, Marlowe toyed with following him, finishing the job he had started and getting the girl out. Then he remembered his mother, his sisters and little Tom and what that would do to them. And he relented.

He had never been so glad to breathe in fresh air in his life. The West Gate had been airless and even though the sun was beating down on the cobblestones of St George's, the stench of corruption had gone. The crowds were still making their various ways home and Marlowe watched Sir Roger Manwood's carriage disappearing along the road to Haw. He felt suddenly sad, knowing that that was a road he would never take and a house he would never visit again. He had crossed the scourge of the night prowler. And no one did that lightly.

'Is that how they do things here in Kent?' someone asked him.

Marlowe turned to find a gentleman standing there, in stylish plumed hat, velvet Colleyweston and elegant Venetians. An impressive Spanish rapier swung at his hip. Marlowe had seen him in the court.

'Sir?' he said.

'I couldn't help noticing,' the gentleman said, 'that you took a dim view of the proceedings just now.'

'It seemed an injustice,' Marlowe said, 'in a place where justice should reign.'

'That's how it seemed to me, too,' the man said. 'You're Kit Marlowe, aren't you?'

'I am,' Marlowe said. 'And you are . . .?'

'Oh, you won't have heard of me.' The man extended his hand with a flourish of his cloak. 'My name is Robert Poley.'

Four

Katherine Marley was used to hard knocks, from the literal ones her husband so often doled out to the ones which left no marks except on her heart; the deaths of her precious babies and now the sight of her beloved son packing his things after only two nights under her roof. She sat on the window sill, her handkerchief pressed to her lips as he emptied the press she had prepared for him, showering the floor with the marigold and lavender flowers she had scented it with. He folded his shirts and hose and put them carefully in his bag. He wanted to shove everything in willy-nilly, to show that he was happy to shake the dust of John Marley's house from his boots for ever. But he loved his mother, and her tears had softened his resolve. So he packed with care, taking his time. And when the last fine sleeve had found its corner in his bag, he turned to her and opened his arms.

'Come, madam,' he said quietly. 'I will not be gone for ever. You can visit me in London, perhaps, one fine day. You can come to the theatre, to the Rose, to see one of my plays. I know Master Henslowe will give you the finest seat, the best in the house. Ned Alleyn will plant the finest words of love that I can write, right here in your ear –' he tickled her lightly – 'come, madam. Let me see a smile.'

She turned her tear-stained face up to his and did her very best. But the lips trembled and the tears spilled over afresh. 'I can't bear it, Kit,' she sobbed.

'But I am probably not even leaving Canterbury,' he protested. 'I have unfinished business here.'

'But where will you stay?' she said, wiping her eyes. That she had to stay with her husband was something she couldn't change. But to have Kit nearby, if only for a while – even John Marley let his wife go marketing and she could still see her ewe lamb until London reclaimed him.

Still holding her close and patting her gently, he said, 'I thought John Moore might take me in. He was my brother-in-law after all, if only for a while.'

'I doubt you will have much welcome there,' she said. 'He is married now to another woman and she doesn't like to be reminded of our Joan, poor dead girl. I should never have let her . . . but, your father would have it.'

'A school friend then. They can't all have moved out of Canterbury.'

'Some are still here . . . but, Kit, why not stay with Master Grijs, Wim Grijs?' There was something about her tone that made the playwright look down at her, startled.

'Wim, madam?' he asked, trying to keep the smile out of his voice.

'Wim and I were . . . could once have . . . But then your father came along and that was it. Your papa was charming once, Kit, and handsome. And now, it's too late. There are the children . . . *you* children, I should say, because you will be my babies till the day I die. So, here I am – but you'll find a welcome with Wim Grijs.'

'*Quod me nutrit me destruit,*' Marlowe muttered into her hair.

'Poetry, Kit?' she asked, the brightness back in her voice now she had had a long cuddle with her boy.

'No, madam,' he said. 'A motto which perhaps will do for you and me. "That which nourishes me, destroys me".'

She looked up and raised a hand to stroke his cheek. 'Enough of that, Christopher, my Kit, or my eyes will still be red when your father gets home; I mustn't cry any more.'

'Or you'll have something to cry about?' Some things you never forget.

'I have that already,' she said, pushing him away. 'Now, do you know how to get to St Thomas's Lane? Of course you do. Wim Grijs lives at the house at the end, the one with the rose pargeting. Now, be off with you.' She reached up and kissed him. 'Don't leave Canterbury without letting me know, will you?'

'No,' he said. 'I won't leave without letting you know, madam. Perhaps you will visit me at Wim's. If you know the way.'

She gave him a playful smack on his backside. 'You're not too big to be put over my knee, you know,' she said. And so it was a smiling Katherine Marley who saw her son out of her husband's house for the very last time.

The Night Watch had called the hour and a pale moon lent its rays to the gabled rooftops of

54

Canterbury. Kit Marlowe watched his father's men patrolling the walls, their halberds at the rest and the wisps of smoke curling back from the silhouettes of their pipes. The moon silvered the highlights of their faces, giving them a ghostly appearance; an imaginative watcher might almost take them for ghosts, back for a short while from beyond to warn of what was to come.

Marlowe padded his way along St George's Street where the shadows gathered under the tower of the church where, long years ago, in a freezing February, they had christened the son of John and Katherine Marley. They had named him for the carrier of Christ, but Marlowe had seen too many things done in the Lord's name of which he was ashamed and he carried no light for the Son of God on his shoulder now. He carried no lantern either because he knew these cobbled streets like the back of his hand, every twist and every turn. The smell of the tanneries reached him as he neared the gate, a low black space in the grey wall of chalk and flint. Wat Tyler and his rabble had passed this way many times in Marlowe's great-grandfather's day, chanting their songs of hate and striking down anyone who stood in the way of their rebellion. Unlettered men who had lived through the plague and the wars, they had been on their way to London to see the boy king who would make all well because he was the Lord's anointed.

'Who goes?' Marlowe stopped at the challenge and saw the halberd point gleaming in the half light.

'A friend of Her Majesty,' he said.

'What colour of friend?' the voice asked.

'Silver,' Marlowe answered. 'Would it could be gold but these are hard times.'

A guard emerged grinning from the gateway, catching Marlowe's coin as it spun in air. 'They are indeed, pilgrim,' he said. 'What's your business?'

'The serving girl, Alice Snow,' Marlowe said.

The guard sniggered, weighing the coin before slipping it into his purse. 'You could find a cheaper mort in the Star,' he said, 'and cheaper still at the Cross Keys. You turn left—'

'I know where the Cross Keys is,' Marlowe said, 'but I want Alice Snow.'

The guard shrugged. There was no accounting for taste. The girl in irons inside was too skinny for him. He liked them large – you only had to look at his wife. But that was precisely the point, he didn't have to look at his wife; which was why he always volunteered for night duty with the Watch, leaving the other onerous task to the lodger.

'I shall have to search you,' he said.

Marlowe's dagger was now gleaming in his hand in a second, the tip tantalizingly near the man's throat. 'No, you won't,' he said and, spinning the weapon in the air, held it hilt first to the guard.

'This way.'

He followed the man up the tight spiral twist of the stair, the stones slick with the passage of many shoulders leaning in for balance. He waited while the guard took a torch from the wall-bracket

56

and continued along a wooden landing before dropping down again into the oubliette.

'Mind your footing,' the guard said as Marlowe gripped both uprights of the ladder and stepped on to the rungs into darkness. He felt his feet land on soft straw and he waited until his eyes grew accustomed to the blackness. Slowly, the shape in the far corner became clear, coalescing from the shadows. Alice was sitting pressed into the niche, iron shackles on her wrists and with a long chain holding her fast to the slime-green wall.

He knelt beside her on the mouldy straw and pulled a crust of manchet bread and a piece of cheese from his doublet. He watched while the girl ate ravenously, glancing up occasionally to make sure the guard had gone.

'Thank you, sir,' she mumbled around a mouthful of food. 'It's good of you. How did you get past the guard?'

'My usual boyish charm,' he whispered to her, smiling. He looked closer at her face, brushing away a lock of her hair, grimy from the wall, salty from her tears. There were cuts and bruises and she had the beginnings of a black eye. 'Who did that to you, Alice?'

'No one, sir,' she said, touching the tender skin above her eye. 'I tripped and fell.' She looked down at her lie; she knew he wouldn't believe her, but she hoped he wouldn't make a fuss. It would only be the worse for her if he did. Then, she looked up at him again, fear darkening her eyes even more than a guard's fist had done. 'What's going to happen to me, sir?'

'That depends,' Marlowe said.

Alice had finished her smuggled supper now and understood. She knelt up as well as she could and began to haul up her skirts. Marlowe stopped her, smoothing the sodden cloth back into place. 'No,' he said. 'I want to talk to you.'

'What about, sir?' she whispered, eyes wide. Men had been talking to her, jabbing her with their fingers, slapping her about, for hours. She had nothing left to say.

'What was missing from your mistress' house?'

'Sir?'

Marlowe leaned in closer still. The walls of the West Gate had ears, he was sure of that. And if they didn't, the guard certainly did. 'Someone ransacked Mistress Benchkyne's house, Alice,' he said. 'Someone who was looking for something. It's my guess she heard him wandering the house. She surprised him and he killed her. Why was there no furniture in the house?'

Alice licked her lips. She wasn't good at secrets, especially when they were somebody else's. 'The mistress, sir, she wasn't right. Not right in the head.'

'In what way?' Marlowe asked.

'The Lord was coming, sir. The Day of Judgement.'

'A lot of people believe that, Alice,' Marlowe said.

'No, I don't mean at the End of Time, sir. I mean now. Well, All Hallows, to be exact.'

'The end of October?'

Alice nodded. 'She spoke of it often, sir. To me, that is. She said she must sell all her worldly

58

goods, against the day the Lord would call her to Him.'

'On All Hallows Day?'

Alice nodded.

'It seems the Lord's timing was a little off,' Marlowe muttered.

Alice looked horrified. 'That's a wicked thing to say, sir,' she said. 'You have been kind to me and I've no right to say it, but taking the Lord's name in vain . . . you risk damnation, sir.'

'Every day,' Marlowe chuckled, but there was no mirth in his voice. 'What did she mean in her will, Alice? "And the movables thereof, with the whole world"? What was she talking about?'

'I told you, sir,' Alice said. 'She wasn't quite right in the head.'

'Alice,' Marlowe growled, sounding at once like her father, her priest and every demon in Hell she'd ever read about. The girl's lip trembled. She was afraid and alone in this darkness, listening as she had been to the rustling of the rats and the whispering of the ghosts. How many of them, she wondered, had sat where she sat now, alone and afraid?

'One thing, sir,' she spoke so quietly he could hardly hear what she said. 'She kept it in her linen chest, the one with the false floor. She said it was mine.'

'What is it, Alice?' Marlowe asked.

'The world, sir, like the mistress said. It's silver with a single jewel. She said it was worth more than all the riches in the world yet known.' She looked up at him and tapped her temple, wincing as she touched a bruise. 'Not right in the head.'

'And where is this world now?' Marlowe wanted to know.

'In the well, sir, in the little graveyard by St Rhadegund's Hall.'

Marlowe knew it. 'You threw it down the well?' he frowned. The pit was deep and small and the boys of the King's School had believed it led right down to Hell.

'No, sir, I lodged it there . . . two days ago now. It's five stones from the top, on the west side, beneath the angel.'

'You took it two days ago?' Marlowe asked. 'Before your mistress died?'

'She gave it me, sir. Said it should be mine one day anyway, but that it was cursed and she wasn't sure I could cope with it. Then she said someone was coming to get it and could I hide it somewhere. And I was not to tell her where it was hid, no matter how she might ask me.'

'Who was coming to see her, Alice?'

'The Lord, sir,' she said. 'Who else?'

'Who indeed,' Marlowe said with a smile and got up to go.

'Oh, take care, sir.' The girl reached up to him as far as the chains would let her. 'I've only had that thing in my hand for moments at a time and since then the mistress has been cruelly murdered and I'm here facing the rope.'

He stretched out his hand and stroked her cheek. 'Not if I can help it,' he said and turned for the ladder, climbing up to the light. He knew his way along the landing without the help of a guttering torch and was soon back at the gate. The guard passed him his dagger.

60

'Did she give good service, sir?' the guard asked with a grin.

'The best,' Marlowe told him and flashed another coin.

'A *gold* friend of Her Majesty.' The guard was impressed. 'She *must* have been good for that.'

But before his fingers could reach it, Marlowe had snapped shut his hand. 'This,' he said, 'is to get the girl to an upper room. I know you have other cells, Master Keeper. Find one with a window. And clean straw. Two square meals a day. And take those damned chains off. Alice Snow's a danger to no one.'

'I couldn't do that, sir,' the guard wheedled. 'I've got my orders from Sir Roger Manwood himself.'

'And now –' Marlowe took the man's hand and pressed the gold coin into the palm – 'you've got your orders from me. Weigh it up, Master Keeper – all life's about balances, isn't it? Roger Manwood pays you every year what you hold in your hand now. And if you displease him, he'll sack you and flog you with the cat. Whereas I . . .' Marlowe beamed. 'I will slice off your pocky, your bollocks, your ears and your nose and I will feed them to the fishes in the Stour. Followed by the rest of you. So . . . are we clear about life's little balances?'

Marlowe would have preferred the night to be moonless, but beggars cannot be choosers and so he kept to the shadows. He still knew the streets of Canterbury like the back of his hand; no matter where a man travels, the world of his boyhood will always be the most real to him, where he goes in his dreams. So he had no difficulty in finding the church of St Mary, tucked in the corner of the city wall and the side wall of the dilapidated St Rhadegund's Hall. The Hall had been a wonder in its day but now the timbers were grey in the moonlight and the pargeting was hanging loose under the eaves. Marlowe stood sunk in blackest shadow and held his breath, listening beyond the night noises for signs that he might have been followed from the gaol. Somewhere out towards the river, a low cry rose to the mad crescendo that was a tawny owl on the hunt. No doubt some water rat or vole had met its end tonight and Marlowe let his ears settle in again to the quiet as the bird crossed the garden on silent wings, its prey dangling from its beak.

Keeping low to the ground, he ran across the open space to the wall of St Mary Northgate and waited again, listening hard. Still nothing. The well was over in the corner of the little overgrown plot. Not many graves had markers here. The priest of St Mary was known to be a kind man, gentle and sympathetic to the mothers of dead babies, of the friends of suicides and others not welcomed in other churches. So Marlowe knew, as he sprinted across to the well on soundless feet, that he trod on the unshriven if not the unloved.

The well was a perfect hiding place, that much was clear. The grass around it grew rank and high, new shoots of bindweed crawling up the rope blending with the old, dead tendrils of last year. Marlowe counted down from the edge the requisite number of stones and then carefully felt around the groove that time had worn in the pediment of the well. Dry mortar fell with a tiny splash into the distant water and spiders ran from his probing hand. Snail shells, grown delicate in the safety of the stones, crushed as he went by. Then, in a deeper cavity, cleaner and smoother than the rest, his fingers brushed something that was neither live nor crumbling. Taking a risk, he leaned over and used both hands to extricate it. Now was not the time for fumbling and losing Alice's world in the water below.

As soon as he had it in his hand, he dropped below the level of the crumbling well wall and held up his new-found treasure to the feeble light of the moon. What he held was a small circle, etched with some design he couldn't see in the semi-dark. Feeling with his fingertips, he could detect a stone of some kind, set off-centre. It was sharp; a cut gem, he guessed. It didn't seem like something to die for but he couldn't judge by moonlight. Slipping it into his doublet, he checked carefully left and right and slid out of the church-yard again, leaving the dead to their thoughts of mortality.

Joining the main roads again, he mended his pace and strode out like any Jack the lad around town. With his Colleyweston cloak and rich doublet, he looked every inch the rich reveller, out looking for what fun was to be had in Canterbury on a balmy June night. Women melted in and out of the shadows as he passed and although he gave each one a dazzling smile, he had no intention of carrying verisimilitude to the extent of actually hiring one. He wanted to get back to the light of his room to examine his prize. More than that, he wanted daylight and a strong lens – this was no ordinary gewgaw to have caused such mayhem. What had Alice said? 'It was worth more than all the riches in the world yet known.' He caught the swing of a skirt ahead of him and took a step out into the roadway. He did not mean to even pass the time of night with the drab who was in his path but as he passed her, he started.

'Annie?'

The woman stopped in her tracks. 'Kit,' she muttered. 'What are you doing here?'

'*I?*' He was amazed at her effrontery, he who had known her all his life and never yet known her obey any kind of social more. 'I'm out for a walk. A gentleman may do that, you know, even here in Canterbury. But you? What are *you* doing here?'

She sighed and stuck out one hip, her hand upon it in the old, truculent, childhood way. 'I don't have to tell you, Kit. You are not my master, not you or any man.'

'Father might have something to say,' her brother observed, without inflection.

'I dare say he might. But what he doesn't know won't hurt him. Will it, Kit? And as the two of you don't appear to be on speaking terms any longer . . . well –' she smiled at him blithely – 'I will be on my way.' She took a step forward, but he had her elbow in a vice-like grip before she could move so much as an ell.

'Where are you going, Anne?' he asked, the politeness just a veneer now.

'I'll tell you where I am not going, Kit,' she said, her chin thrust pugnaciously forward. 'I am not going to my grave, like Joan. Little more than a child herself and dead of birthing another. As I said to you, no man is my master.'

Marlowe picked up a pinch of her skirt between finger and thumb and rubbed it thoughtfully. 'Silk,' he said. 'Are you still telling me that no man is in this story? I have never known you wear silk before, no matter what the occasion.'

She pulled herself loose and stepped back from him, shaking her arm and he let her go. 'Kit,' she said, crooning, wheedling, 'if I want to meet a man, let us say in the old churchyard of St Mary Northgate for . . . some reason, then why should I not?'

'It's a nice enough night for spooning,' the playwright agreed. 'But why there?'

'It's quiet,' she said. 'It was his idea, if I am honest with you, Kit. I prefer somewhere a little more comfortable, given the choice. He's a stranger here in town and is in a lodging house.'

Her brother raised an eyebrow.

'No privacy in a lodging house. Although he was telling me this afternoon . . .'

'Where was this?' Marlowe didn't see his family much, but brotherly affection could still raise its head.

'Er . . . nowhere. I just . . . bumped into him and we seemed to have much in common. He was telling me, anyway, that his bedfellow is an uncouth lout who brings drabs back to the room most nights and . . .' In the faint light of the street, Marlowe could tell she blushed.

'Please, Annie,' he said, holding up a hand. 'Spare us both the detail. So, this man . . . Do we have a name, by the way?'

'Robin.'

'This Robin, he has decided to take *his* drab to a nice flat slab in St Mary's churchyard.' This was harsher than even Marlowe had intended but the words had flown unbidden into the warm June night.

She stepped back another step as if he had spat at her. Then, she flew at him, slapping and scratching like a mad thing. 'How dare you, Kit Marlowe?' she hissed. 'How dare you? I am not a drab. I am no man's whore. What I do and where I do it and who I do it with is my business.' Finally, her anger spent, she dropped her arms and stood there, her face, tear-streaked, turned up to his.

'Oh, Annie, Annie, my little Nan,' Marlowe murmured and drew her into his arms. 'I'm sorry. I didn't mean what I said.' This was a great admission for a man whose every word was gold. 'Go to your Robin and do what you must.' He could feel the loneliness and despair coming off her in waves. Living with John Marley was not something he could manage; why should he assume it was easy for her?

'I don't want to, now,' she muttered into his shoulder and he knew, as a brother will, that she was wiping her nose on his brocade.

'Yes, you do,' he said. 'A good cry and a fight with your brother always did put fire in your belly, Annie. Go now and use that fire on your Robin.' He pushed her gently away from him and wiped her eyes with the corner of his cloak. 'I hope he lives to tell the tale. Now, run, or you'll be late.'

'Kit . . .?'

'Yes?' He could see the old fire in her eye and wasn't sure what was coming next.

'I'm not a drab, am I?'

'No, my love,' he said, leaning in to kiss the tip of her nose. 'Not a drab.' And he pushed her gently in the direction of St Mary Northgate. 'Not a drab.'

And, turning once to wave, she walked fast, off to meet her Robin.

'Not a drab,' he muttered again. 'Just a Marley. May Heaven save you.' If there was such a place. And if it could.

The Queen's Spymaster was at Placentia that day, walking in the rose garden there. Francis Walsingham was not the man he had been. Years of guarding Her Majesty and Her Majesty's possessions had taken their toll. He had trouble sleeping and his left eye let him down in candle-light. No sooner had his Puritan God dispersed the Armada with His wind than the Spymaster had gone down with the ague and it had taken him weeks to recover. But all that was last year. What would the year of His Lord 1589 bring? What it had already brought him, and he held it in his hands now, was *The Principal Navigations*, a handy little volume glowingly inscribed to Walsingham by the younger Hakluyt. All right, the man had outrageously pinched the scholarship and hard work of almost everybody, but he meant well and was a staunch clergyman to boot. Many was the hour that Hakluyt had spent in Walsingham's study at Barn Elms, with tall tales of the sea and the strange peoples who inhabited the lands to the far west. He usually got so carried away that he slopped his wine in all directions, pointing and gesticulating until the Spymaster didn't know which river flowed where or even how many beans made five.

The volume was handsome, bound in calfskin and beautifully engraved with maps and pictures of the painted people Columbus had called Indians. But that was in the days of Walsingham's grandfather, when men believed the earth was flat. Dear old Francis Drake had stopped that nonsense of course. It took an Englishman to have the guts to sail around the world. Magellan? Never heard of him.

Walsingham could hear Hakluyt's words ringing in his ears: 'We must educate these heathens, Sir Francis, the smokers of tobacco and the growers of potatoes. They must see God.'

'Indeed they must, Richard,' Walsingham had agreed, but it was odd that the would-be explorer had lighted on the two crops that would make England a fortune. Hakluyt cared nothing for that, but Walsingham did. Besides, he had his own fortune to recoup. He had lost his shirt not long ago backing the voyage of that idiot Frobisher, looking for a passage through the Ice Sea. Mountains of gold he had promised everybody and he had brought back worthless tat, shining emptiness. No, Walsingham was ever ready to invest in the untold riches of this world, but he had learned his lesson. It would have to be tangible and it would have to have a real value.

'Um . . . about Francis Kett.' Walsingham heard a mumbled voice behind him. So engrossed had he become with Hakluyt's *Navigations* that he'd forgotten his long-suffering secretary, shuffling behind him with an inkwell, quill and parchment. The Secretary's secretary knew the great man's proclivity for giving instant dictation wherever he was, be it rose garden or the chase.

'Yes.' Walsingham slammed the book shut. 'Kett. Send a message to Christopher Marlowe. Try Norton Folgate first, failing that, the Rose. I want to know what he knows about our friend Kett.'

'Isn't he dead, sir?' The secretary saw no point in putting quill to parchment unless he had to. The contraption he carried in lieu of a desk was heavy and awkward.

'As a nit,' the Spymaster confirmed, 'but that's not the point. Humphrey, how long have you been in my employ?'

'Eight years, Sir Francis, give or take.' The secretary beamed. Was this it? The Day? He had well and truly served his apprenticeship. Was it time for the pay rise of which he had so often dreamed?

'Then you should know there is a world of difference between extinguishing a man and extinguishing an idea. Master Kett affirmed there is no God. Dangerous blasphemy, you'll agree?'

'Oh, I will, sir, I will.' Humphrey bobbed. His

financial hopes were dashed, but he still had his life and all his limbs. Best not say anything that might jeopardize either happy condition.

'Kett and Marlowe overlapped for a few months at Corpus Christi. It's likely that they met each other at some time. In any case, even if they didn't, Marlowe's exact contemporaries at Cambridge may have been infected by this madman's ideology. I need names, Humphrey. See to it.'

'Sir Francis,' he said with a nod and braced his back as he swung his contraption in front of him and began to write. 'Dearest Kit . . .'

'Dearest Kit . . .' Marlowe read the Spymaster's letter. When Walsingham began letters like that, there was something in the wind.

'Wim . . .' He found his host at his loom in the workshop along the Stour, where the ducks flapped noisily in the clattering reeds of summer and Great Harry clanged his voice over cobbled Canterbury. 'Wim, I've been called away.'

Wim Grijs popped his head out of the jacquard frame, wiping his hands as his apprentice hauled him upright. 'Back to London, Kit?' The man's face was running with sweat. For all the windows over the river were open, the sun was fierce again today and a weaver's workshop was not a place to keep cool. Dust flew in the slightest breeze and the floor was ankle-deep in tight-curled wool and tangled yarn. In the courtyard outside, snorting donkeys steamed as Grijs' people unharnessed their panniers and hauled the new yarn inside. With the cries of the men and the animals' braying and the hum and clatter of the looms, it was like some version of Hell.

'The Rose,' Marlowe lied, dexterous as ever, dusting the weaver down. 'I don't know what Henslowe would do without me. Promise me, Wim, that you'll never become a playwright.'

'What?' the weaver replied with a laugh. 'And give up all this? Apprentices who don't know their warp from their weft? Donkeys shitting all over my Dutch tiles? Trust me, Kit, life doesn't get any better.'

Marlowe laughed and gave the weaver one last pummel and was rewarded by a cloud of linty dust.

'You'll say goodbye to your mother.' Wim was suddenly serious. 'She worries about you.'

'Mothers will.' Marlowe nodded. He looked at the man. 'Wim,' he said, 'you've been kindness itself over the last few days and I thank you for that. Tell me . . .' He paused to find the right words. 'You and my mother . . .?'

The weaver's hand was in the air, as though for silence. 'Better to leave some stones unturned, Kit,' he said softly. 'Let's just say she was dear to me once. She is dear to me still.'

Marlowe nodded again, leaving the metaphorical stone where it was. 'Say my farewells for me, Wim. Tell her . . . well, you'll know what to tell her.'

'Yes,' the weaver said with a sad smile. 'Yes, I will.'

'Tell me about Francis Kett.' The Queen's Spymaster leaned back on the Turkish ottoman that had cost him a fortune. It lent an exotic touch to his otherwise drab little office at the Queen's palace of Whitehall.

For the most fleeting of moments, Marlowe was back in the Cambridge of his University days, when he was Secundus Convictus standing on Parker's Piece with his grey-gowned fellows listening to the ravings of a madman. That was nine years ago, but he could recall as though it were yesterday Kett's words echoing around the colleges. 'And what was Moses,' he heard the dead man say, 'if he was not a conjuror, a fairground charlatan performing cheap tricks to amuse the children? It took the man forty years to find the Promised Land that you and I could reach in as many days.'

'What's there to tell?' Marlowe asked, sampling the Spymaster's excellent Rhenish. 'I've heard he's dead.'

Walsingham leaned towards his projectioner, his smile twisted in the candlelight. 'And I've heard that Machiavel has flown over the Alps. What's that to do with the state of the nation?'

Marlowe paused, then laughed. 'Machiavel is dead,' he said. 'Silly boys called me that when I was a silly boy myself. My salad days, when I was green in judgement.'

'But that's precisely the point,' Walsingham said. 'It is the greenness of scholars that parasites like Kett prey upon. Who stood with you on Parker's Piece? Whose heads were turned by his atheist drivel?'

Marlowe looked hard at the man. Walsingham was his bread and butter. Certainly, the scribbling of plays barely kept a roof over his head, toast of London though he may be. But if the Spymaster was asking Marlowe to betray his friends . . . that was a step too far.

'I remember Dr Norgate was there,' he recalled with a smile. 'God rest his soul. Yes, I know what you're thinking; Master of Corpus Christi, an atheist? Whatever next?'

'Don't trifle with me, sir,' Walsingham snapped. 'Never forget, scribbler, you are eminently expendable, Muses' darling or no. There are plenty more where you came from; the line behind you stretches on to the crack of doom and beyond, believe you me.'

'Sir Francis.' Marlowe put down his goblet and leaned forward so that their noses almost touched. 'You are asking me to betray friends I loved.' He leaned back. 'Or faces I barely remember. Either way, you'll get no names from me. If I remember aright, we went along to laugh at Kett, not to listen to him. There were those of us who poked the wretches in the madhouse too – and paid a fortune to see the three-headed lady on Midsummer Common. Kett was nothing more than entertainment.'

For a moment, silence filled the rooms of the Queen's Spymaster, then Marlowe broke it. 'No, if it's a *real* atheist you're after, you should look to Giordano Bruno.'

'The priest of the sun?' Walsingham looked grave.

'The same. I heard him in Oxford a while back. He told us he had pierced the air and penetrated the sky, travelled among the stars and overpassed the margins of this world.'

'Gobbledegook, surely?' Walsingham frowned.

'Undoubtedly,' Marlowe replied with a smile. 'But not bad imagery. I might use it myself one day.'

The door crashed back and a large man stood there, his boots and gown travel-stained, his ruff awry and his face scarlet.

Walsingham was on his feet. 'Walter?' he frowned, taking in the man's ragged appearance. 'Whatever's the matter?'

'I've been robbed, Francis. Here, in the Queen's England.'

'Here?' Walsingham was puzzled.

'Well, not here exactly, no. At my place. St Albans.'

'Oh, dear.' Walsingham dithered a little before offering the traveller a chair and a draught of Rhenish.

The newcomer looked Marlowe up and down, then turned to Walsingham. 'Who's this?' he asked. Marlowe was unimpressed. Clearly St Albans was not the place to go if one required manners and good breeding. The man was an oaf.

'Oh, forgive me,' Walsingham said, extending a hand. 'Marlowe was just leaving.'

'Marlowe?' The stranger downed his wine in one and held it out to Walsingham for a refill. 'Aren't you the playwright fella?'

'I've had some modest success in that quarter.' Marlowe half-bowed. 'Master . . .?'

'This is Sir Walter Mildmay, Marlowe. You know – the Chancellor of the Exchequer.' Marlowe smiled and nodded. At least that explained the manners. Walsingham looked pained – things were not going too well today.

'Forgive me, my lord,' Marlowe said, reaching for his cloak from the back of his chair. 'As Sir Francis says, I was just going.'

'No, no,' Mildmay said as he stayed his arm. 'No, my dear fellow, I may have need of you.'

'You need a playwright, Sir Walter?' Marlowe asked, with a raised eyebrow.

'Playwright be damned.' Mildmay attacked his second goblet of Rhenish. 'They tell me you're good with that.' He pointed to the rapier at Marlowe's hip. 'I have reason to believe my life may be in danger. I had come to ask my brother-in-law here for help and he may, unwittingly, have provided that already.'

'Oh, yes.' Walsingham suddenly remembered their family link. 'How are my nephews and nieces?'

'Very well . . . well, you know, apart from the usual trouble children bring.'

Both men's eyes rolled Heavenwards.

Mildmay spun to the door, checked the passageway for loitering spies – although, of all the places in the Queen's England, Whitehall had more than anywhere else – closed the door and locked it.

'Marlowe,' he said as he sat down next to the man, 'can you keep a secret?'

Five

The Chancellor of the Exchequer's first account was so brusque and, at the same time, rambling that neither Walsingham nor Marlowe understood it. Mildmay was on his fourth goblet of Rhenish before any clarity emerged.

'The rest of the house was untouched,' the Chancellor said, trying to answer his companions' questions. 'I was away for the day hunting and the day became night – you know how these things drag on, Francis?' Walsingham did.

'My steward, Fenchurch, was there to greet me on my return. He was distraught. Kept babbling. I had to slap him to calm him down.'

'What had happened?' Marlowe could do without endless tales of the berating of servants.

'My strongroom had been . . . well, plundered isn't too strong a word. You know the house, Francis . . .'

'Yes, of course, but Marlowe doesn't,' Walsingham said. 'Tell him.'

'Pretty place, near Verulamium, the old Roman city.'

Marlowe knew.

'Conventional building. Like a letter "E". My strongroom is in the West Wing. If you have parchment and ink?'

Walsingham did and the Chancellor sketched a quick plan. To be honest, Marlowe could make neither head nor tail of it. 'Here's the duck pond,' Mildmay said, sensing the man's bewilderment. 'Stables.' He stabbed with a stubby finger on the drawing. 'This bit here –' he looked at it again with his head on one side – 'there or thereabouts at any rate, is Christina's parlour where she and her ladies sit endlessly stitching and bitching about ladies of the county who are not present. Jakes. Kennels. Here –' he tapped again on the vellum – 'is the strongroom. It's double locked and there's only one door.'

'Windows?' Marlowe asked.

'Again, only one. That had not been touched.'

'So the intruder got in by the door?' Walsingham checked.

'Must have,' Mildmay replied with a shrug. 'Damnedest piece of lock-picking I've ever seen.'

'You're sure it was picked?' Marlowe asked.

'Ah,' Mildmay said. 'I know what you're thinking. An inside job, as it were.'

'Who has keys to that door?' Walsingham wanted to know.

'Only Fenchurch and me,' Mildmay said. 'And that was my first thought too. Fenchurch has itchy fingers. But the man's been with me now these twenty years. Anyway, just to be sure I thrashed him within an inch of his life. He didn't crack. And I know Fenchurch. Not made of the sternest stuff, to be honest. If there was any cracking to do, he'd do it.'

'The room itself . . .' Marlowe brought the Chancellor back to the point.

'Contains two . . . no, three . . . chests. One

77

contains the Mildmay papers – deeds, covenants, *inspeximi*, that sort of thing.'

'And the others?' Marlowe asked.

Mildmay hesitated, his narrow eyes flitting between the faces of his listeners. 'Well . . .' he began.

'You insisted that Marlowe stay, Walter,' Walsingham said. 'No time for cold feet now, I fancy.'

'The others contain coin, gold and silver. Oh, nothing excessive. Just my personal fortune and the usual expenses involved with running a great office of state. You know, Francis . . .'

Walsingham knew and he sighed. He sighed because, of all Her Majesty's Privy Councillors, he alone had grown poor in her service. The others lined their pockets so heavily it was a wonder they could walk.

'How much was taken?' Marlowe asked.

Mildmay turned pale. This upstart had the impudence to enquire into his finances. *His*. The Chancellor of the Exchequer. He composed himself. 'The Great Seal was broken,' he said. 'Shattered as an act of pure vandalism.'

'I assume these chests were also locked, Walter?' Walsingham checked.

'Of course. Double, like the door. Again, no smashing of the mechanism. Just the lids left open.'

'How much was taken?' Marlowe asked again.

The silence hung heavy in that candlelit room in the heart of London, the river sliding silver under the fitful moon. 'Only a gewgaw,' Mildmay said.

'A gewgaw?' Walsingham repeated. 'What sort of gewgaw?'

'Er . . . may I draw it?'

He'd made a dog's breakfast of the plan of his house. Walsingham was happy to watch him do likewise with his stolen artefact. The pen slashed this way and that and then, peering closely, Mildmay placed a series of dots across the vellum. 'There,' he said, leaning back and quietly pleased with the results of his penmanship, 'something like that.'

'*Something* like that?' Marlowe said.

'No.' Mildmay took umbrage. '*Exactly* like that, come to think of it.'

Walsingham tilted the paper this way and that and finally Mildmay took it from him and turned it firmly the right way up. 'What is it?' Walsingham had to ask.

'Well, it's the world, of course.' Mildmay was a little hurt. 'Or at least, a map of it.'

'Er . . . I see.' Walsingham was lying. 'What's this bit?'

'Where?'

'This blob here. Some uncharted territory? *Terra Incognita*?'

'It's a diamond, Francis,' Mildmay explained. The people they were appointing as Spymasters these days!

'What is it made of, Sir Walter?' Marlowe asked.

'Silver,' the Chancellor told him.

'And its worth?'

'Damn you, sir!' Mildmay roared. As if this whole business were not disturbing enough, he was obliged to endure the financial probings of a man he knew to be a cobbler's son. It was intolerable.

'I merely ask,' Marlowe said softly, 'because it's odd that the charmer should have overlooked your other valuables and merely taken this.'

'Charmer, Marlowe?' Mildmay bridled. 'A curiously polite term for a blackguard of the deepest hue.'

'Forgive me, Sir Walter,' Marlowe said with a smile. 'In the theatrical world I inhabit, a charmer is a man who picks locks. Yours seems to be something of an expert.'

'Marlowe's point is well made, Walter,' Walsingham said. 'A bit of silver, a small stone. It's upsetting, of course, a man of your sensibilities . . . It must seem that your world is turned upside down.'

'It will be if Drake finds out,' Mildmay muttered.

'Drake?' Walsingham blinked. 'I don't follow.'

Mildmay checked the room again to make sure that Walsingham's rats didn't work for the hero of the Armada. 'Drake gave me this,' the Chancellor said in a half whisper. 'He said it was precious. More precious, he said, than all the perfumes of Arabia.'

Marlowe smiled. 'I hadn't put Drake down for a poet.'

'Do you know him?'

'I know *of* him,' the playwright said.

'Yes,' Mildmay said. 'And if you're wise, you'll keep the distance that that implies. The man is a stone cold killer.'

'Oh, come now, Walter,' Walsingham said with a chuckle. 'Drake can be difficult, I know . . .'

'Difficult? He threatened to fight Frobisher in his shirt. I personally saw him hang sailors at Plymouth. And he murdered poor old Doughty on a whim.'

'That was a case of mutiny, Walter,' Walsingham reminded him. 'Drake was within his rights. Doughty challenged his leadership during the circumnavigation.'

'Yes, well, we only have Drake's word on that, don't we? And as to what he does to Spaniards . . .'

'That *is* what we pay him for, Walter,' Walsingham reminded him.

'Where is he now?' the Chancellor wanted to know.

'Somewhere off Dungeness, I heard,' Walsingham said. 'Although once a captain is at sea, even my intelligencers can't track him.'

'Precisely,' Mildmay said. 'For all you know, he could be at St Albans as we speak. Outside that very door, even.' And the Chancellor of the Exchequer grew paler still.

'Look. Walter.' Walsingham laid a reassuring hand on the man's shoulder. 'Why don't you rest here for a while? It's a long ride from Hertfordshire and you're clearly overwrought. I'll have a bath drawn for you . . .'

'Don't be ludicrous, Francis. The Queen may have one of those a year, but I don't intend to. There are standards, you know. Besides, I have a bed in my own apartments along the river. I can lock myself in there and hope for the best.'

He stood up, straightening his gown and

adjusting his ruff. 'Marlowe. You will attend on me tomorrow. Nine of the clock sharp.'

'Very good, Sir Walter.' Marlowe stood up with him.

'I'll bid you good night, then.' And he bowed curtly before leaving, checking that the passageway was clear before he did so.

'You'll keep all this under your hat, of course,' Walsingham said. 'Don't worry. I wouldn't inflict Walter on you. I'll find a sworder from somewhere to watch his back.'

'Is he right?' Marlowe asked. 'About Drake, I mean.'

'Well . . .' The Spymaster thought for a moment. 'He *does* have a certain look about him. Something in the eyes. Actually, I was less than honest a moment ago. Drake is not off Dungeness – at least, he'd better not be – as he's leading an expedition against Lisbon; well, the Portuguese have had it coming for some time. He's going to put Don Antonio on the throne. Yes, I know the man has less right to it than you do, but what's a little genealogical fudging in foreign affairs. But no, my dear brother-in-law, as you may have gathered, is rather excitable. Lets things get out of proportion. Goes with trying to balance the nation's books, I suppose.'

'And he doesn't know what Drake is really up to?'

'Nobody knows what Drake is *really* up to,' Walsingham said with a scowl. 'But no, Walter is not privy to such information, Privy Councillor or no Privy Councillor.'

Marlowe smiled. He knew more than the

Chancellor of the Exchequer did. He'd always known that that was likely to be true, Sir Walter Mildmay not being noted for his brain, but it was nice to have it confirmed. 'Still,' he said. 'It is a coincidence, isn't it?'

'What is?'

The poet-projectioner slid his hand into his purse and produced the silver disc that had been Alice Snow's and Jane Benchkyne's. 'How similar Sir Walter's awful drawing is to this?'

Walsingham's jaw dropped a little and he took the thing in his hand. It was heavy and gleamed in the candlelight, a diamond sparkling from its centre. He looked at Mildmay's sketch, then at the globe. 'Where did you get this?' he asked Marlowe. 'Not, please God, from Francis Drake.'

'From an angel in a well,' the poet said with a smile. He caught Walsingham's look. 'It's a long story,' he added and accepted another goblet of the Spymaster's excellent Rhenish.

'But I'm still not sure how Jane Benchkyne came by this trifle.' Walsingham had abandoned going to bed tonight. The air was sultry anyway and he found it hard to sleep these nights.

'No more am I,' Marlowe said, 'but it must have meant a lot to her. That much was clear from her will – "All the world" that she bequeathed to her maidservant. And that brings me to another problem, Sir Francis. Alice Snow is languishing in the condemned cell in Canterbury's West Gate – and neither my father nor Sir Roger Manwood is a particularly gentle gaoler.'

83

'What do you suggest?'

'The girl is as pure as her surname,' Marlowe told him. 'Perhaps a word from you?'

Walsingham smiled. If there was one thing he enjoyed, it was kicking the arse of overmighty magistrates. 'Won't that make things awkward, between you and your father, I mean?'

'Nothing could make *that* more awkward,' Marlowe assured him bitterly.

'Very well, then,' he said. 'Consider it done. But in exchange . . .' Walsingham was still looking at the silver globe. 'You say this is identical to the one stolen from my brother-in-law?'

'Not exactly, no.' Marlowe looked at the sketch again. 'But, with all due respect to Sir Walter's artistry, which we must accept is negligible, it is very difficult to tell. The diamond is in a different place.'

Walsingham strained his eyes in the candlelight. 'So it is,' he said.

'"In exchange"?' Marlowe was waiting for the other boot to drop.

'You see this.' He pointed with a quill to a point on the silver map. 'What does it say?'

'It looks like MM.' Marlowe squinted at it, turning it this way and that in the light. 'Two thousand?'

'No.' Walsingham shook his head. 'You are trying to be too clever by half. MM is the man who made this map. Michael Mercator, if I don't miss my guess. You'll find him near the sign of the Fleece in Paternoster Row.'

'And what's this?' It was Marlowe's turn to ask the questions.

'Looks like a "J",' Walsingham muttered. 'Inside a star.'

'And what does that mean?' Marlowe asked.

'When you find Michael Mercator you can ask him.'

It was always easy to find Tom Sledd. A man with ears and a nose all in working order would soon track him down inside the Rose by listening for the sound of sawing – or cursing – or sniffing out the pungent scent of glue which carried more than a slight whiff of the cow's foot from which it was made. Outside the Rose, he could blend with all other men, but in here, in his element, he *was* the theatre. The important bit, the bit that kept the audiences coming back time and again. Playwrights may come, playwrights may go, but Tom Sledd was happy in the knowledge that stage managers would go on for ever. On this particular day, he was standing on the stage, trying to look up into the flies without getting a faceful of paint.

He flinched slightly as he heard voices approaching from stage right.

'Where in Hell is he . . .? Oh, Tom, there you are. Have you seen that idiot Shaxsper anywhere today?'

Philip Henslowe would probably also have been able to blend with all other men, had his face not carried a purple hue in all weathers and moods. The man always looked as if he might explode and now was no exception. Taking his customary step backwards, just in case today was the day the explosion would finally happen, the stage manager shook his head.

'*Someone* must know where he is. He's supposed to be rewriting that final scene. It just doesn't work. Henry the Bloody Sixth! What was I thinking, letting him have his head in the first place?' He was remembering every ghastly, reckless moment and repeated Shaxsper's pleading, Warwickshire accent and all. '"I think I'm ready, Master Henslowe." *Master* Henslowe; what a crawler! "Marlowe's all very well, but I have a few ideas of my own." Why, oh why, did I say yes?' He looked up, shielding his eyes against the light. 'You! You, up there! Have you seen Shaxsper at all?'

The muffled answer was not very helpful but the gist appeared to be that the man with the paint pot wouldn't know Shaxsper if he bit him on the leg.

'You must know him,' Henslowe said, exasperation oozing from every pore. 'About so high . . .' And he sketched a wide arc that meant the playwright from Stratford could be a dwarf or a giant. 'Big head . . .'

Tom Sledd shuffled his feet. 'He may be a bit pleased with himself . . .' he muttered, 'but that's a bit unnecessary, Master Henslowe.'

Henslowe spun to face his stage manager. 'What?' he barked. Then, he realized the misunderstanding. 'No, no, I mean, he actually has a big head.' Again, he sketched the feature in the air and there was no arguing with that. Shaxsper really did have an unusually big head, especially now he was parting company with his hair.

There was a louder answer from above, accompanied by a large gob of white paint which missed Henslowe by the merest whisker.

86

'Sorry!'

'Do that again,' Henslowe yelled, 'and you'll be looking for other employment. Now, have you seen Shaxsper or not?'

He strained upwards to try and hear the answer but with no success.

'Come down, you cokes!' he yelled. 'And mind that paint.'

Above the two men, the ladder creaked and, with much panting and muttering, with joints whose clicking almost drowned out the ladder's complaints, the scene painter came down to stage level.

Tom Sledd could only sigh. There were never enough hours in the day at the best of times, without Henslowe ordering his men around to further order. The job at hand wasn't to do with scenery per se, he would admit, but the ceiling certainly needed a coat of paint. In the last scenes the previous night, so much whitewash had fallen on the players they looked as though they had been caught in a snow-storm. Bad enough when the snow actually did come in, but this was the hottest week of the year so far, so a coat of paint was overdue.

'Now, then,' Henslowe snapped. 'Have you seen Shaxsper?'

'About so high.' The painter waved an arm and sent a random spray of paint across Sledd's chest from his paintbrush. 'Sorry, Master Sledd. Big head.' He held his brushless hand above his own head to show the extent of Shaxsper's undoubt-edly stupendous brow.

'That's him,' Henslowe said, almost hopping from foot to foot in frustration.

'No, Master Henslowe, Master Sledd. I haven't seen him today.'

'And that's *it*?' Henslowe roared. 'That's *it*! You came all the way down that ladder, sprayed Master Sledd with paint, for *that*?'

The man was dumbstruck. 'You told me to come down,' he said, mildly. 'I said up there I hadn't seen him.'

Henslowe was reduced to incoherent howls and Sledd thought it was probably time to step in.

'Back you go, Dick,' he said kindly, patting the man on the arm. 'No harm done.' Except perhaps to his second best doublet, but it would wash. 'Master Henslowe is a little . . .'

'Mad?' Dick said, edging away towards his ladder. He was dubious about climbing it with this crazy man at the bottom but he trusted Tom Sledd and so scrambled back aloft and was soon spreading the limewash over the ceiling. He could hear Henslowe below, still ranting and thought a few harsh thoughts of his own. These men, the ones with the money, they didn't know what it was like to live from hand to mouth, never knowing where the next crust was coming from. He gave a little chuckle. He, Dick the Painter, was not short of an angel or two either. And, his day was coming. Oh, yes. And then the paint would fly.

A large globule of limewash plummeted to the stage.

'Oy!'

'Sorry, Master Henslowe.' Oh, yes, his day was coming all right.

* * *

Nicholas Faunt took the old pilgrim's way out of London, skirting the Forest of Blee and taking his repast at God's House in Ospringe. Then, as the sun burned across this shoulders and on to his velvet-covered head, he clattered under the West Gate in Canterbury and slid out of the saddle.

'Who goes?' the guard challenged him, emerging from the cool shadow of the tower wall.

'A friend of Her Majesty,' Faunt said.

'What colour friend?' the man asked, looking him up and down. Faunt rummaged in his satchel and whipped free a blade that nicked the man's nostrils. 'Silver in a certain light,' Faunt said. 'Blood red in another.'

The guard staggered backwards, howling and bleeding.

'I am on the Queen's business, lickspittle. Take me to Alice Snow.'

Faced with officialdom on this level and faced with that officialdom's dagger-point, the guard could not move fast enough. He slid bolts, hauled open doors, moved ladders and dripped blood all the way. Even so, he tipped the wink to a colleague pouring water over his head in an attempt to keep cool and the colleague hurried away, dripping wet, to the constable's house by the Bull Stake.

Alice Snow leapt to her feet at Faunt's entrance. She was a frail-looking little thing, her eyes red with crying and there were the marks of iron fetters around her wrists and ankles.

'Leave us,' Faunt ordered and the guard was only too happy to comply. Marlowe's money and

Marlowe's threats had bought Alice an upper room, with daylight through a solitary window high in the wall. Even so, there was no furniture and the straw on the floor was wet and soiled in one corner.

'Are you him, sir?' the girl barely breathed. 'My executioner?'

Faunt smiled. He took her hand. 'I have been in my time, mistress,' he said, 'and may well be again. But yours? No. Master Marlowe sent me.'

'Master Marlowe?' Alice's eyes lit up, brimming with tears as they were. 'Is he coming back for me?'

'No need, Alice,' Faunt said. 'I am to take you to him.'

'You're going nowhere,' a gruff voice snarled in the doorway.

'Who are you?' Faunt asked.

'John Marley, constable of Canterbury. You?'

'Nicholas Faunt, Queen's messenger.' He took the girl by the arm and led her towards the door, but Marley still blocked it. 'That means,' Faunt whispered in his ear, 'that I outrank you so far that it's like a tree top to shit. So, if you'd be so kind as to stand aside? So kind and so sensible?'

'Show me your papers,' Marley grunted.

This time, Faunt produced nothing but parchment from his wallet. 'Er . . . you *can* read?' Faunt checked.

Marley snatched the document. He saw the Queen's cypher and Walsingham's and he stood aside. 'Sir Roger Manwood shall hear of this,' he snarled into Faunt's right ear.

'I have no doubt of it,' Faunt said and brushed

past. At the top of the stairs, he turned. 'Just a moment,' he said cheerily. 'You're Kit Marlowe's father, aren't you?'

'What if I am?' Marley asked, never keen to be reminded of the fact.

'I've got a little message for you, from Kit.'

Nobody but Nicholas Faunt was ready for what came next. The projectioner's knee jerked up into the constable's crotch and as he doubled up, Faunt's fist slammed down on his head and he lay, poleaxed, on the cold stone.

'Kit says "Hello". Tell Sir Roger,' Faunt said to the quivering guard, 'he need not fear treatment as rough and vulgar as this. Loss of his title, lands and privileges are far more likely. Good afternoon, lickspittle.'

And, tucking Alice Snow's hand into the crook of his arm as though she were the most gracious of ladies, Nicholas Faunt swept out.

Hog Lane ran like a dog's leg north from Bishopsgate between the greens of Moorfields and Spitalfields, the windmills' sails still in the windless air of summer and the grass a gleaming white with the spread of the tenter sheets. Dawn was gilding the gateway as Marlowe walked his horse beneath its dark arch, the portcullis rusted open over his head. For a moment, he looked at the two heads rotting on the spikes above the parapet and wondered who they were. Both men were bearded, but their skin was the colour of boiled leather now and their eyes and lips had gone, tasty morsels for the crows. Whoever they were when they were alive, they must have looked funny at Francis Walsingham or perhaps Lord Burghley and that was never a wise thing to do.

The poet-projectioner patted his horse's neck and let the groom take him on to the rest and comfort of his stall. Marlowe had avoided the river as he would the plague. The tide was low this early in the morning and all along the Queen's wharves the stench was indescribable. Filthy urchins, naked from the waist down, waded up to their knees in the brown ooze, looking for scraps of anything that might keep them alive, foraging shoulder deep with questing fingers. Instead, he had cut through the Cheap, already bustling with the setting up of stalls and the cries of the street hawkers. He had paused to buy some bread and cheese and slung half a hogshead of ale over his saddle. Gallants dressed like this rarely ventured along the Cheap so early in the morning, but the stallers knew Kit Marlowe. For all his fine clothes, his Greek and his Latin, he was one of them. From Canterbury, men said, and his father was a cobbler. Nothing wrong with that.

He was at the bottom of the outer steps in the courtyard along Hog Lane as she reached the top. For a woman who had spent the night with Tom Watson, she looked surprisingly fresh and elegant, her hood pulled forward over her face so that any unduly nosy passer-by would not recognize her.

''Morning, Eliza.' Marlowe sketched a bow, difficult with a barrel of ale on one shoulder.

'Hello, Kit,' she replied with a smile.

'How is the Studiosus this morning?'

'In fine voice last night,' she said. 'This morning . . . well, all I got was a grunt. Does that give you a clue?'

Marlowe laughed. He watched her cloak sweep the flagstones dappled by the morning sun and heard her talking to the manservant Watson paid to take her home. It was high time, he thought, as he climbed the steps, that Thomas Watson, Studiosus et Generosus, made an honest woman of that girl. And how long her father would continue to believe that nonsense of her visiting the sick three nights a week was anybody's guess. Then, he suddenly remembered Watson's wife and realized the problem.

He kicked the door open and dropped the keg loudly on the table. 'Is there a poet-musician in the house?' he asked loudly.

There was a groan from the far corner.

'May I take that as a "yes", Master Watson?'

'Go to Hell, Marlowe,' a voice croaked.

'I've been there,' the projectioner said. 'It isn't all it's cracked up to be, take it from one who knows.' He hauled back the coverlet and Watson buried his head under the pillow. 'Hair of the dog, Tom?'

Watson emerged like Lazarus from his cave. He wasn't sure which was the more painful – the morning's sun streaming in through the window or Marlowe's hideous bonhomie. 'What have you got?' he asked, trying to sit up.

Marlowe smiled. 'A vast amount of talent. More good looks than any man has a right to own. And a coy modesty that forbids me to mention either.

But, more relevant, I suspect, to your question, a quantity of Goodman's ale.'

Watson threw the pillow at him. 'Just a threat, then,' he said and watched Marlowe draw the beer. 'Do I owe you any rent, Kit?' he asked.

'We're square up to June,' Marlowe told him, passing him the beaker. 'June of *last* year, that is.'

'What did Sir Francis want?'

Witty Tom Watson didn't miss a trick. He had known Walsingham for longer than Marlowe, having met him in Paris not that long after the massacre there. He was a lute-player of skill, a poet after Marlowe's own heart and an expert in the Roman law. His plays? Well, you couldn't have everything.

'He wants me to find the man who made this.' Marlowe threw him the little globe.

Watson rubbed his eyes and tried to focus. The ale tasted sour on his tongue, but then his tongue felt like a barber's strop. 'That's pretty,' he said, turning it over in his palm. 'What is it?'

Marlowe paused slightly before he sat down. 'It's a map, Tom,' he said as though to the village idiot.

'Yes, yes.' Watson's head was throbbing so hard he felt sure that Marlowe could hear it too. 'But what does it show?'

'Apparently, the voyages of Francis Drake.'

'Ah, yes.' Watson turned the little jewel to the light and tried to look as if he knew what he was talking about. 'I see that now. When did he get back? Eighty, was it?'

Marlowe nodded. 'I was at Corpus Christi then,'

he said. 'It set the cat among the pigeons with some of the older fellows; they didn't like the fact that a man could gad about the world like that and not get eaten by anthropophagi.'

Watson chuckled. 'I was working on the Sophocles then,' he remembered, wistfully. 'And . . . Betsy, I think it was. Yes, that's right. Betsy.' He smiled into the middle distance for a moment, then gave himself a shake and returned to the here and now. 'I did take time to read the reports, though. These events don't come into every life-time, after all. A man sailing around the whole world. Marvellous! But what's the significance of this?'

'I don't know,' Marlowe said. 'Not until I have talked to Michael Mercator, at any rate.'

'Who's he?'

'He's a map-maker, Tom,' Marlowe patronized. 'Look, write a madrigal or whatever it is you do. I'm going to get some breakfast. Join me? Soft quail's eggs, thick butter, goat's milk?'

But Tom Watson's head was back under the pillow again and he sounded quite muffled when he said, 'Go to Hell, Kit Marlowe.'

Six

Michael Mercator welcomed Marlowe to his rooms at the sign of the Fleece, near Paul's churchyard, but cautiously. As a visitor to London he had, of course, seen all the sights, from the heads on the Bishopsgate parapet to the menagerie at the Tower. For much of the time he had been scowled at and jostled by the apprentices of London, who viewed any foreign visitor with ill-disguised contempt. And he had, naturally, been to the theatre called the Curtain. Sadly, he had not been to the Rose and had no idea who his visitor was – for once, Marlowe could enjoy some moments of anonymity, rare at this level of society, in this city. Because Michael Mercator was a personage, of a sort. His home was along the Rhine, so he felt at home in the watery city where the Thames cut such a swathe through the teeming thousands that filled the streets. But he still felt like a stranger, wiping the spittle off his gown, though his English was easily as good as any that could be heard anywhere in London. He was the son and grandson of map-makers who had, quite literally in his grandfather's case, changed the world. But he wondered if, these days, there were many more lands to discover. He had come to England to curry favour with the great sailors who lived along her shores – the fact that they were self-serving men who in any other land would have been hunted down as pirates was something he was beginning to realize as time went on. Sir Francis Drake, to take the greatest example, gave him the shivers every time he thought of him. Not for nothing did the Spaniards call him El Dracque, the Dragon. And now, here was this popinjay in velvet and brocade who must surely be more than he seemed, extending his hand and smiling. He was surely the smiler with the knife.

'Master Mercator,' Marlowe said. 'I'm not sure why, but I imagined you would be older.'

'You are thinking of my grandfather, perhaps. Or my father even. They are still at home; they travel little these days, not even by the pen.' He looked like a man who had been taken for his grandfather or father once too often. 'My maps are more for the people than for those who can afford to pay for whole voyages to be undertaken in their name. I believe that the whole world should be able to know what . . . what the whole world looks like.'

'A laudable aim,' Marlowe agreed. The rooms that Mercator was living and working in were very pleasant, with large windows over Ludgate Hill, so that the bustle of London passed by in full array. The trestle was loaded with parchment and inks; pens and charcoal sticks were regimented in racks to one side. There was no sign, however, of anything to do with metalworking of any sort. Perhaps he had come to the wrong place. After all, MM was not an unusual combination of initials. They were those of Marlowe's own sister, to name but one.

'At the moment,' Mercator went on, 'my maps are still out of the reach of the man in the street. But I am working on processes – still very secret, I am afraid, Master Marlowe, by which I can create maps in almost any medium. Parchment. Paper. Silver. Gold—'

'It is your silver maps I am here about,' Marlowe cut in. As a theatre man these days, he knew someone who liked the sound of their own voice when he met one.

Mercator looked shifty and slid the papers on his trestle together into an untidy heap, turning them over so that only the charcoal-stained back page was uppermost. 'Oh?' As an attempt to sound unconcerned, it was a very dismal failure.

'Yes.' Marlowe rummaged in the breast of his jerkin. 'I have one here.' And he brought out the little chamois pouch he had taken to using to protect the globe.

Mercator's eyes popped. 'Where did you get that?' he asked, breathlessly.

'I am afraid I can't tell you that,' Marlowe said. 'I was going to ask you if this was your work, but I see from your face that it is. Can you tell me something about it? Why it was made? When and for whom?'

Mercator had control of himself now and prefaced his next remark with a small cough and a condescending smile. 'Oh, you Englishmen! You always think you can guess what a person is thinking. I did *not* say that this was my work. I was merely . . . overcome with its beauty. I asked where you got it so that, well, so that I too could purchase one.' He smiled again and twisted round to look out of the window, as if the whole conversation was of no importance.

Marlowe tossed the globe up and down in his hand a few times, as though playing Jacks. 'It's not really that beautiful,' he said. 'In fact –' he peered at it, leaning on Mercator's shoulder to reach the light – 'it's a bit of a rough little devil. Just here, look . . .'

Mercator spun round. 'How dare you criticize my . . . oh ho, Master Marlowe,' he said, shaking his finger. 'I see what you are at. You tricked me and cleverly too. Yes, this is my design. Not my workmanship, though. I would love to be able to work in silver like this, but –' he spread his hands ruefully – 'these are not artisan's fingers.' He looked at Marlowe, challenge in every line of his face.

'I didn't mean to trap you, Master Mercator,' Marlowe said, putting the globe back into the confines of his jerkin. 'But it is important that I know who owned this globe and why it was made.'

'It was made to a commission,' Mercator said. 'I can say no more.'

'Francis Drake's commission?' Marlowe asked, blandly.

Mercator stepped back and looked mutinous. 'If you know that, why are you here asking me? The next thing we know, it will be . . . what are they called? Skeffington's Gyves? The Sister of the Duke of Exeter?'

'Daughter.'

'I beg your pardon?'

'Daughter. The Duke of Exeter's Daughter.

99

But I don't think it will come to torture machines.'

Mercator came close to Marlowe, so close that the playwright could feel the map-maker's breath hot on his face. 'That, Master Marlowe, is what they all say. Your Queen's England is not a place for the faint-hearted. Papists go in fear of their lives. But I, for myself, will say no more, as a God-fearing Protestant. The man who made the globe, and I do not say for who, remember that, is Joshua the Silversmith. You will find him in the Vintry. Now, Master Marlowe, I must ask you to leave. I have work to do.'

'Well, thank you, Master Mercator,' Marlowe said, backing away. 'I will certainly visit . . . Joshua, you say?'

'In the Vintry, yes.'

'I'll wish you good day, then.' Mercator seemed to have no more to add to the conversation, so Marlowe let himself out, down the vertiginous stairs to the street. He paused beneath the over-hanging window for a moment, weighing up the best way to go, then turned left. Cutting across St Paul's churchyard would cut a few moments off the journey and suddenly, moments seemed to matter.

Up in his window, Mercator watched him go. Then he called for his manservant. 'Johannes! Johannes! Pack our things. We're leaving.'

Joshua's quarters were not as palatial as Mercator's and here the smell was not of paper and ink but the clean, sharp smell of metal, solder and char-coal. A fierce fire could be seen out in the yard, adding to the heat of the day and a downtrodden-looking lad was watching a crucible balanced on a tripod over the flames. He wore huge leather gauntlets which reached to well above his elbows and a mask over his face, also leather, with a mica window let into it. He seemed lost in his gloomy, underwater world as he peered out through the dim lens and Marlowe decided not to disturb him. There was something about his grim grasp on the crucible's handle that spoke of a man on his last chance to get it right; it wouldn't be fair to go near. Marlowe looked around for someone else who may be able to help him in his search for the jeweller who had made Mercator's design live in metal and precious stone.

The light from the bright doorway into the yard and the red-hot heart of the fire had dulled Marlowe's eyes so he jumped when a voice suddenly asked, 'Can I help you, sir?'

He looked around and finally made out, over in a corner by a window, a hunched form. The face was turned to him, an interrogatory eyebrow lifted above a dark and glittering eye. 'I apologize,' he said, bowing. 'I didn't see you there.'

'Few do,' the man said with a laugh. 'Over here in my quiet corner, I get more work done than I would on the counter by the door. But, as I said a moment ago, can I help you?'

'I'm looking for a man named Joshua,' Marlowe said.

'May I ask what you want with Joshua?' the man said, twirling round on his chair and straightening up with a crack of bone.

101

'Only if you are Joshua,' Marlowe said. 'Then, you may ask away. But if you are not he, then perhaps we could stop playing games and you could either fetch him or tell me where I might find him.'

'Testy, aren't we?' the man said, sliding off the stool. He was about sixty years old, perhaps a touch more, but he wore his years well. He had a slight stoop, but without it he would have been Marlowe's height, but without his breadth of shoulder. His hair was worn long, tucked behind his ears to keep it away from his work. He wore a pair of highly magnifying lenses in a wire frame pushed up for now on to his forehead. His nose jutted before him like a beak and the mark of the lens frame was deeply incised on either side of it. He looked Marlowe up and down and appeared to come to a decision. 'I am Joshua,' he admitted.

Marlowe wanted to yell at the man. But he wasn't to know that he had not had an easy day so far, so he pasted on a smile and bowed again, this time rather deeper. 'So, I have found you at last,' he said. 'But before I get too fulsome, tell me, did you make this?' He held out the small flat globe to him on the palm of his hand.

The jeweller stepped forward to see more clearly. Closer to, Marlowe could see that his calling had taken its toll. His eyes were red and sore and he was clearly very short-sighted indeed. He snatched his hand away as the man reached out to take the globe. He still didn't know what it was, but that men were willing to kill for it was clear enough.

102

'Look, but don't touch for the moment, Master Joshua, if you don't mind. This little jewel has a chequered history.'

The jeweller stepped back and straightened his back again, with an even more resounding fusillade of clicks. Marlowe looked startled.

'Forgive my old bones, Master . . .'

'Marlowe,' the playwright muttered.

'Marlowe. I have enjoyed your plays at the Rose.' He looked closer, peering through short-sighted eyes. 'If you are indeed he.' He cocked his head, like an inquisitive bird and with his beaked nose, the resemblance brought a smile to Marlowe's lips, against his better judgement.

'I am he,' he said. 'Although the current production is not one of mine.'

Joshua tossed his head and dismissed it. 'Henry the Sixth. Shaxsper, isn't it? I was not impressed by his footling rubbish. Though, sometimes . . . sometimes there is a spark there. But still, the jewel. Why chequered?'

Marlowe wasn't used to other people being able to revisit several sentences back in the conversation. He had thought it a skill confined to playwrights and projectioners. 'It has . . .' To say 'caused a death' sounded too melodramatic. 'It belonged to a woman, now dead.'

'A woman?' The old jeweller seemed surprised.

'The woman surprises you, but not the dead?' This didn't seem to be the right way round, somehow.

The man chuckled and paused. In the silence, the hiss of the fire sounded louder than before and the man's head came up. 'Ithamore! Ithamore!'

103

'Yes, Master Joshua?' The voice was muffled by the helmet, but its plaintive note was not to be missed.

'You've got the fire too hot. Cool it down. Is the silver ready to pour?'

'Not yet, Master Joshua.' The boy sounded terrified and puzzled all at once.

Joshua sighed and shook his head. 'Poor lad. He will never make a silversmith if he lives to be a hundred.'

'Ithamore?' Marlowe said. 'I don't believe I've heard that name before.'

'No, nor those of his brothers and sisters, who are legion, believe me. His mother is . . . too friendly for her own good. Unfortunately, she gives away for nothing that which most women of sense barter for money. So she has many children and nothing to feed them on but her own good nature. She ran out of names years ago so she makes them up as she goes along. What she hasn't run out of is . . .'

'Friendliness?' Marlowe asked.

With a chuckle, the silversmith nodded. 'Those of us who can, help her out sometimes. I needed an apprentice. But instead of that, I got Ithamore. A pleasant lad, but . . .'

'He seems frightened of something.' Marlowe was good at seeing fear – it had saved his life more than once.

'Only me. He is on his last chance.'

Something about the man's face made Marlowe ask. 'How many last chances has he had so far?'

The jeweller counted on his fingers. 'As of today, almost five hundred. But he always forgets the others. But, yes, it was the woman that surprised me.'

Again the skill at recalling word for word.

'Although, there is no reason that it could not have been given to someone else as a gift. But . . .' He wandered back to his bench and reached beneath it for a box, which he pulled out and carried over nearer to the daylight. 'I got the impression, you see, when I was given this commission, that these little things were some-what special.' He opened the lid of the box and rummaged inside. 'Ah, yes, here we are. Yes, I am right. All men. See.' And he waved the paper in front of Marlowe.

The poet grabbed it as it whipped past his nose. It was a closely written document but he could make nothing of it. Then, focusing more clearly, he recognized it. 'Hebrew?' he asked. He had already forgotten most of the Hebrew lectures at Corpus Christi; it all seemed so long ago.

'My apologies, Master Marlowe,' the silver-smith said. 'I have an English copy here some-where . . .' He pulled out a sheet of paper and peered closely at it. 'Yes. This is it.' He held it out and took the other sheet from Marlowe in one movement.

'I didn't know . . .' Marlowe felt he should apologize, but was not sure for what.

'Don't concern yourself, Master Marlowe,' the Jew said. 'I haven't apologized for not recog-nizing you as a Christian.'

There was good reason for that, but Marlowe acknowledged it with a smile.

'I have lived here for many years now, but I

come from far away. All Jews come from far away, you might say, but I really do.' He looked proud for a moment. 'I speak nine languages. Living ones. Eleven if you count Latin and Ancient Greek.'

Marlowe raised an impressed eyebrow.

'But I still return to Hebrew when putting down notes. Master Mercator was very specific and I needed to write quickly. He wanted eight of these little worlds made, all the same except in one particular.'

'Eight?' Marlowe had known there was at least one more, but eight in total? That was unexpected.

'Yes. May I look closely at the one you have there?'

There seemed to be no reason to withhold it now and so he handed it over. The jeweller pulled his eyepieces into position and held the jewel out to the light, looking closely. 'Yes, I remember this one, I think. But perhaps you could check for me. Hmmm. Yes. The diamond is positioned . . . so . . . I think you'll find . . .' And without looking up he pointed with an amalgam stained finger to the paper in Marlowe's hand. 'I think you'll find that this jewel was sent to a Master . . . Gray of Canterbury.'

A small bell rang in Kit Marlowe's head. He didn't know everyone in Canterbury but he knew Master Gray. The locals knew him as Wim Grijs and Marlowe had not so long ago accepted his hospitality along the Stour. He looked down the list. 'There is someone of that name here,' he said casually, 'but how do you know it is this one?'

'Ah!' The jeweller held his finger in the air. 'Turn over the paper. There. Do you see?'

Sketched on the back of the sheet was a rough facsimile of the world jewel. Rough as it was, it was still by no means as rough as that drawn by Walter Mildmay. It was marked with numbers one to eight and these, Marlowe saw on turning the page back over, corresponded to the list of names. 'I see. But these numbers are very close together. How can you tell?'

'The sketch is rough,' the man agreed, 'but don't forget I made these with my own hands. I know my work and which jewel is which. If you were to bring them all to me, I could tell you which one went where, to perfect accuracy. You see, not only were the jewels in a different place on each, but there were different jewels to be set. Master Mercator gave them to me. They were only chips, but beautifully cut.' He sighed the sigh of a craftsman. 'Beautifully cut. It isn't my skill, you see. Silver and gold is my medium.'

'So, they weren't all diamonds?'

'Oh, by no means. I felt that they may have come from another piece, which had been broken up. I wondered if they might be for keepsakes. In memoriam, as you might say.'

'I see.' Marlowe grasped at the straw. It didn't sound likely but it was all that made sense so far. 'What were these stones?'

'They're all listed there,' Joshua said. 'Look.'

'*Rubinus* . . . um, ruby,' Marlowe began.

'Your Latin is good, Master Marlowe.' There was no hint of irony in the man's voice. 'But I don't think I am testing you much with this list.

107

Perhaps we can have a chat later – English is too easy, when you speak it all the time.'

'*Et erit in voluptate,*' Marlowe said, politely.

'*Omnis voluptas assumenda est, per meam.* Next.'

'Er . . . *amethistus* – amethyst.'

'Only semi-precious, of course. But very pretty, nonetheless.'

'*Opalus.* You are right, Master Joshua. This is easy. Oh – two of those.'

'Yes. Correct. And two diamonds also. This is why I assume the stones come from another piece. Why have such a strange combination otherwise?'

'Hmm. Two diamonds. One . . . lapis, is that?' The man nodded.

'And one . . . *smaragdo*? Oh, emerald.'

'Well done, Master Marlowe,' the Jew applauded softly. There was a small crash from out in the yard, followed by an ominous silence. 'Excuse me a moment, if you will?' and, trying not to run, the man swept out through the open back door.

Marlowe looked around the small and cluttered room while the man berated his apprentice out in the yard. Eavesdropping was not really a problem as it was clear that anyone within a half-mile distance could have heard the shouting. Eventually, it seemed to come to a natural conclusion and the boy, without his gloves and helmet now, rushed through the workshop and out into the street, sobbing.

'One last chance?' Marlowe asked the jeweller. He shrugged and his shoulders popped in protest. 'Perhaps just one,' he said, with a smile. 'But I have to let him worry for a while. It is good for his soul.' He stepped back behind the desk and continued, 'Emerald, yes. So, would you like to make a fair copy of my list?'

'I would indeed,' Marlowe said. If only every job that came the projectioner's way could be so easily accomplished.

'But wait, there is no need. Have that one, do.' The silversmith waved the paper away as Marlowe held it out to him. 'I have my Hebrew copy and –' the man winked and tapped the side of his nose – 'perhaps it would be best if we didn't leave too many clues along the way.'

'Clues?' Marlowe smiled thinly. 'I'm not sure . . .'

'Oh, come now, Master Marlowe. A "chequered history" you said. What can that mean but death and disaster?'

'Theft?'

'Well, yes,' the Jew agreed. 'But if theft, how do you have the jewel still? And I doubt whether mere theft would set you on the trail. So, death, then. And not the death of the owner, or you would know who it was. No!' He held his hand in the air. 'Tell me nothing. The less I know, the less I can tell when put to the test.'

'Master Joshua, I can assure you . . .'

'You can assure me of nothing, Master Marlowe. I come of a people long dispossessed. I know all there is to know about the knock on the door in the dead of night. But if I don't know your secret, it is safe enough with me.'

There was no denying the logic of that and so

Marlowe folded the piece of worn paper into four and slipped it inside his doublet. 'Well, thank you, Master Joshua,' he said. 'May I come and see you again, if I need to know more?'

'You may, of course,' the silversmith said. 'Or I may see you one day in the theatre, perhaps.'

'Perhaps. I am working on a new play, but it isn't going well. People always expect more of the same and I fear that Tamburlaine has played his last act. I need something new.'

Joshua shrugged on his coat. 'Let us walk together for a while, Master Marlowe,' he said. 'I suppose I should go and fetch back that stupid boy, offer him one last last chance. We can talk as we go.'

Marlowe smiled. 'That would be pleasant, yes. I confess I know very little about your people.'

'That is hardly a surprise, Master Marlowe. None have lived here for three hundred years. I am not here as a Jew but as a silversmith and the best there is. That is how I manage to remain. But if I were to wish to marry, to have children and a normal life – then, I think, things would be different. I was married once.' The man looked thoughtful and briefly closed his eyes. 'But that was in another country; and beside, the wench is dead. As long as I remain an old man, good to poor boys, generous to my neighbours, even to the church, when I am asked, then I can stay. But under sufferance, Master Marlowe, a stranger in a strange land.'

'Gershom.' The word popped out before Marlowe knew he knew it.

'That was quick. You know your Testament, then?'

Marlowe smiled. 'It seems I do,' he said. 'But that doesn't make me less of a stranger here than you.' He waited while the jeweller locked his door. 'Where has the boy gone, do you think?' he asked, looking up and down the street.

'Oh, not far, not far. He always goes to the same place when he uses up his last chance.' He turned to the left and stepped out well for someone of his years.

'Back to mother?'

The man clapped a hand on the playwright's shoulder. 'Back to mother, indeed. Where eventually all men go that are lost.'

Marlowe nodded but couldn't speak. Going back to mother was always possible. Back to the father, not so easy.

Seven

Francis Walsingham felt the cold these days, but even he had allowed the fires to be left unlit at Barn Elms in the hottest June that anyone could remember. He had tired of telling all who would listen that the country was in the grip of an ice age and being profligate in taking off layers of clothes just because the weather was warm was the best way to catch something horrible and die in agony. His family patted him fondly and removed their cloaks, candles melted in their sconces and, eventually, he had had to give in. Even so, he sat close against the cold grate and read the piece of parchment Marlowe had put into his hand.

'So,' he said as he thought he had better get it right, 'you got this piece of paper from a Jew in the Vintry and he told you it was a list of all the men who have one of the globes. Firstly, there are no Jews in England, not in the Vintry or anywhere else.'

Marlowe shrugged. 'I definitely know of at least one.'

'If you say so.' Francis Walsingham would far rather not know. 'Is this a copy?' He turned it over in his fingers.

'No, an original. I have this one, he has one written in Hebrew.'

'Hebrew?' Walsingham closed his eyes and

leaned back. No one in England had met a Jew. The last one had been ejected from the country three hundred years before, driven out as a Denier of Christ and an Eater of Babies. But even yet the stories rang around the rafters of many of the great houses. It would be much better if this man was not Jewish and so Sir Francis Walsingham gave himself a shake and saw that it was so. 'Hebrew, eh? A scholar, then.'

'Yes,' Marlowe agreed. 'And a Jew.'

There was a long pause in which the silent hearth clicked as the bricks deep within its heart finally cooled. Marlowe was used to long pauses when in conversation with Sir Francis. Nicholas Faunt was easier to meet with, being quick to the point and also willing to jump on a horse and go and get his hands dirty. Sir Francis was more of a delegator than a doer, but Marlowe was not fazed by that. He knew his place. And hopefully, Sir Francis would soon tell him what that place was.

'Hmm.' The queen's Spymaster bent forwards and looked at the list. 'What do these numbers mean?' He pointed.

'I understand that they refer to the small differences between the globes,' Marlowe paraphrased Joshua's explanation. 'Where the different stones are placed, that sort of thing.'

'Yes. These stones. Do they have a significance, do you think?'

'Well . . .' Marlowe had been mulling that one over and had come up with no better explanation than the one the jeweller had had to give. 'They were provided ready cut and in that combination.

Perhaps they come from another piece. Perhaps these globes are all memento mori.'

'For Jane Benchkyne, certainly,' Walsingham said sharply. 'And for my brother-in-law, if things had been a little different and he had caught his night prowler in the act. What did Mercator have to say on the subject?'

'He was difficult to read, Sir Francis, if I am to be honest.'

'Why start now?'

The new voice made both men turn.

'Ah, Nicholas,' Walsingham said as his left-hand man strode down the room, sweeping off his cap and cape. 'I was wondering where you had got to. What news of that lunatic Drake?'

'As we understood, Sir Francis, he, Sir Francis . . .' Faunt stopped in some confusion.

Walsingham flapped an impatient hand. 'Yes, yes, very amusing. The Queen can laugh for hours over the coincidence. Just call him Drake. That Mad Bastard. Whatever works for you.'

'Er . . . Drake,' Faunt said, hardly missing a beat. It wasn't like the Spymaster to be quite this testy, but Drake put everyone on their mettle. Nothing was quite what it seemed with Drake in the mixture. 'He is still at sea. As I understand it, and this is from someone who just saw his signal, he is having trouble with . . .' He foraged inside his doublet and brought out a scrap of paper. 'Excuse me, Sir Francis, these nautical terms are rather incomprehensible . . . trouble with his ballywrinkles at his bitt end. Also, from what I gathered from a rather half-witted old sailor who seemed to be the only one who could read signal flags, his boom vang is giving him –' he consulted the paper again – '. . . gyp.'

'And this means?' spat the Spymaster.

'I have no idea,' Faunt said. 'I think in general terms we may assume that Sir F . . . Drake will be at sea for a while longer while he attends to –' and he waved the scrap of paper vaguely – 'things.'

'You don't have to be cryptic in front of Marlowe, Faunt. He *is* one of us, after all. I assume Drake's assault on Lisbon has petered out?'

'It has,' Faunt acknowledged with a nod. That round-the-houses explanation was five minutes he'd never get back.

'So,' Marlowe butted in, 'we can't ask Drake about these globes, but should we, anyway? If the Chancellor is right and he will be moved to anger when he finds one or even more of these globes have fallen into the wrong hands, then perhaps the least said to him, the soonest mended?'

Faunt agreed, nodding. 'Marlowe's right, Sir Francis. Why trust Drake?'

'Oh, I don't,' Walsingham said. 'Never have. Never will. But Marlowe was about to tell me about Master Mercator when you came in, were you not, Christopher?'

Marlowe had hoped to dodge that particular projectile. Mercator had not taken his fancy as the silversmith had. He had been rather secretive and although he had finally shared the jeweller's name and whereabouts with him, it had taken all of Marlowe's powers of persuasion to tease out

115

the facts. 'I can certainly tell you of what he said, Sir Francis,' he said, 'but it was nothing we didn't know already. The list of the owners of the globes will surely take us further.'

'List?' Nicholas Faunt pricked up his ears. 'How many are there, then?'

'Eight, or so we believe.' The Spymaster took back the initiative. 'I don't believe we know the gentleman in Canterbury who sold his globe to Mistress Benchkyne.'

'Or had it stolen from him by her or another,' pointed out Marlowe. He was quietly glad that Walsingham didn't know Wim Grijs. Men known to Walsingham tended to end up twisting in fires or dangling at the end of ropes.

'Precisely so. But he will no doubt be easy to investigate, Nicholas. My brother-in-law, Walter Mildmay we know. The other six –' and he glanced again at the list in his hand – 'I know perhaps one of them. You may know more, Nicholas.' He handed the paper over and Faunt read it carefully.

'What do the numbers signify?' he asked, looking from man to man.

Walsingham raised a hand to his forehead. 'Kit,' he muttered. 'All this and the risk of having to deal with Drake is giving me a headache. Take Nicholas somewhere, share some Rhenish and tell him all about it. Then, choose one person each and go and squeeze him until there is not a drop of juice left in him. There is more to this than meets my eye. And I don't like being purblind. Let me know how you get on. And . . .'

'Yes, Sir Francis?' They spoke in unison.

116

'Get someone to come and light this fire. It's perishing in here.'

'Yes, Sir Francis.' And, wiping a thin film of sweat from their brows, the two went off in search of Rhenish and a cooling breeze.

The breeze on the water was indeed cooler than that on land and Marlowe settled down in a quiet place on deck of the little barque that Faunt had summoned up to take him to Lowestoft, the furthermost eastern location of a globe. He and Faunt had drawn lots as to which of them went to the coast, all other means of making the decision having been exhausted, bar actual combat. Wim Grijs had fallen to Marlowe with only minimal sleight of hand, but Faunt had quite reasonably pointed out that a visit to him was unnecessary as yet because they already had his globe, though by circuitous means. Faunt was off to Hertfordshire, which he claimed was hardship enough. Marlowe had pleaded prior engagements galore but the straw didn't lie and so here he was, a few essentials in a knapsack and nothing but time until they dropped anchor in Lowestoft. The crew on the little ship were all busy as they wove their way down the Thames, with its sandbars and deadly currents. The tide was running high and fast and soon they were shooting past Tilbury and the Essex marshes and were out in the open sea.

Marlowe didn't mind travelling by sea. He had some happy memories of going out on boats with his mother's family out from Dover when he was a child. But other memories crowded in too and he didn't close his eyes for fear that the image of the wooden walls of Spain engulfing him and consigning him to the drumming deeps of the Solent should jerk him awake with a scream.

A hand on his knee made him awake with a scream.

'Master Marlowe.'

He looked up into a weather-beaten old face, not a handspan from his own. 'I wasn't asleep,' he said, hurriedly. 'Just thinking.'

'Ar.' The old man sat down on a coil of rope alongside Marlowe's perch. 'They said as how you were some kind of a writer man. Tells stories, they said, for them players.'

As a brief job description, it couldn't really be bettered, so Marlowe nodded.

'I'm a bit of a writer myself,' the old man said.

Marlowe steeled himself to be polite. After all, he was in the hands of this old man and the rest of the crew up the treacherous east coast where, he had heard, doomed ships were lured on to the hidden sands by siren songs and were lost. 'I don't think I have met a sailor with a tale to tell before,' he lied. 'Have you got anything you would like me to read?'

The old man looked surprised. 'Read?' he said, looking puzzled. 'Read? I'm not a hand for reading.' He looked sharply at Marlowe. 'Oh, ar, I see where we've got a bit mazed, like. When I says *writer* what I should have said was *teller*. I tell tales, to them as wants one.'

'Oh.' Perhaps there was a chance that the old

man would go away, if he said no more and a companionable silence fell, broken only by the soft flap of canvas and distant sailorly calls.

'So,' the ancient mariner said, eventually, when it became clear to him that Marlowe was not going to say more. 'Would you like a story, master?'

Marlowe sighed. There didn't seem to be much choice and beside, he had had ideas for plays from stranger men than this. 'Why not?' he said.

'What would you like, master? They've all happened to me, you know. All first-hand stuff. I've had all sorts ask for my stories. I bin everywhere, I bin.'

'Oh,' Marlowe said, kindly. 'You choose, why don't you? Tell me your favourite.'

'Now that's a tough 'un,' the old sailor said. 'I bin everywhere, I bin.'

'Have you, indeed?' Marlowe looked over the old man's shoulder, hoping to be rescued by a passing deckhand or even perhaps a sighting of a whale, mermaid or similar sea creature. 'Still, you choose.'

'Well,' the old storyteller said. 'I was at the Siege of Malta. Course, that was back in '65. I wasn't a youngster even then, though you might not think it to look at me. No, but I was still putting in my years before the mast for any as'd pay me. It was a day much like today, June it was an'all, when the call came up, All hands on deck. So I got on to the deck and . . .'

Marlowe slept, but it didn't matter. The old man was back before the mast, his face sprayed with the warm Mediterranean water and the blood of his fellows, with all manner of djinns bearing down on him. As always when he reached the end of his story, he had to be led away by kindly sailors, to lie in his hammock, weeping for the dead.

'I wish he wouldn't always tell that one,' the Master said to his Mate. 'He's much easier to manage when he tells the one with Drake in it.'

'True,' the First Mate said, nodding and twirling the wheel to catch the wind. 'But then we get the crying for all the gold he had to leave behind. I don't know which is worse.'

The Master shook his head and sighed. 'Poor old beggar,' he said. 'And the only sailing he's ever known is a crabber out of Lowestoft. I only bring him along of us to get him out from under the wife's feet. I know blood is thicker than water and all, but I'm going to have to stop bringing him out.'

'It'll kill him,' the Mate remarked.

'Ar.' And the Master fixed his eye on the horizon, a small smile on his lips.

A single candle lit the room. Shadows advanced and retreated, trying to extinguish the light. But still the flame held out and it flashed on the brass buttons of a doublet, a doublet worn by a man on a mission.

'Are you there, Benedict?'

'I'm here, Shakespeare. I'll always be here. Until the job's done, anyway.'

The newcomer eased himself down, his hand never far from the dagger hilt hidden in the folds of his cloak. He had met this man once only and he trusted him about as far as he could throw him.

'Wine?' When it came to trust, the risk of poison had to be taken into account, but the job wasn't finished yet, so taking a proffered drink was probably still safe.

'Thank you, I will.' He laid his cap on the table in front of them and waited while the cup was poured. Then, despite everything not being yet over, he took the other one. Old habits die hard.

'My, my,' the host chuckled. 'Aren't you the trusting soul?'

'My soul's got nothing to do with it. You've bought the money?'

'Let's see the merchandise.' The smile had vanished now from the host's face and he held out his hand.

The other reached inside his doublet, past the metal of the dagger hilt and he laid the leather bag on the table. The man called Benedict opened it with one hand. The other lay on the butt of a wheel-lock pistol cradled in his lap. The candle-light flared on the silver. He saw America, Asia and Terra Australis. And he saw the emerald glowing green along the dotted line carved carefully into the metal.

'This precious stone,' the newcomer murmured, 'set in the silver sea.'

The other grunted, snatching the jewel and replacing it on the table with a purse of gold. 'Very poetic, Shakespeare,' he said. 'Where next?'

'That depends.' The thief leaned back, tucking the purse safely away next to his dagger.

'On what?'

'On why a silver trinket should be worth so much more in gold? In any bourse in Europe you'll find it ought to be the other way around.'

'You agreed. No questions.'

The thief took another sip of his wine. 'That was before . . . Canterbury.'

'Why? What happened in Canterbury?'

'A woman died, Benedict. The woman who owned the gewgaw that got away.'

'You killed her? A thief *and* a murderer?'

'I do what I have to do. She was old and the jewel wasn't where I had thought it might be and someone got to it first.'

'Who?'

'His name is Marlowe. We are in the same line, he and I.'

'Does he know you? For what you are, I mean?'

'No.'

'Can you retrieve the jewel, Shakespeare? That is the main thing.'

'I can, but meanwhile, you have another now. Fortunately, Hertfordshire was easier.'

The man patted his breast where he had safely stowed the globe. 'In what way?'

The younger man smiled, knowingly. 'Let's just say the lady of the house has a . . . weakness.'

'Oh?'

'Men,' he said with a grin. He smoothed down his doublet and stood a little straighter. 'Not just any man, but I took her fancy.'

'So,' the other said thoughtfully, 'you kill the old ones, lie with the young ones?'

'I didn't say that, but in these two cases in point, you are right, Benedict. But you did say, did you not, as we embarked on our little transaction, that I was to obtain the globes. How I do it is my business. And –' he poked the other painfully in the chest with his forefinger – 'my private life is, after all, my private life.'

When Marlowe woke, he couldn't for the life of him remember where he was. He was moving, he could tell that, in a series of bumps and knocks which resonated up his spine. His head was at an unnatural angle and felt too heavy for his neck to carry. He was under some foul-smelling cover, redolent of fish and grime. People were shouting in the distance and it was dark. Was this Hell? He had been damned to there by so many people in his short life already, perhaps he had been transported there in his sleep. He opened his eyes, gritty and hot though they were and prepared himself for the sight of the eternally damned to be spread before him in all their legions. But everything was dark. He tried to move, but his leg appeared to be severed from his body. At least, when he tried to move it, nothing happened. Then, suddenly, there was a light, so bright and piercing that he flinched from it, squeezing his eyes closed again.

'Come along, Master Marlowe,' a gruff voice said. 'Lowestoft.'

'What?' It all started to come flooding back. An old man and a story. The list. The globes. Lowestoft! He jumped to his feet and regretted it as his leg buckled.

'Leg gone to sleep?' the Master chuckled. 'Sorry, Master Marlowe, not to have woken you last night but you were well away. Old Jem was telling you some yarn and you dropped off. We just covered you with yon tarpaulin and left you sleeping like a baby. Only other place to sleep would've been along of old Jem in the hold so we thought you'd be better off up a'top, especially on a lovely night like the one we've just had. Calm as calm and warm as a whore's tits, begging your pardon, sailors' term, like.'

'Thank you, Master,' Marlowe said, taking a tentative step along the deck. 'Whores' tits are warm on land as well as at sea.'

'Oh, no,' the Master was shocked. 'No women on board. We goes and finds us what we needs on land, when the devil drives.'

'I see.' Marlowe remembered now what it was that he disliked most about going to sea. The sailors. 'I believe Master Faunt paid you in advance?'

'Well, now . . .' The Master scratched his head. 'Not sure . . .' He looked around aimlessly. 'Perhaps the Mate knows . . .'

Marlowe reached into his jerkin front. 'Perhaps a little . . .' And he passed a gold coin into the Master's open hand.

'That's very kind of you, Master Marlowe,' the Master said, with a small bow. 'Very kind. Will you be wanting a passage back to London?'

'I'm not sure when I will need to return,' the playwright said. 'But I assume I can ask here for you?'

'Yes, we're allus here, here or on the way back.'

The Master stood aside. 'I'll let you be on your way, then, Master Marlowe. Safe journey.'

'Thank you,' Marlowe said, and shouldered his knapsack. 'Do you know where there is a livery stable in the town?'

'Right ahead, up the street, turn left, you can't miss it.'

'I'll say you sent me,' Marlowe said.

The Master smiled and nodded. For a land-lubber, Marlowe knew a sailor's ways. 'God speed.'

Marlowe inclined his head in a way which could show consent to the wish and edged down the gangplank, carefully failing to make eye contact with old Jem, who sat on a capstan on the harbourside, pregnant with tales. With his customary glance behind and to either side, to check for possible assailants, Marlowe set off up the street to the livery. He knew before he even turned left that there would be no livery stable and turned with a sigh back to the harbour.

Everyone but old Jem had gone and there was no point in asking him anything, not because he would have no answer, but because he would have so many. Before Marlowe had to grasp that particular nettle, a door opened just as he walked past and a man who looked as though he might just know how many beans made five stepped out.

Marlowe grabbed his sleeve and the man flinched and his hand reached instinctively round his back for the dagger he doubtless wore there.

'My apologies,' Marlowe said quickly, letting go and spreading innocent hands. 'I did not mean

125

to alarm you, but I am in a hurry and need a livery stable, if Lowestoft has such a thing.'

'Lowestoft folk are a seafaring lot who have little to do with horses,' the man said, smiling now the threat of attack seemed to have receded. 'Inland to them is terra incognita! But there is a small stable at the edge of town, not ten minutes' walk from here, if you were to step out lively, as I think you probably will, being a strong young chap. They will let you have a horse for a reasonable fee, but make sure you haggle the price.'

'Are their prices too much, then?' Marlowe asked.

'Not at all,' his helper told him. 'But they distrust all foreigners here and if you don't haggle they will be suspicious and won't lend you even a sway-backed nag.'

'I'm not a foreigner,' Marlowe protested. 'I am from Kent.'

'*I* know you are not a foreigner,' the man said with a laugh. 'But you're in Suffolk now, master, and things are different here. Anyone not from the town is a foreigner. Anyone not related to you is a foreigner. That makes you a foreigner on two counts, so watch your step. They're a funny lot round here.'

Marlowe had to ask. 'And you? Are you a foreigner?'

'As foreign as the day is long, master, but I mingle. That's the key around here. Blend and mingle and you will get on. Stand out and they'll kill you where you stand. They're a funny lot round here.'

'You said.'

'And for a reason. It isn't something to forget if you want to live to go back to Kent or wherever it is you come from.'

'Well . . . thank you.' Marlowe wasn't sure whether he had perhaps just met one of the funny lot or not and before he could find out, the door opened again and the man looked round.

'Yes?' he asked the shadowy figure inside, who muttered something indistinguishable. Turning to Marlowe, he said, 'Good luck with your quest, Master . . .'

Something made Marlowe reply, 'Watson.'

'Master Watson. Don't forget to haggle, now.' And with that, the door slammed shut behind him and Marlowe was alone again, standing in the street. He looked back and forth and there didn't seem to be anyone else to ask, so he stepped out lively, in search of the stable. He didn't know what he might find at Ness End Hall but he felt that time was of the essence. A black dog was on his shoulder and he needed to solve this conundrum before it bit him.

Eight

The evening sun glowed a fierce orange over the trees of Starkey. Nicholas Faunt could see the lights of the Hall like fireflies in the distance. All day he had trotted north, through Bishopsgate and Moor Fields to take the road through Hertfordshire. There was a hunt in full cry in the fields south of Lord Burghley's Hatfield and Faunt rested to watch the gallants and their ladies, a flutter of colour riding through the pale gold of the ripening corn. He saw no sign of the doe, but the dogs knew where she was and they howled in the afternoon, dashing blind through the barley stalks and leaping the low walls of the covert. He heard the bells on the wrists of the hawkers and saw the grey- and white-streaked birds high against the blue. Hind and hare were both at risk today.

Faunt had ridden on, moving north-east along the old legions' road with its ruts iron-hard in high summer. He had stopped under the welcoming gables of the Fat Ox, tethering his horse to a post there and won himself a few groats at tables. His opponent was the innkeeper, so bewildered by the speed of Faunt's pieces over the board that he ended up paying for the man's luncheon and the water for his horse.

'What did you say brought you this way, sir?' the innkeeper had asked as Faunt swung into the saddle again.

'I didn't,' he replied with a smile. He leaned low over the horse's neck to murmur in the man's ear, 'But let's just say I'm looking for a crock of gold at the end of a rainbow.'

'Good luck with that, sir,' the innkeeper had called and had carried on grumbling about the ruinous monopoly on wines of that bastard Sir Walter Ralegh.

Now Faunt let his bay amble through the sheep pastures where the hurdles stood at lazy angles and ducks quacked at him from the safety of their reeds. He heard dogs barking and saw torches suddenly burst into life at a side door of the Hall and saw men come running. There were three of them, armed with staves and an arquebus.

'Ho, stranger!' one of them called. 'What business have you at Starkey?'

'Private business, sirrah!' Faunt told him. 'With Sir Oliver.'

'That won't do, sir,' a female voice called from the doorway.

Faunt could not make out her face, silhouetted as she was with the Hall's lights behind her, but there was no doubting the outline of her form. He swept off his cap and swung out of the saddle, glad to be able to flex his legs.

'Well?' She stood facing him now. The girl was perhaps twenty, with long dark hair piled high under a simple cap of lace. Her eyes smouldered at him and she placed her hands on her hips, the farthingale swaying as she waited.

'I am Nicholas Faunt,' he told her. 'Queen's messenger.'

'Show me your papers, Master Faunt,' she said,

her voice as cold as the nose of the wolfhound that now snuffled round the messenger's leg.

He obliged, drawing the parchment slowly from his doublet in case one of the serving men, the one with the gun, should be of a nervous disposition. 'You know Her Majesty's cypher?' he asked her.

She nodded and smiled. 'You are most welcome, Master Faunt. Will you come this way?' She led him into the entranceway to the Hall. 'Stable Master Faunt's horse, Stewart,' she ordered. 'You *will* stay the night, Master Faunt?'

'That would be a kindness, lady,' he said.

'Lady,' she giggled. 'You can call me Marie.'

'A French name?' Faunt asked her. Years in the service of Francis Walsingham had taught him to be as suspicious of foreigners as any London apprentice. Too many of them were Papist projectioners, still bent on claiming the head of the Jezebel of England.

'A Maltese name,' she told him. 'Won't you take some supper, Master Faunt?'

'Nicholas,' he insisted.

She led him into the main chamber where a huge oak table filled half the room and the wolfhound circled back to his bed in front of the stone fireplace, black and empty now in the summer's heat. It was cool here and the room glittered with candles, glowing on the Gobelin tapestries that hung from the walls like memories of another world. But it was the huge portrait above the mantle that caught Faunt's eye. A fierce warrior stood there, in fluted Maximillian armour of a half a century ago and wearing a scarlet cloak emblazoned with a white cross and holding a shield that bore the devices of a star and a key.

'Grandfather,' Marie explained as she saw Faunt looking up at the canvas, 'in his heyday. And for God's sake, Nicholas, don't get him started on his war stories or you'll be up all night. I'll fetch him. I'll also get Cook to find you something – it'll likely be cold mutton, I'm afraid.'

'I can't think of anything I'd like better,' he replied with a smile.

'Your business with him –' Marie turned back and looked the man in his strange, grey eyes – 'I will have to be present while you discuss it.'

'As you wish,' he said politely and she swept away.

Faunt took in the portrait in more detail. Behind the warrior's legs a fortress blazed, black clouds billowing into the blue of the sky and a fleet of infidel galleys bore down from the right. There were various shields and designs along the canvas's edge, the arms of Starkey that Faunt had already seen over the gateway and the front door. But the oddest emblem was a hand, upright and facing the viewer. That looked like the Red Hand of Ulster, that Papist Hell across the Irish Sea. What was it doing here, on the portrait of an old soldier in deepest Hertfordshire?

'Nicholas Faunt.' He turned at the sound of his name. Marie was walking down the broad stairs into the chamber slowly, leading a white-bearded old man by the hand. 'May I present my grandfather, Sir Oliver Starkey?'

Now Faunt understood why Marie had insisted

she be present. Oliver Starkey was as blind as a worm, groping his way forward with one hand outstretched and the other firmly fixed to his granddaughter.

'Welcome to Starkey Hall, Master Faunt,' he said.

Faunt bowed and took the man's hand.

'We don't get many visitors from Her Majesty. It has been a while since I was at Court. How fares Gloriana?'

Nicholas Faunt, who had seen her recently, was not seeing the same woman that Oliver Starkey had in his mind. To the old man, the queen of England was everything the poets wrote about. She was Eliza, Pandora, Cynthia, Astraea and Belphoebe. Her face was pale as all beauties should be, her forehead broad and intelligent. She danced the volta with the grace of the Muse. Her voice was the tinkling of bells that rang from her horse's harness and her laughter could melt ice. In reality, the woman was old, tetchy, more difficult by the day. Her friends were dying around her. Her chest was scrawny and her teeth black. To watch her flirting with courtiers who could have been her grandsons was nauseating and Faunt kept away from the Presence as much as he could.

'She fares well, Sir Oliver,' he replied with a smile. 'A brighter light I could not hope to serve. And she sends you her remembrance.'

'Oh!' The old man clasped his hands together and tears filled his pale, sightless eyes. Faunt looked closely at them. This was no ordinary blindness, the failing of the light that comes with old age. There were old scars across the bridge of his nose and down his left cheek. 'Tell me all about it, Master Faunt.' Starkey let his granddaughter help him into a huge chair by the fire and he kicked the dog out of the way. 'Nonsuch, Placentia, Whitehall. Tell me, is that old rascal Christopher Hatton still up to his old tricks?'

'You mistake me, sir,' Faunt said. 'I have been sent by Sir Francis Walsingham.'

Starkey's face fell. 'Ah, the Queen's Moor.'

'Even so,' Faunt said and smiled, vaguely tickled that the man's detested nickname should have got this far.

'I'll be honest with you, Faunt –' Starkey's voice was harsher now – 'I've never liked your master. An outsider. Not one of us.'

'He has Her Majesty's safety at heart, sir.' Faunt thought he ought to defend the man. 'As have we all.'

'Yes,' Starkey said with a sigh. 'Yes, indeed. Well, what does he want?'

'Forgive me, Sir Oliver –' Faunt shifted in his chair – 'I must ask you whether you own a certain gewgaw.'

'Gewgaw?' the old man repeated.

'It is a small disc, sir, made of silver and representing the world.'

The Lord of Starkey frowned and looked vaguely in the direction of his granddaughter. She looked blank.

'Ah!' Starkey's face brightened. 'Yes, I remember now. It was a memento sent to me by Francis Drake. Showed his circumnavigation of the globe. What is your interest, Master Faunt?'

133

Walsingham's man checked that the three of them were alone. He was good at this. Priest holes, chinks in the wall, plastering that did not match up – little things like that spoke volumes about the secret world that men like him inhabited. Rats squeaking behind the Arras, a careless tread on a loose stair – he knew all the sounds.

'I hardly know where to begin,' he said. 'Why did Drake . . . Sir Francis . . . give this little gem to you?'

'Why shouldn't he?' Starkey countered. 'I invested rather heavily in the man's adventuring. As I believe did Walsingham, not to mention Christopher Hatton, Robyn Dudley and the Lord Admiral. It was a token of his appreciation, I suppose.'

'Sir Walter Mildmay?'

Starkey blinked, his milky eyes flickering from side to side. 'Yes, I understand he contributed. But I don't understand . . .'

'Could I see the globe, Sir Oliver?' Faunt asked.

'Er . . . yes, I suppose so. Marie . . .'

'Don't bother Stewart, Grandfather,' the girl said, patting his hand. 'I'll get it for Master Faunt. Ah, supper.'

The cold mutton had arrived, with wine, bread and cheese. To a man who had been on the road all day, it tasted like Heaven. But while he was eating it and Marie had gone in search of the gewgaw, Nicholas Faunt made a fatal mistake. To make small talk, he referred to Sir Oliver's portrait and that unleashed such a torrent of memoirs that Faunt's head was reeling with it all and his arse was numb with lack of movement.

'St Elmo,' the old man began, settling himself back with a large cup of wine in his hand. 'Malta. Back in '65. You know, of course, that I am a knight of St John?'

It had crossed Faunt's mind.

'Well, the Grand Master, de la Valette, told us to hold the fort at all costs. And it *did* cost, Master Faunt. Many a good man. My eyes. I remember it as if it was yesterday.'

And after several hours, as tomorrow made an appearance in the midnight courts of Starkey Hall, Nicholas Faunt did too.

Dawn would be creeping over his window sills before long, but Faunt was still wide awake. He had lost track of the wild goose chases the Spymaster had sent him on over the years. What had Marlowe told him? A woman was dead in Canterbury on account of this trinket. Well, people were killed in Elizabeth's England for far less worth every day – a couple of groats, a loaf of bread, a look, a chance word, a quarrel over a bill. But there was something else about this, something that involved the highest in the land. Walter Mildmay had owned one and had been robbed of it. What would be the tale of woe here, he wondered, from a hero of the siege of Malta and the knights of St John?

He didn't know this house. Starkey Hall was Hatfield writ small, with wings and stables, kennels and outhouses. Who knew where the old man kept his valuables? In a double strongroom like Walter Mildmay? Perhaps, but Mildmay was Chancellor of the Exchequer, a man obsessed with the colour of money and the need to keep it safe. Would Faunt have to wait until breakfast and listen to yet more of Oliver Starkey's interminable stories before he got round once again to the jewel he had ridden for a day to find?

Then he heard it. A click. Two. All houses sang a different song and the night was the time to hear the counterpoint, the small notes that make up the whole. He had not had time to learn the harmonies of Starkey Hall, but he knew this noise wasn't just the music of the night. Someone was creeping into his room, unannounced, unheralded and trying their level best to be undetected. Had the man in the bed been other than Nicholas Faunt – or Christopher Marlowe, with his fine-tuned ears and almost seventh sense – the intruder might have got away with it. The curtains around the high tester were velvet and brocade, heavy and thick but the night was so hot that Faunt had left them open on the window side, so his eyes were accustomed to the moonlight filtering through the leaded panes. He heard the soft shuffle of footsteps cross the bare floorboards. He had counted sixteen paces from the door to the bed, but that was with his usual purposeful stride. Someone trying to catch him by surprise would take smaller steps. He knew that they were barefoot – he could hear the soft thud of the heel go down, the pause as the foot rolled on to the toes, for the next stealthy pace. His rapier lay at an angle against the bottom of the bed, but he had no need of that. His dagger lay unsheathed under his pillow. Nicholas Faunt slept with his wife when the fancy took him. But he slept with his knife every night, the cold steel companion of his dreams.

He reached out with his left hand, grabbing a handful of the four-poster's hangings. The footsteps had stopped now. Whoever it was was standing just beyond the velvet. Neither soul in that little room dared breathe. Then, Faunt struck first. He hauled the drape down, tearing it off its rings on the bed-frame and threw the heavy curtain over the figure that stood there, pulling it aside as quickly, disorienting his visitor. There was a muffled cry instantly stifled and the projectioner's blade-tip was nicking the pale throat of Marie Starkey. She looked at him with terror in her eyes, her mouth open in a silent scream. He relented and the dagger was back under his pillow as if it had never been.

He stood beside the girl, looking down into her face. 'You only had to knock,' he said, quietly. The servants would be up and about soon and he didn't want to compromise her position in the house. He knew better than most men how much the servants loved to gossip about the mistress of the house – he had often used scurrilous, scuttled butt tales as his source of information. 'The whereabouts of the silver globe could have waited for the morning.'

He looked down. The girl's nightgown had partly fallen open and her firm breasts were in full view. She covered herself up quickly and it was her turn to look down. Nicholas Faunt was as naked as the day he was born, his shirt and Venetians thrown with his doublet and buskins on to a linen chest under the window. He made no attempt to cover himself but slid back the remaining curtain and looked at the girl in the first rays of light creeping from the east.

'The whereabouts of the silver globe,' she said. 'That's precisely the point. It's gone.'

'Gone?' Faunt repeated. This was sounding depressingly familiar. 'Don't tell me. You were burgled and the curber used his hook to fish the thing out of Sir Oliver's window.'

'Curber?' she repeated.

He smiled. 'Oh, it's an old and dishonourable profession,' he told her. 'Curbers lift things out of windows with a specially made hook. Other people's things, naturally.'

'I could lie to you,' she said softly.

Faunt reached out and stroked her cheek with the tips of his fingers. 'You could,' he nodded, and he kissed her. She kissed him back, hard and passionate and let him slip her linen gown off her shoulders. 'On the other hand,' he said, 'you could lie *with* me.'

He pulled her gently towards him as he dropped back on to the bed. Now she was straddling him, her legs widening as their tongues entwined. Her breathing was jagged as he started to move against her and his fingers ran over the curves of her body. When she was ready he gave a gentle thrust and buried himself in her, letting her catch her breath before starting to move rhythmically. She moved with him and he noted with the cool, projectioner's part of his brain which was always alert, no matter what the rest of his body might be doing, that he was not the first man whose bedroom she had visited.

'The silver globe,' he whispered in her ear as their mouths parted.

'A keepsake,' she hissed, her breasts rising and falling. 'Given to a friend.'

'The friend asked for it, specifically?'

She nodded, unable to speak for a moment.

He slowed his pace and she looked at him with eyes wide and pleading. 'When was this?'

She wriggled against him and her answer came on her ragged breath. 'I don't know. A week ago, perhaps. What does it matter?'

'It matters, Marie.' He held her to him and thrust deeper. Her body was shuddering now and it was unnecessary to withhold from her what she clearly needed so badly. Even after all this, she would tell him what he wanted to know. 'This . . . friend. Does he have a name?'

'How . . . how do you know it is a man?'

'Marie,' he said, chidingly. 'Lie with, remember, not to; does he have a name?'

'Robyn,' she panted, her hips heaving against him.

'Just Robyn?'

'That's all I know. He was like you . . . a passing stranger. What . . . will you take? As a keepsake?' She was staring into his face now as her pleasure overtook her. She arched her back and threw back her head, her body jerking convulsively. He let himself go with her and then lay still, stroking her hair as it cascaded over his face.

'Nothing,' he said, smiling. 'Just this memory.'

Marie Starkey found it difficult to look Nicholas Faunt in the face in broad daylight, especially as she was sitting with him and her grandfather at their breakfast table. He was not helping her in her discomfiture either, as he kept smiling at her and raising a conspiratorial eyebrow. She kept her head down and crumbled her bread with shaking fingers.

'By the way, Master Faunt,' said the old man as he took a deep draught of his morning ale, 'I fear your journey was wasted.'

'How so, Sir Oliver?' he asked, helping himself to more honey and treating Marie to an extra sweet smile.

'Marie reminded me earlier. My old memory isn't what it was. The gewgaw you seek was stolen from us – only the other week. Damndest thing, though. Stewart!' he clapped his hands and his man came scuttling.

'Sir Oliver?'

'Bring the Hand.'

'Very good, sir.'

The man clattered up the stairs while Marie stared pointedly out of the window. The glow she had felt not two hours ago had left her now and if her cheek burned, it was with embarrassment.

'Sir Oliver.' Stewart was back, carrying a glass dome under a velvet cloth.

The old man fumbled with it and whipped the cloth away. 'Behold!' he announced.

Faunt peered at the shrivelled thing which lay under the glass. It was hard to make out, but looked like a finger, long dead, mounted in what seemed to be gold.

'That,' the old man said proudly, 'is the index

finger of the hand of St John the Baptist. The Grand Master gave it to me when we held Malta in the siege. "You've lost your eyes, Oliver," he said to me, "but our blessed saint will always point the way for you".'

'Fascinating,' Faunt murmured. For this relic alone, he could have the old man burned at any of Walsingham's stakes across the land. Beside him, Marie stiffened with apprehension, but Faunt simply repeated the word, for all the world as though he were enthralled. 'Fascinating.'

'Doubly so,' said Starkey. 'Doesn't it strike you as odd that our thief stole a piece of cheap silver and left this behind? It's worth a fortune. The gold housings alone . . .'

'Yes, Sir Oliver,' said Faunt, with a last smile at Marie. 'Odd indeed.'

Nine

Ness End Hall had clearly seen better days, as had the spavined nag that Marlowe was astride as the Hall came into view. All around, the land was flat and Marlowe wasn't surprised to see that, although geography had never been a favourite study of his. But Ness End Hall was so determined to hide from prying eyes that it seemed to nestle into the ground, and it lurked there, grey and damp-looking, despite the low sun which gilded its roof. The windows were small and mean and looked out suspiciously from under the eaves. The front door was deep in the thickness of the wall and to Marlowe it seemed that it had sealed itself shut with years of repelling visitors. He would not have been too surprised had the whole house shied away from his hand as he raised it to the enormous knocker hanging crookedly on the age-greyed oak. The noise echoed through the house and came back to Marlowe on a wave of mildew and hopelessness. He did not hold out much hope of hospitality here. He knocked again and suddenly the door was wrenched open and a man stood there, tall and beautiful. Marlowe had allowed his imagination to have full reign and so he had expected a bent and wizened family retainer, should the door open at all. He had even adjusted his gaze to where this mythic creature's face would be, so he had to hurriedly raise his eyes.

'Who're you?' The golden creature might be handsome, but his voice was of the corncrakes over in the water meadows to the east. In his eyes, not even a small candle burned to show that any soul was at home.

Marlowe bowed, sweeping his short cloak behind him with a practised hand. 'Christopher Marlowe,' he said. 'Here on the Queen's business.'

Somewhere deep in the house, a door slammed and running feet were to be heard by diminishing returns as they disappeared out of a distant back door.

The golden giant looked vaguely over Marlowe's shoulder, almost as if Gloriana might be waiting behind him, impatient to come in. When no one was there he seemed to lose interest and bent a lacklustre gaze back on to Marlowe. He neither moved a limb nor spoke.

Marlowe tried again. 'So,' he said, 'if I may speak to your master, perhaps.'

The lovely face, as calm and stupid as a Botticelli angel, didn't move a single muscle.

'Or mistress, even.' Marlowe thought that the time was right to start to make a move to at least enter the house and edged forward. But the angel stood his ground, not pushing back, just not moving an ell by dint of staying totally still, like an ox in the furrow.

'Ain't no mistress here,' the corncrake said eventually. 'Master's out.'

'Perhaps . . .' Marlowe was wondering, looking

around at sagging pargeting and wood spongy with age and damp, whether this benighted place would run to many staff, but it was worth a try. 'Perhaps I might speak with your master's steward?'

'Ar,' said the man, at last. A tiny furrow of thought creased his lovely brow. 'I dunno where he is, though.'

'Perhaps I could come in,' Marlowe suggested. 'Come in and wait. Then, you could go and find him and bring him to me.' Keeping things simple seemed to be the key and the giant nodded ponderously.

'Ar. I'll go and find him,' he agreed. He stepped aside and let Marlowe in through the door, into the dimness of the Hall. After the day's bright sun, it was like walking into a barrel of pitch, if barrels of pitch smelled of mould, last year's apples, dust and wet dog. The man gestured woodenly to a settle against one wall and Marlowe sat down, gingerly. It was surprisingly comfortable, though, and when the cloud of dust had dispersed, Marlowe found his companion had gone. He could hear him outside, calling.

'Master Barnet! Master Barnet! There's a furriner come. Master Barnet!'

Marlowe smiled to himself in the darkness. So his adviser back in the town had not been wrong. Then he pricked up his ears. There were two voices outside and then, suddenly, all was action, light and sound.

A man came in through the doorway, bringing the sun with him. Smaller than the giant by almost a foot, his face was just as lovely, but with the light of intelligence giving it a soul. His golden curls escaped from under a shapeless hat and his clothes had seen better days, but he crackled with energy and grasped Marlowe's hand in both of his own, pumping it up and down as he introduced himself, in breathless gasps of excitement.

'Master . . .'

'Marlowe,' Marlowe began, ready to explain further, but was cut off.

'Marlowe. How wonderful. We get so few visitors out here at Ness End. You're welcome, my dear man, so welcome. Did Micah take your cloak? No, I can see not. A cup of ale?' He tutted to see the total lack of refreshments. 'No, no, I see he failed in that small courtesy also.' He smiled and looked down at his feet for a moment as though in embarrassment, then looked Marlowe candidly in the eye. He buffeted him lightly on the shoulder. ''Fraid Micah is my own fault, my own cross to bear. His mother was a nice girl, very accommodating, not much up here though.' He tapped his own forehead. 'Might be a bit of inbreeding. Not so many families of any quality around here, you see. Have to fend for ourselves a bit, especially in the winter, when the fens are in flood. But no matter –' and he cheered up again – 'nothing to be done about it now and he is a damned useful fellow when there's any heavy lifting to be done.'

While he was telling Marlowe the kind of secret which in London men would kill to keep, he was shepherding the poet into another room, rather as a dog would chivvy a recalcitrant sheep. On this side of the house the windows were bigger, and Marlowe could see the extent of the land in which Ness End Hall stood. There was a rough paddock, grazed by a mixed herd of oxen, sheep and a few skittish-looking deer. At the far horizon, the land sloped sharply away into dunes and, eventually, the sea, glittering and shifting. Even behind the glass, Marlowe could almost taste the salt and thought he had never seen anywhere so lonely in his life. He realized why this man was so relentlessly cheerful; without this facade, he would probably just turn his face to the wall and fade away.

'Master Marlowe,' he had begun again and Marlowe turned to face him. 'I am remiss. I am Leonard Morton, the master of Ness End.' He wrinkled his perfect nose and smiled. 'Not that being master of Ness End is what it was, I fear. Father – and grandfather, if it comes to that – was not a good manager. Wine, women, cards, dice . . . if it costs money and makes none, then they were to be found in the vicinity. By the time I got my hands on the tiller, there was little left to manage, to tell you truly, Master Marlowe. I ran away to sea, you know –' and the little man leant forward with a twinkle in his eye – 'but they found me and brought me back.' He sighed and for the first time looked genuinely downcast. 'And here I am. But, don't let's be downhearted. No, indeed. A little wine, I think, will be pleasant, while you tell me why you are here.'

Marlowe was getting used to the man's style. A lot of flummery and then suddenly, something very pertinent at the end. A simple enough rule of thumb, if only there was a clue as to when

the end was coming, so it would only be necessary to listen to the last sentence. But he was a
pleasant enough fellow and a goblet of wine
would be very welcome after the journey Marlowe
had had. He could still faintly taste fish, right on
the back of his tongue. His host walked briskly
along the solar and shouted through the door at
the end. His voice echoed and re-echoed down
the stairs into the nether regions of the house and
it was just possible, in the pauses, to hear the
corncrake response of Micah. Morton trotted back
down the room and sat opposite Marlowe, hands
cradling one knee.

'So, Master Marlowe. We see so few strangers
here I can't think you are here by accident. So,
it must be by design.' He tilted his head and he
looked like a good-natured faun, eyes sparkling
and curls almost sparking with lightning bolts.
Marlowe was reminded of his reading of the
Greek myths and thought that it must have been
meeting one such that had started Homer on his
writings. Olympus had come to earth in deepest
Suffolk.

'Design indeed,' Marlowe said. 'I am here on
Her Majesty's business . . .'

Morton blenched. 'Not . . . not a Progress?'

Marlowe patted the air in front of him, calming
the man down. 'No, no, well, that is to say, I am
not privy to the Queen's travelling arrangements.
But that is not why I am here, I assure you.'
Marlowe could hardly suppress a grin. Belphoebe
had bankrupted better men than Morton and then
gone back for more. She would not even think
of crossing the threshold of Ness End Hall.

Micah appeared at Morton's elbow with two horn goblets on a battered tray. 'Wine,' he croaked, almost as if he were giving an order.

Morton turned and flashed him a brilliant smile and praised him as though he had transmuted base metal to gold. '*Micah*!' he patronized. 'Well done. Thank you, thank you. Now, give one to Master Marlowe, there. That's right. That's right. Thank you.' He looked at the golden oaf and then flapped a hand, dismissing him. He turned to Marlowe and lowered his voice. 'I try to praise him when he does things right. He *is* improving.' He sipped his wine and put the goblet down, making small smacking noises with his lips. 'Delicious.'

Encouraged, Marlowe took a deep draught. He had been in many a poor house where the wine cellar spoke of better days. Tears sprang to his eyes as almost neat vinegar soured his tongue and it was as well that Morton was yet again in full cry, because he was not at all sure that he would be able to speak for a while.

'I am relieved to hear you say it, Master Marlowe,' Morton said. 'My coffers would not withstand a visit from Her Majesty, not even a passing one as she went on her way elsewhere. You may have noticed –' and he swung a hand around above his head – 'we have seen better days.'

Marlowe cleared his throat as best he could. 'Do you have *no* treasure here?' he asked.

Morton chuckled. 'I have but one piece of precious metal left, Master Marlowe and I suspect you know that already. I am not a stupid man, you know, though I may play the fool at times. I find fewer people bother us here if I seem a simple soul. I have but this . . .' He reached into his shirt and brought out a silver globe, the twin, it seemed of the other, threaded on to a thick chain. 'I was told to guard it with my life. Shutting it in a strongbox is not guarding with my life, in my opinion, so I keep it here, next to my heart.' He twisted it around and looked at it fondly. 'It reminds me of my time at sea. I was happy then, Master Marlowe. Happy and free from care.' He looked at it for a few moments more and then wiped a single tear from his cheek.

Marlowe leaned forward. 'May I see it, Master Morton, if you please?'

'Of course, my dear fellow. Of course you may. But you will have to come nearer, because I do not let it leave my person.'

Marlowe stood and went closer still, holding the globe in the palm of his hand and turning it to the light. It was just like Jane Benchkyne's and, allowing for some artistic license, Walter Mildmay's. In this one, an opal gleamed, its myriad colours winking and crawling through the surface in the hot summer light streaming in.

'That's it, Master Marlowe,' Morton said. 'Turn it this way and that. You'll see the fire at its heart that way.' He looked down at the globe lovingly. 'Sometimes, I sit out in the paddock and take it off its chain. I can hold it in my hand and watch its colours come and go.' He looked Marlowe in the eye and, in their close proximity, Marlowe could see that the iris was as blue as the flower, dark and clear.

Morton's tone grew wistful. 'They say,' he said, 'that opals can make you invisible. You have to wrap them in a bay leaf and . . . sadly, I have never found out what the other part of the spell might be.' He sighed. 'I sometimes think that invisibility would be a wonderful thing, don't you, Master Marlowe?'

But before Marlowe could answer, he was hit amidships by what felt like one of the white oxen browsing peacefully outside. He was borne to the ground and lay there prone, under what felt like a ton of bricks, but bricks which lived and breathed and all too obviously, sweated. In the distance, he could hear Morton shouting and after a while, his load removed itself, but not without kneeling rather heavily on one of his thighs, driving out all feeling from his leg below the knee. He sat up, groaning.

'I do apologize, my dear, dear man.' Morton hauled him to his feet and propelled him gently to a chair. 'Here, let me cover you with this coverlet. You must be shocked. Brandy?'

Marlowe waved away the coverlet but gratefully accepted the brandy. 'What happened?' he asked, although he thought he knew what had occurred.

'Micah, I fear,' Morton said, fanning Marlowe absent-mindedly with the edge of his tattered jerkin. 'He looked in and saw us near the window with your hands near my throat. He feared the worst and . . . well, he charged. He isn't perhaps very quick-witted, but he is loyal.' He looked anxiously at Marlowe, frowning. 'You *are* unhurt, I hope.'

Marlowe raised a sardonic eyebrow. How

anyone could be unhurt after being knocked flying by someone the size of Micah he couldn't begin to imagine.

'Of course you are hurt! How foolish of me. Not *badly* hurt, perhaps I should say. Stay the night, please say you will.' The little man looked quite stricken. 'Then, in the morning, we can look again at your injuries and see what, if anything, needs to be done. Will you stay? Hmm?'

Marlowe paused long enough to make it look as though he was giving it consideration, then nodded. It would be hard to part Morton from his jewel, but another twenty-four hours would give him a fighting chance at least. And his leg *did* hurt.

'Micah will be punished,' Morton promised. 'He has gone too far this time.'

This time? Marlowe wondered how much of a habit this was with him. It was something else to consider if taking the jewel turned out to be more brawn than brain. But, he was not a vindictive man at heart. 'No, he was only doing what he thought was right. Don't punish him.'

Morton looked thoughtful. 'I will compromise,' he said. 'He normally sleeps in the kitchen. Tonight, he can sleep in the stables instead. He does like his comfort, does Micah. And sleeping in the kitchen means he is never far from food, which suits him also. So, Master Marlowe, is this a plan? You sleep here tonight and Micah sleeps with your horse.'

Marlowe smiled and extended a hand, but carefully. His ribs were rebelling at pointless movement.

151

'I will get Barnet to bring in your bag and then we will put you to bed, when it has been aired. A bowl of frumenty and an early night will soon have you right as rain.' Morton stood back smiling, his cherub's curls bouncing around his face. Marlowe almost felt sorry for what he must do, but what was a little breaking and exiting, for the good of the country?

Just knowing where the Spymaster was at any given time was half the art of being a projectioner. He was rarely at home at Barn Elms where the trout rippled under the cool brown waters. More often he could be found at Placentia, its gilded turrets standing tall over the river at Greenwich. His second home was the palace of Whitehall, with its labyrinth of tunnels and gloomy passageways.

But today, Francis Walsingham was at Nonsuch, the fairy palace at Cuddington where the towers shimmered in high summer like hoar frost in their whiteness. The Queen's Spymaster felt uncomfortable here, if only because he, like his Mistress, was an unwelcome guest. In one of her increasing fits of meanness, Her Majesty had sold the great house her father had built to John, Lord Lumley, three years ago, yet she couldn't stay away.

'Whither thou goest,' as the highfalutin Biblical and poetic phrase of the day had it, so did the Court. So a less-than-enchanted John Lumley bowed low whenever the Queen arrived and decamped to a hunting lodge in the grounds. And if the Queen was at Nonsuch, so was Walsingham. And so, after hard riding, was Nicholas Faunt.

The golden clock in the Inner Court was chiming the hour as the projectioner swung out of the saddle and handed the reins to a groom, wearing the livery of the Queen. The sun sparkled in the fountains where living water tumbled from the gargoyle mouths of sea monsters, splashing over stone griffins' wings to whirl and bubble in troughs of pure marble. Hercules gazed down at Faunt as he dashed for the steps and the Queen's guards clicked to attention as he passed.

He found Walsingham wandering in Lumley's Italian garden, the long-suffering clerk trotting behind him like a marionette on a string.

'Make this quick, Faunt. She's planning a Progress.' It had been a while since Her Majesty had gone a-wandering. She rode her white horse, with bells on her fingers and bells on her toes, her musicians fluting and luting behind her. Tall gentlemen in their velvets and silks carried her canopy, to shield her from sun and rain. And among those gentlemen, armed to the teeth and watchful as hawks, Walsingham's men mingled. They might look like fops and popinjays but to a man they were trained killers, ready for any and every eventuality. For nearly twenty years now there had been a price on the head of Elizabeth Tudor. The Pope himself had given absolution in advance to any good Catholic who chose to end her days and with them, the Protestant heresy. Walsingham's men had to watch for them *and* the odd maniac Puritan, or the mad atheists like Francis Kett; who knew what murderous design any of them had on the Queen?

But the woman was maddeningly, infuriatingly optimistic. Her people loved her, she assured Walsingham, and they had a right to see her; their fine lady, their Gloriana. George Gower's Armada portrait had said it all – the exquisite face below the flaming red hair and above all the ropes of pearls. Her hand lay on a globe, a world that belonged only to her and the galleons of Spain sank at her merest gaze.

'A Progress?' Faunt nodded briefly at the secretary who bowed while still steadying his portable writing desk.

Walsingham bent to pick one of Lumley's roses, then thought better of it and merely sniffed it. He sneezed loudly. 'Nothing too exotic, apparently. You know she never goes north of Kenilworth. But you know, too, what this means?'

Faunt knew. All leave cancelled. All projects halted. Every man jack of Walsingham's people on high alert.

'So . . .' Walsingham was struggling with the inner demons of his nose that demanded he sneeze again. 'What news of Starkey's globe?'

'Gone, Sir Francis.'

Walsingham stopped walking. 'Gone – like Walter Mildmay's?'

'Not exactly,' Faunt said and smiled at the memory. 'Rather, it was given away.'

'Generous man, is he, Oliver Starkey?'

'You don't know him, sir?'

'Oh, I've met him, of course, but a long time ago. He must be a hundred. Blind as a bat.'

'He has a granddaughter.' Faunt was remembering still.

Walsingham frowned, his Puritanical streak widening in the rose garden. 'And the relevance of that?' he asked.

'It's the granddaughter who is generous,' Faunt told him, damping down the reminiscent gleam in his eye; Walsingham could read him like a book and he had no intention of going into detail. 'She gave the gewgaw to a . . . friend. Robyn.'

'Robyn who?'

Faunt shrugged. 'Just Robyn.'

'Well, that narrows it down to only a few thousand men in this great country of ours. Tell me, Faunt; anything *odd* about Starkey? Anything I should know?'

Faunt knew exactly what the Spymaster meant. The old man was a member of a Papist society, albeit rather retired. He had the finger of John the Baptist under a glass dome in his house. He had the hand of John the Baptist painted on his portrait. And his granddaughter was a whore, albeit a beautiful one who gave her wares for free. Faunt could smell one of Walsingham's fires crackling into life. 'Nothing, sir,' he assured his master. 'The Starkeys are as loyal a family as you could wish to meet.'

'How did he come by the globe in the first place?'

'A present from Drake, sir. He invested in the circumnavigation.' At least this part could be the truth and Faunt did prefer to keep a little kernel of that rare commodity in his tales if he could; it made them easier to remember afterwards.

'I also invested,' Walsingham said with a frown,

'but I didn't get one of those. Who's next on that wretched list?'

'Charles Angleton, Sir Francis.' Faunt had committed Joshua's names to memory. 'He's a merchant in the City.'

'All right. Pay him a call and find out what he knows. But that's the last of it. This whole thing is a wild goose chase. And I have more pressing matters.'

'Any news of Marlowe, Sir Francis?' Faunt asked.

'Not yet. But I've a feeling he's chasing shadows too.'

In his room under the eaves, Kit Marlowe waited until the last light of the August day had gone. There was the palest of moons, a crescent that slit the purple curtain of the night. He eased himself out of bed and hauled on his doublet, fastening the dagger at his back. He had spent the day familiarizing himself with the house. He had wandered the knot garden, rundown and tatty, its once-intricate designs a tangle of weeds. He had seen the harvesters in the golden fields that sloped to the sea, their scythes flashing against the dusty stalks, the ears bouncing on the hard ground as the blades sent them tumbling. Women scurried along behind them, building stooks of armfuls of corn and behind them came the gleaners, the old and the young, squealing toddlers and toothless gammers, picking through the furrows for the grain and short stalks left behind. By the time they burned the stubble, there would be not a grain to be found; the funeral pyre of another year would drift over the world, promising the Fall and the decay of all things.

Marlowe knew the stables where Micah was sleeping and hoped he slept the sleep of the just. What Marlowe did *not* need tonight was a man with the strength of ten who would wake at the merest whisper of the wind. He had counted three maidservants and knew that they slept under the eaves like him, but in the far wing of the house. He had heard mention of a steward, Barnet, but he had seen no men other than Morton and his ox-like lackey. Stewards usually had reasonably well-appointed quarters, not far from the kitchen and always on the ground floor. During the day, by a combination of observance and casual conversation, he had found out that Leonard Morton's chamber lay at the front, over the main door with its crumbling archway.

There was no Mistress Morton. The sorrowful owner of Ness End had explained that she had gone in childbed years before, her child with her, and no one had taken her place. Marlowe padded along the passageway, passing the leaded windows as quickly as he could and keeping to the shadows. He half-turned to watch the white ghost of a barn owl glide over the garden, hunting for its supper. Tonight he was a hunter too. He *could* have explained to Morton his mission, tried to explain the mystery of the globes that a woman he knew had died for, but Kit Marlowe was a shrewd judge of men. Morton might understand. He might even sympathize. But he would not part with the jewel, not even for a Queen's messenger, not even for a moment.

Marlowe reached the head of the stairwell where portraits of older Mortons glared down at him from their shabby, once-gilded frames. Who was this stranger in their midst? This thief in the night. The thought had been bothering the projectioner-poet for some time. If Leonard Morton hung the globe on a bedpost or laid it down on a press, all well and good. But if it was still around his neck . . .

But Marlowe had no more time to wrestle with the problem because he heard a sound in the darkness behind him. There was a hiss he knew all too well – the sound of a sword blade slicing through air. He staggered back and the weapon missed. At the other end of it, a middle-aged man stood there. He was fully dressed and had a murderous look in his eye. Walsingham's man had done this before, facing a rapier with a dagger, and he knew it was an unequal contest. If the rapier was in the hands of someone like Nicholas Faunt or even Ned Alleyn when his blood was up, it was suicide. And Marlowe had no idea who this man was. He retreated slowly down the stairs, his dagger still sheathed at his back, his hand sliding down the smooth oak of the banisters. He expected Micah to come crashing through the house like a rampaging bull. At the very least he expected his host to be standing there, demanding to know what was going on. Instead, the swordsman was advancing as slowly as Marlowe was retreating, like the slow practice passes at a fencing school, his blade tip glittering in the soft light.

'I know why you're here,' the man said. He was whispering.

'Do you?' Marlowe whispered too.

'It's been a long time.'

Marlowe frowned. There was a cross purpose here, unless all men at Ness End Hall were as limited as Micah the ox. 'Has it?' Perhaps he could humour the man.

'Years,' the swordsman said. 'I forget how many. But I've been waiting all this time.'

Marlowe had reached the first landing now, where the stairs fell away to his left into the darkness of the great hall. He looked beyond the sword to the man carrying it. He was . . . what . . . fifty or so and he had a bunch of keys at his waist. 'You are the steward here,' Marlowe guessed, his voice still low. 'Barrett?'

'Barnet,' the steward snapped. 'And don't pretend you don't know. *He* sent you, didn't he?'

'He?' Marlowe was descending the last stairs now and once on the flat he knew this madman would strike.

'Don't play games,' Barnet hissed. 'Oh, you may indeed be the Queen's man, but you are here because of Oliver Starkey.'

'Oliver Starkey?' Marlowe played for time. A name from Joshua's list, whispered at him in the dark of this stairwell of all places, was beyond the bounds of coincidence. Marlowe had more than one problem before him now; the first was how to find out what this man knew, the second, how to live to make use of the knowledge.

'Yes. Oliver Starkey. Do you think me slow-witted?' Barnet seemed to relent a little as

159

Marlowe reached the ground level and his blade tip dropped. 'It was all so long ago. Could he not have forgiven and forgotten?'

Marlowe stood still. It was time to stop retreating. This nonsense had gone on long enough. 'Forgotten what, Master Barnet?' The sword hissed forward in a deadly lunge. Marlowe's entire body still ached from his collision with Micah and he was slow on the turn. He heard the rip of his doublet and a clatter as a button was hacked off and dropped to the floor. He spun sideways, grabbing Barnet's sword-arm with one hand and bringing the other down hard on his wrist. The rapier fell, clattering on the flagstones and Marlowe twisted the man's arm up behind his back, forcing him down on to his knees.

'Now,' he said, letting his voice grow a little louder, 'suppose you tell me what all this is about?' He hauled the man up and frogmarched him across the hall and into the kitchen. The place was only lit by the dying embers of the fire in the huge grate, where black pans hung from the racks in the chimney space. Marlowe pushed his man into a chair and stood behind him, his dagger blade horizontally across Barnet's throat.

'Get on with it,' the steward hissed, his eyes closed tight, waiting for the inevitable, the slice across the windpipe which would send his life-blood spraying across the chopping block in front of him. Marlowe could not have chosen a better place for his work.

'If I'd wanted to kill you,' the playwright said, 'I could have done it on the stairs. Your wrist action –' he sheathed the dagger – 'definitely needs work.'

Barnet was astonished. His would-be assassin had disarmed himself and was suddenly sitting cross-legged on the block in front of him like some goblin in the woods. 'You haven't come to kill me?'

'No.' Marlowe smiled.

'Starkey didn't send you?'

'No.'

'And Starkey didn't tell the Queen about me?'

'What is there to tell?'

The silence that followed was ended by a laugh from the steward. Marlowe knew relief when he heard it.

'My God,' Barnet said. 'I thought . . . as soon as I heard you were here on the Queen's business, I thought . . . oh, it's been years. In here . . .' He tapped his head. Then he tapped his heart, and continued, 'And in here. Wherever we keep our souls, Master Marlowe.'

'And your soul is troubled, Master Barnet?'

'That it is,' the steward said.

'Why?' Marlowe asked, the globe and his purpose for being abroad tonight momentarily forgotten. 'And what is Oliver Starkey to you?'

'Oliver Starkey,' Barnet said with a sigh, 'is a knight of St John.'

'The Hospitallers.' Marlowe didn't want to give anything away until he knew what the link between the two men might be.

'They were once called that, yes. He commanded the English contingent at St Elmo.'

'St Elmo?'

161

'Malta. We were besieged there by those bastard Turks. Oh, it was years ago.'

'1565.' Marlowe nodded. 'I was barely in hanging sleeves.'

Barnet snorted. 'I was a soldier of fortune. I was a young man then and I wanted to see the world.'

'And all you saw was St Elmo?'

'That bloody fortress on its bloody rock. It was hopeless. We were outnumbered, four, five to one. I stood it for as long as I could, but one day . . . well –' there were tears in the man's eyes – 'one day I broke. The Turks were pouring in through the gate, with murder in their hearts. Black faces, black hearts. I thought to myself, "Why am I here? What's this all about?" I didn't want to die, Master Marlowe, not in some foreign land under a Papist flag.'

'So you ran?'

'I did. My friends, Harry and the rest, they stayed. But I ran and as I ran, I heard Sir Oliver yelling at me. "Come back, you coward," he said. "Stand and fight like a man."'

'But you didn't.'

Barnet sighed and shook his head. 'I swam for it. Found a fishing boat and lay in it all that day and half the next. Then I rowed away, out into the sea roads, away from that cursed island. Don't ask me how, with a torn arm.'

Marlowe smiled again. 'That explains your wrist action,' he said.

Barnet smiled too, in spite of himself. 'That and the years,' he said. 'You never forget the moves, but you do get rusty. Ever since that day

I've heard that man's voice in my head, echoing and re-echoing down the years. "Come back, you coward." I did a bit of this, a bit of that, always watching my back, jumping at the click of a door. At first I thought they'd all died, all the defenders of St Elmo. But when news came through that it was a victory, that the Knights had held Malta, I thought – I still think – I am a marked man. That Sir Oliver would come looking for me himself. Or at least report me to the authorities. Hiding out here in this wilderness was my best chance.'

There was a sudden crash somewhere in the Hall, beyond the kitchen.

'The strongroom!' Barnet was on his feet, dashing across the flagstones and scuttling across the hall, snatching up his fallen sword as he went. Marlowe followed him. 'Someone's breaking in,' he heard the steward shout and saw him disappear up the stairs to his right, along the landing towards the maids' rooms. He whipped his dagger free and gave chase. Ahead of him was a window, blank in the early morning grey light and it was a dead end. To Marlowe's right, another passage ran the length of the east wing and startled maids popped their heads out of doors.

'Stay there!' Marlowe shouted at them and took the passage to the left.

There was utter darkness here. And silence now. This must have been the way Barnet had gone, but there was no sound. Then he saw him, on a half-floor above, silhouetted against a window. 'Barnet,' Marlowe called. 'Anything?'

The man just stood there, his sword still in his

hand, the blade tip trailing the floor. There was a gurgling sound and as Marlowe reached him and Barnet half-stumbled into the light, he could see that the steward's throat had been cut and dark blood was oozing over his shirt and doublet, his left hand, pressed to his neck, doing nothing to staunch the flow.

Marlowe caught Barnet as his knees buckled and the playwright cradled the dying man's head. There was a crash, a splintering of glass and Marlowe was on his feet again, following the sound and bursting into a darkened room. The window, glass and frame, had gone. He peered out to see a running figure, his left leg dragging as he limped over the cobbles where he had landed badly. Shouts of 'stop, thief!' seemed superfluous as the figure grabbed his horse's reins and swung into the saddle. Marlowe watched transfixed as the horseman clattered for the gate to be confronted by the huge figure of Micah, stumbling half-awake out of the stable. The horseman batted him aside and the ox went down with a groan.

'Jack!'

Marlowe turned back to the landing. Leonard Morton knelt there, his wooden staff abandoned at his side. His hands were red and sticky with the blood of his steward.

'Oh, Jack!'

Barnet's eyes fluttered and his chest heaved one last time as his self-imposed life sentence finally came to an end.

Ten

He limped into the alleyway that ran by Queen's Hythe to the river. Drunks lurched past him on their way home, clattering over the cobbles damp with early morning dew. He saw the spars of the galleons black against the coming dawn. He tapped on the door three times, then once: the appointed signal.

He lifted the latch and went inside. This was another new meeting place, the fourth, or was it fifth, he had been told to find in the space of the last two months. There was no doubt about it, Benedict was a careful man.

'Your usual, Shakespeare?' The voice was like velvet in the darkness. A candle spluttered into life and lit the man's face. Two goblets lay on the table. There was one jug.

'It's a little early for me, Benedict,' he said. 'Or is it late?'

'Never too late,' and he poured a drink for himself. 'What do you have for me?'

The visitor sat down. 'A tale of woe, I fear.'

'Leonard Morton . . .?'

'Wears an opal around his neck.'

There was a pause. 'And does he wear it there, still? Or did you hack it free?'

'I slit the throat of his man,' came the answer, 'but I was interrupted.'

'By his people?'

165

'By Kit Marlowe.'

Benedict paused in mid-sip. 'That name again. Is the man everywhere?'

'He would like us to think so, fire and air as he is.'

'He is a man!' Benedict slammed the cup down so that the jug jumped. 'And I want him stopped.'

There was a silence between them.

'Charles Angleton,' Benedict said. 'Not a stone's throw from here. That's where you'll find the lapis lazuli. And no mistakes, this time, Shakespeare. I'm beginning to wonder what I pay you for.'

'Lowestoft was expensive,' the man replied, by way of a hint. 'In more ways than one.'

'I know,' Benedict replied with a smile, but no purse appeared on the table. 'Lowestoft always is. They're a funny lot round there.'

Ithamore had only heard old Joshua use that word once before and that was when he had driven a spike into his thumb in a careless moment at his bench. Now he used it again, but he was not working. He was looking in disbelief at the state of his workshop, the hapless boy standing in the middle of it. Joshua scowled at him. What was it about the boy that made him look so guilty? He could be as innocent as a lamb, as pure as the first new snow that fluttered on to the roofs of the Vintry in the depths of winter, but there was something about his face that screamed a furtive guilt.

Joshua hit him around the head.

'Ow!' The boy's breaking voice shot skyward

with surprise – although perhaps he shouldn't have been surprised at all. 'What was that for?'

'This!' Joshua threw his arms wide to indicate the chaos. Every drawer had been wrenched open, every lock smashed, every pot overturned. Papers lay strewn in scrolls across the floor.

'I didn't do it!' the boy protested, suddenly not caring whether the old Jew gave him his notice or not.

'No,' Joshua spat as he rummaged through the papers, checking corners, nooks and crannies. 'But you didn't stop it, either.'

Ithamore did not live in, like most apprentices. He lived with the unholy brood his mother had spawned, they whose fathers were some sailors and the children's skin was of the colours of the rainbow, sired as they had been by Turks, Chinamen, Levanters and Mongols. Joshua knew perfectly well that the boy had to wade through the shit of the Vintry's streets to get here from the Tower. It was half an hour's run. And Joshua was insistent that he ran. How long it took the boy to get home after work was his own affair.

Joshua was actually angry with himself, but slapping yourself around the head was not half as satisfying as slapping the next man; and Ithamore was the next man in this and every situation.

'Well, don't just stand there, boy,' the Jew snapped. 'Clear it up.'

Ithamore hopped to it, righting furniture and replacing drawer contents. Joshua's brain whirled. He couldn't see anything obviously missing. The

167

gold was where it had been, give or take a lock or two. So was the silver. Had the thief been so blind that he had overlooked that? Surely not. If you're going to turn over a silversmith's, isn't it precious metal that's uppermost in your mind? Unless, of course . . .

'Ithamore . . .' Joshua had no sooner taken his cap off in disbelief and astonishment than it was back on his head again. 'Who came to see us the other day?'

'Er . . .' Ithamore was at a loss. He spent most of his time out in the yard; he didn't know who the people were who came and went. His master had always made it clear that the less he knew, the better it would be for him.

Joshua gave him another clip around the ear for good measure. 'Marlowe,' he said. 'Christopher Marlowe, the playwright.'

'Oh, yes.' Ithamore remembered vaguely. He had been there when Ithamore had spilled the silver. Again.

'And where do you find a playwright, Ithamore?'

'Er . . . at the theatre?' Ithamore could never be sure whether Joshua's weren't trick questions.

'Right,' said the Jew and he wagged a warning finger at the boy. 'Last chance, mind. How many is that I've given you now? Last chances, I mean.'

'One or two, sir.' Ithamore saw his chance to minimize things.

'Well, let this be the last. When I get back, I want this place spotless.'

*   *   *

168

'Well, we've got to do something.' Ned Alleyn slapped his thigh. There was a crown at a rakish angle on his head and he was well into his second bottle of wine. He was the foremost actor of his day, everybody said so, but he'd been daft enough to take on the role of the king in *King Henry the Sixth* because Philip Henslowe had begged him to do it. And why not? Alleyn had dared God out of Heaven with Kit Marlowe's *Tamburlaine*. Obviously, only Alleyn could play the lead in any play at the Rose, but this was not just *any* play – it was the first, fumbling, faltering attempt by Will Shaxsper and it needed work. A lot of work.

'It's like Marlowe without the Marlowe.' Tom Sledd was drinking too, nodding his agreement and sympathizing. 'Pentameter, just not very iambic, somehow.' He sat in full plate armour with a long skirt under his taces, as unhappy with his role as Joan la Pucelle as Alleyn was with Mad Harry.

'I just assumed,' Alleyn went on in his booming stage voice that carried to the Bear Garden across the road, 'that the king would be a heroic character, something I could get my teeth into. Instead, he's as mad as a tree and crawls around people – anything for a quiet life. Well, that's just not *me*.'

La Pucelle wasn't Tom Sledd either. There was a time when he *always* played the female leads. He had the face for it, the innocent eyes, the high voice. Some said he had the legs as well, but they said it softly because buggery got you burned in Elizabeth's England. Now, though, he was stage manager at the Rose and had thought all that was behind him. Then that useless boy Ben August had gone down with something nasty he'd caught from one of the Bishop of Winchester's geese, so here Sledd was, back in the petticoats again.

'Would he do a rewrite, do you think?' Mad Harry asked the Maid of Orleans. 'Marlowe, I mean.'

'Restore the mighty line?' Sledd took a hefty swig before hauling up his skirts to scratch under his codpiece. 'That would be favourite.'

'I wouldn't mind so much if Shaxsper had even finished the bloody thing,' Alleyn lamented, hanging the crown of England on the chair behind him. 'At least I'd have a death scene. Go out on a memorable note.'

Sledd saw the man's point. No one died on stage quite like Ned Alleyn.

'Where the bloody hell *is* Shaxsper?' Alleyn asked, somewhat plaintively.

But before Sledd could answer, there was the loud clearing of a throat in the darkness of the auditorium. The morning sun lit the alien features of Joshua, as he stepped forward into the centre of the yard like a groundling with the plague.

'Show doesn't start for another two hours, mate.' Sledd was in no mood to be civil, even to a paying punter.

'I'm looking for Kit Marlowe,' Joshua said.

'Aren't we all?' Alleyn sighed.

'Try Henslowe.' Sledd refilled his cup and Alleyn's. 'Up there,' he said and pointed to the gallery. 'In his counting house. You can't miss it.'

Joshua smiled. Counting house was a phrase he understood all too clearly. 'Henslowe?' For that he needed more information.

'Runs the place,' Sledd told him.

'Our Lord and Master.' Alleyn bowed; he who never acknowledged he had such a thing; he who bowed to no one. And he broke into his lines – '"And poise the cause in justice' equal scales, Whose beam stands sure, whose rightful cause prevails". Mother of God, you couldn't make it up.'

'Unfortunately,' Sledd sighed, 'Will Shaxsper could. And has.'

Halfway along the gallery, the Rose became confusing. Flats blocked the only obvious access and a man was sitting there, painting one of them.

'Would you be Master Henslowe?' Joshua asked politely, a little surprised to find the owner of a Southwark theatre carrying out so menial a task.

'Not for ready money. He's along there, second door on the right.'

'Really?' Joshua was lost. 'I was told it was this way.'

'By who?'

'Er . . . the lad in the dress, down on the stage.'

'Oh, him; yes, well, they're actors. Funny lot around here. I don't mingle with them any more than I can help it.' The painter dipped his brush into a pot of rose madder and swept a sunset swathe across the top of the flat, stepping back and looking at it critically, his head on one side. He clearly had no more to add on the subject.

'Quite,' replied Joshua and followed his new instructions.

He heard the rattle of coins before he reached the room and recognized the muttering sound of someone counting money under their breath.

'Master Henslowe?'

Philip Henslowe stopped counting and crouched over the table like a naughty schoolboy caught stealing sweetmeats or a lunatic chained to a wall in Bedlam. 'Who's there?'

'My name is Joshua. I am looking for Kit Marlowe.'

'Joshua?' Henslowe half rose from his chair, careful to scoop all the takings out of sight first. 'How Biblical.' He took in the man's odd robe, the ringlets tucked behind his ears. 'Er . . . Joshua of . . .?'

'All points east.' Joshua shrugged. 'My home, I suppose, is in Venice.'

'Italian!' Henslowe beamed, clicking his fingers. 'I thought so. I never misplace an accent. What news on the Rialto?'

Joshua shrugged and looked skywards, seeing only the cobwebs shimmering in the sun shafts that lit Henslowe's inner sanctum, up here beyond the Gods. 'I haven't seen that for years. There's a rather good little brothel at the eastern end of it.'

'Is there?' Henslowe said, ever a man of the world. 'I did not know that.'

'Master Marlowe?' Joshua reminded the man why he had come.

172

The theatre manager suddenly became very paternal. 'May I ask why you wish to see him?'

'I'm afraid that's my business,' Joshua said.

'Yes, yes, of course. It's just that, well, in this business, actors, playwrights, they draw their creatures, you know, their following. Fanatics, some of them. We can't just give out details will-they, nil-they.'

'I owe him some money,' Joshua said, sliding a bulging purse from his sleeve.

Henslowe's eyes glittered in the reflected sunlight. 'I see. Well, I'm afraid Marlowe's not here at the moment. I could look after it for him, if you would like to . . .'

Joshua replaced the purse and shook his head. 'His address?'

Henslowe's face fell. 'Oh, no, I couldn't possibly . . .'

Joshua let a silver coin clatter on to Henslowe's table, where it rolled in a diminishing circle before it was joined by one more, then another.

'Hog Lane,' Henslowe said to the coins.

Another two followed.

'Number sixteen. By the sign of the Grey Mare. You can't miss it.'

By the time Joshua had reached the Liberty of Norton Folgate, the sun of that endless summer had reached its height and Moorfields lay parched under it, its grass yellow, its windmills still; no wind to ruffle their sails. A strumpet offered him her services outside the Grey Mare, but Joshua's mind was elsewhere and he rapped sharply on the low, studded door of number sixteen.

173

A dog barked at Joshua as he waited and a couple of apprentices, their leather aprons dirty and their hair cropped short, looked at him with distaste. Then the door was opened and a handsome young man stood there in his shirt and Venetians. He looked Joshua up and down. 'Not today, thank you,' he said and made to close the door.

The Jew was faster and he wedged his foot in the way. 'I'm a friend of Kit Marlowe,' he said. 'Is he in?'

The man frowned at him. 'So am I. And no, he's not.'

'I'll wait,' and Joshua barged past both door and man.

'Now, look . . .' But the man never finished his sentence because Joshua was holding the tip of a knife blade under his chin. He flashed a glance around the hall. It was clean and neat with a flight of stairs leading up to the first floor. There was no sign of a servant. Conversely, there was no sign of Kit Marlowe.

'Who are you?' Joshua wanted to know.

'I am Thomas Watson,' the man replied with a gulp. He was not a coward by nature, but in the lifelong battle between discretion and valour, it was usually discretion that won in the world of Tom Watson.

'What are you?' Joshua probed, both with his questions and his blade.

'A poet,' Watson told him. 'Musician. Philosopher of sorts.'

'And Marlowe?'

'Er . . . a playwright. University wit. The Muses' darling. All fire and air.'

'Yes, yes,' Joshua hissed. 'I read his handbills too. I mean, what is Marlowe to you?'

'A friend. And my landlord, I suppose. I live with him. Or he with me. In the nicest possible sense of the term, of course.'

'Of course,' Joshua said. 'Where is he now?'

'Er . . . I don't know. He hasn't been here for a night or two, but we are our own fellows, you know. We come and go as we please.'

Joshua relaxed his grip on Watson's sleeve and the poet drew his first free breath in some minutes. 'So, are you expecting him?' he asked.

Watson felt his throat. Thank God. No blood. 'No. I told you . . .'

'You are your own fellows; yes, I know. Give Marlowe a message from me, will you?'

'Of course.'

'Tell him he has the list. Tell him he has all I have to give. Tell him there was no need to turn my place upside down. Give him this.'

'What it is?' the poet asked.

'It's a bill,' Joshua said. 'A reckoning up of the damage he caused to my workshop. He's got until cock-shut on Thursday to pay me. He does, of course, know the address. After that, I shall take it out of his flesh.' And he slid the dagger away.

Nothing much had changed on stage at the Rose, except perhaps the addition of another bottle, well on the way to being empty. Ned Alleyn was now lying on the floor, one knee bent and the other leg in the air, a crown twirling on his extended toe. Tom Sledd was still in his skirts, but they were now hauled up with no pretence at modesty and he was sitting on the apron of the stage, a sullen pipe in his mouth, smoke trickling out despondently. They scarcely looked up as the door at stage right crashed back and Thomas Watson stormed into their midst.

'Where's Kit?' he gasped, hand to his chest.

Alleyn snorted. 'Kit who?' he said, finally.

Watson kicked him non-too-gently in the ribs. 'Christopher Marlowe, playwright and poet,' he said.

'Oh, *him*,' Alleyn said nastily. 'The playwright and poet who should be here, rescuing this rubbish of Shaxsper's from disaster and me from death by turnip.'

Watson listened carefully. Had the generation's greatest actor just said turnip? 'I beg your pardon, Master Alleyn,' he said.

'Turnip.' Alleyn kicked the crown up in the air and reached out to catch it. It clattered somewhere behind some scenery and he lost interest in it. 'I say turnip, of course. Generic vegetable.'

'Yes.' Sledd got up and shook out his skirts. 'It was half a cabbage nearly got me the other night, but still . . . this play *is* a disaster. They just come to throw things, that's what I think.' He sucked furiously on his pipe, which had gone out.

'It can't be that bad,' Watson said, dismissively, 'but, look, this is important. I need to find Kit . . .'

'We *all* need to find Kit,' the two actors said in perfect unison.

'A man is after him. He says Kit . . . well, I'm

not sure what he has done, but I know that this man is angry. *Really* angry.'

Alleyn seemed to see Watson for the first time. 'You're Thomas Watson, aren't you?'

'Yes!' Watson could have screamed with frustration. 'But . . .'

'You're a writer, aren't you?' Alleyn nodded at Sledd, who moved forward, putting an avuncular arm across Watson's shoulder.

With Alleyn on the other side, Watson had been caught in a perfect pincer movement. 'I dabble,' he said, looking at each man dubiously.

Alleyn treated him to his musical laugh, which had women the length and breadth of London swooning. 'Dear boy,' he said, dropping his voice now to its deepest timbre. 'More than dabble, or so I hear.'

Sledd grimaced. He had heard Watson's stuff but any old port in a storm.

'I'm more of a poet, really,' Watson offered. 'Musician, I should say. Lyricist.'

Alleyn waved his protestations away with a languid hand. 'This will be a simple task for anyone who is imbued with Marlowe's mighty line every day,' he said.

As the last conversation he had had with Marlowe had been through a haze of alcohol, Watson was not so sure, but Alleyn's voice had a way of creeping under the skin, making a man feel all was possible and, almost without his conscious intervention, Watson's head began to nod, at first slightly, then enthusiastically. 'I'll do it!' he cried.

'Good man!' Alleyn clapped him on the back.

'Tom –' he smiled at the stage manager – 'get someone to clear that little room at the back, you know the one.'

Sledd knew the one. The only one in the theatre with a lock.

'Get Master Watson here some ink and parchment, some bread, some wine . . . perhaps not wine, some water. A copy of the play so far, if we have one.'

Sledd was pretty sure there was one somewhere about – he would try to find one with the least defacing; the company had become a little critical of Shaxsper over the last week or so and had taken it out on the pages.

Watson stood there smiling. Something momentous had happened to his life, though for the life of him he couldn't work out how. But he thought of his many months of unpaid rent and made up his mind to do this job, take the payment and never come near Ned Alleyn again. The man was some kind of magus, his words did things that shouldn't be allowed. Then, a thought struck him.

'I will be paid, will I?' he asked. 'For my work.'

Sledd and Alleyn exchanged a look. Then, again in perfect unison, they turned to him and spoke.

'Of *course* you will,' they said. 'You just need to see Master Henslowe and he'll see you right,' Alleyn added, speaking solo.

Sledd turned away. He didn't have Alleyn's skill of hiding a smile and he didn't want to give the game away.

In keeping with his role as Privy Councillor and Queen's Spymaster, Francis Walsingham owned more books than his royal mistress had wigs. But there was one of those volumes that could not be found in his library at Barn Elms, nor in his study at Whitehall, nor any of the other palaces within the Verge, the visiting circle of Her Majesty. That was because it never left his side. It was usually tucked discreetly into a secret panel in his purse, with a dagger to protect it. At best it was on whatever table was nearest to the man. And it contained the names and current addresses of every man in his employ, from high-ranking projectioners like Nicholas Faunt, to the humblest intelligencer who listened at keyholes and lurked on staircases. All of them were listed in Carolingian Miniscule, a centuries old script that only Walsingham and his Code Master, Thomas Phelippes, could understand.

He was flicking through its well-thumbed pages that Thursday. It was Lammastide, the first day of August, although the Church of England made little of that these days and an old Puritan like Francis Walsingham hardly noticed.

'All right,' he said after a considerable silence. He looked at Nicholas Faunt, sitting alongside him in his oak-panelled chamber in the bowels of Whitehall. 'Catlyn it is.' He got up suddenly and crossed the room to the map pinned to the wall. It showed Gloriana's England in all its greatness and on it was a dotted line, the route that the Queen intended to take on her Progress later that month.

Faunt was less than positive. Of all Walsingham's men, Maliverny Catlyn was the one he liked least.

The man was no fool and he was straight as a die, but he could – and did – whinge for England. Whatever Walsingham paid him, it wasn't enough. Did the Spymaster not realize he had a family, expenses, a certain lifestyle? Even when Faunt had pointed out to him that that applied to almost everybody, it didn't shut the man up. Did no one realize, that he lived in Buckinghamshire and Buckinghamshire as everybody knew (except the Spymaster, apparently) was the most costly county in the kingdom. Faunt had permanent jaw-ache yawning at that one.

'She insists on Buckingham –' Walsingham was frowning at the map, imagining a mad assassin at every fork in the road, on every bend – 'so it has to be Catlyn. He'll be in charge for that part of the Progress.'

There was a knock at the door and Kit Marlowe swept in. He half-bowed to them both. 'Masters.'

Faunt snorted, suppressing a laugh. The cobbler's son had not acknowledged a master for years – why start now? The subtlety of it was lost on Walsingham.

'Ah, Marlowe. Yes, those wretched globes. Look, I've already told Faunt. Forget it.'

'Forget it?' Marlowe echoed, looking at both men for an explanation.

'I visited the next man on my list,' Faunt told him. 'Charles Angleton. He was less than helpful.'

'Does he still have his jewel?' Marlowe asked.

'God only knows. I didn't get over his threshold.'

'He owns that big place, doesn't he? By the Bridge?'

180

Faunt nodded. 'Fishmongers' Hall stands to its right.'

'What did he say when you asked him about it?' Marlowe wanted to know.

'I didn't see him. Angleton didn't get where he is today without serious support. The man owns a private army. I haven't seen so many halberds in one place outside the Tower.'

Marlowe raised an eyebrow. 'You mean Nicholas Faunt couldn't think of a way past all that?'

A little muscle jumped in Faunt's jaw. He liked Kit Marlowe. But the man was an over-reacher and one day he would tread on the wrong toes.

'I told Faunt and now I'm telling you,' Walsingham snapped. 'Forget this nonsense about the jewels. All very entertaining, I'm sure . . .'

'Entertaining?' Marlowe strode forward, staring the Spymaster in the face. 'Two people at least are dead because of these jewels. We owe it to them to—'

'You forget yourself, sir!' Walsingham bellowed. He didn't lose his temper often but when he did, half of Whitehall knew about it. Outside in the passageway, Her Majesty's guards checked their weapons, just in case. The Spymaster had turned an unusual shade of puce, but he recovered himself and turned back to the map. 'At the moment,' he said quietly, 'I have my hands full with Her Majesty's plans for the Progress. Faunt is part of those plans.'

'And I?' Marlowe asked.

Walsingham looked the playwright up and down. He had no time for insubordinates today.

181

'No, Marlowe,' he said coldly. 'I have no need of you.'

For a moment, Marlowe stood there, then Faunt jerked his head silently towards the door and the over-reacher left.

Eleven

Marlowe knew that he had overreached himself, something he usually took care not to do, especially around Sir Francis Walsingham. But his heart had ruled his head this time and he had spoken out of turn. Since the death of Jane Benchkyne he had felt that he had a personal axe to grind in this matter. And the more he delved into it, the more the threads tangled and wove themselves around him and he knew that soon, unless he found his way out of the labyrinth, a Minotaur would come roaring out of the dark and take him down into a pit from which there may well be no escape. He needed to clear his head and for that, he needed to go to the Rose.

To many, the Rose was a place of entertainment, but by and large they left as soon as the lights went out. For all who worked there, it could still be a place of enchantment, but more normally it was a place where they could expect to have the very life sucked out of them and to be spat back out on to the cobbles, old before their time and reeking of sawdust and greasepaint. Marlowe was drawn there in spite of himself; what did not kill him made him stronger and he was in need of some comfort and validation. Not that he would receive either at the Rose – for Philip Henslowe, you were only as good as your last play; for Ned Alleyn, you were only as good as your last death scene; for Tom Sledd . . .

'Oh, Kit, Kit, thank Heavens above you're here.' He was suddenly draped in the theatre manager, being hugged and squeezed and, yes, kissed on both cheeks. 'Where have you been?'

Marlowe took Sledd's forearms in a firm grip and unwrapped them from around his neck. He held him at arms' length. He had removed the skirts but still retained La Pucelle's plate armour above the waist, presenting a rather unusual picture. Like everything behind the scenes of the Rose, there was likely to be a good reason for what Sledd was wearing, so Marlowe decided to overlook it. 'Busy, Tom.' It was impossible to explain where he had been and why. It made him realize, however, how long he had been away. 'You know me; hither, thither. All places are alike and every earth is fit for burial.'

'There you *are*, you see!' Sledd punched him in the shoulder.

'Ow. There what are . . . is?'

'You. You speak better lines when you are just talking than Shaxsper can conjure up after days with a quill and parchment.'

'That's good of you, Tom, but why bring Will into it?'

'Because we've been looking for him for weeks, to try and do something about this play he has left us with. He wrote most of it and we rehearsed. I can't say we were very excited by it, but it was going as well as you might expect. Ned grabbed the king's part, only to find that he wasn't the hero.'

184

Marlowe looked across at the wall of the auditorium, which had a handbill pasted to it. 'It seems to be called –' he leaned forward and squinted in the poor light – '*Henry VI*.' He straightened up and looked back at the stage manager. 'That seems straightforward enough.'

Tom opened his mouth to explain, then gave it up as a bad job. 'Kit,' he said, 'nothing is straightforward in this farrago. It doesn't seem to have a proper start, even. We spent days looking for the missing pages, until someone said they thought this was all there was. And the ending . . . diabolical.'

'Well, that's good. The groundlings love a bit of fire and brimstone. That's why Master Henslowe had that trapdoor built, wasn't it? For a bit of Demon King work.'

'Yes,' Sledd said with a sigh. 'But I don't mean "diabolical" –' he put two fingers to his head like horns and gave vent to a spine-chilling laugh – 'I mean diabolical.' This time he turned down the corners of his mouth and slumped his shoulders. 'As in terrible, awful, they throw vegetables.'

'Ah.'

'So that's why we've been looking for you.'

Marlowe backed away, hands up. 'No, Tom, oh, no, you don't. Let the lad win his spurs. He wrote it, let him put it right.' He paused, his head cocked like a dawn-treading sparrow after a worm. 'Did I hear someone calling?'

Sledd listened and then said, 'No, I don't think so. Where was I? Yes, well, we would love to let him put it right, Kit, but he seems to have disappeared.'

That didn't sound like Will Shaxsper to Marlowe. Here was a man for whom no ripple of applause was too small. It seemed unlikely that he would not stay around for his first play's opening. 'Was he well when you saw him last? Not in love, or anything?'

Sledd smiled. 'Will is always in love, Kit,' he said. 'But no more than usual, no. You wouldn't think he was a married man with three children, would you?'

Marlowe thought back to other married men he knew, with or without three children, and could come to no consensus as to what made typical behaviour. 'He's an actor, Tom,' he said. 'No one expects actors to be normal.' He stopped again. 'There definitely *is* someone calling, you know.'

'Probably someone out in the street,' Sledd said, hurriedly. 'But, Kit, have a heart. Now you're here, and Will is not, couldn't you just look at his last few pages?'

'I can never read his writing,' Marlowe hedged.

'Nor can we,' Sledd agreed. 'Watch the play tonight, then. Tell me what you think. It may be that it just needs . . . oh, I don't know. Another character. Just one more speech, perhaps. It just isn't working as it is.'

A large glob of paint suddenly fell from the flies and landed between them.

Sledd looked up. 'Dick!' he yelled. 'If you do that one more time, you'll be looking for new employment.' He turned back to Marlowe. 'Sorry, Kit,' he began. 'You just can't get . . .'

But Marlowe had gone.

He had slipped out between two leaning flats

and was treading slowly and silently down the corridor that ran behind the stage. He was listening intently and pausing every step or so, triangulating on the sound which he now knew for sure he could hear.

'Kit? Kit, is that you?'

He couldn't be sure, but it sounded a lot like Thomas Watson.

'Tom?' He spoke quietly but still the answer came.

'Oh, thank God in Heaven. Kit, I'm in here.' A tapping sounded from along the corridor and Marlowe moved towards it.

He put his mouth to the keyhole. 'Tom? Tom Watson? What on earth are you doing in there?'

'It's a long story . . .' Watson sounded weary and there was something else odd about his voice that Marlowe could not quite place for a moment, then it fell into place. For the first time in many a long and bibulous month, Thomas Watson was stone cold sober.

'Tom, stand away from the door,' Marlowe said. 'I'm going to break it in.'

'NO!' Watson's voice came out as a hysterical squeak. 'There isn't room to swing a cat in here. You'll hurt us both if you do that. Go and get a key.'

Marlowe thought for a moment. It had to be Alleyn – no one else would do this. But Tom Sledd would have the key. 'Hold on, Tom,' he said to Watson through the door. 'I'll be back.' He just stopped himself from telling Watson not to go away; he wasn't sure how much of his sense of humour was still intact.

Tom Sledd was overseeing the swabbing of the

stage to remove the paint blob when Marlowe reappeared.

'Oh, there you are, Kit,' he said, with a smile. 'Call of nature?'

'No.' Marlowe's voice sounded like the thud of a coffin lid and Sledd looked up, anxiously.

'Problem?' he said, quietly, shooing the maid-servant and her bucket away.

'Why?' Marlowe said, speaking with unnatural calmness, the calm before a storm. 'Why do you have Thomas Watson locked up backstage?'

'Thomas Wa . . .? He's not locked up,' Sledd said with a laugh. 'That door sticks sometimes, he's just . . .'

'Locked. In.' Marlowe looked dangerous.

'Kit, I can explain.' Sledd was already scurrying off the stage, rummaging for his keys. 'We needed someone to finish Shaxsper's play. And Watson came looking for you.'

Marlowe held the man back. 'Looking for me? Why?'

'Something about a man looking for you. Something like that. Anyway –' Sledd pulled away and started off towards backstage again – 'I'll have him out in two shakes of a lamb's tail and then you can ask him yourself.'

Marlowe stood behind the flustered stage manager as he struggled with the keys. After a lot of muffled oaths and confusion, Watson was finally free. He turned to Sledd and took a deep breath, but thought better of it. He thrust some inky pages at the man and then turned on his heel. 'Kit,' he said, 'there's a man after you. He's *really* angry!'

* * *

'But apart from angry, Tom.' Watson had calmed down a little after a few tankards of ale at the Mermaid and Marlowe was trying to pick the facts from the embroidery. 'And allowing for the fact that he couldn't really be *that* tall –' he waved his hand in the air high above his head – 'can you give me any other clues?'

The problem with being Kit Marlowe was that the list of men that were *really* angry was a long one. He needed it to be fined down a little: age, height, colour of hair. A name would have been more help still, but Watson had little to add on any level. His incarceration with only props, parchment, ink, bread and water for company seemed to have driven things he once knew completely from his head. He spread his hands apologetically. 'I really am so sorry, Kit. I'm a bit flustered, to be brutally frank. One minute, I was looking for you at the Rose, then the next minute, Ned Alleyn is muttering in my ear. After that, it's all rather a blur.'

'Yes. Alleyn will do that to a person.' Marlowe clapped Watson on the shoulder and took a draught of ale. 'I actually pretended to be you, just briefly, the other day.'

Watson spilled his drink in his agitation. 'Kit! Who to?'

The playwright chuckled. 'Don't worry, Tom. It was a long way from here. And it wasn't to a husband, as far as I know. But it just goes to show; I meet a lot of people. A lot of them end up angry. We'll wait and see if he turns up again but, Tom, if he does, try and find out who he is, please!'

'Sorry, Kit.' Watson buried his nose in his tankard. 'Are you home now, for a bit? Only, there is no food in the house, and I have no money . . .'

'Tom!' Kit reached for his purse and passed across some coins. 'Living with you is a little like being married, I should think, but without even the smallest fringe benefit.'

'Married!' Watson suppressed a shudder. Least said, soonest mended on that score.

'As for me, I am home now for a while, I think. Sir Francis is arranging a Progress . . .'

'A Progress?' Watson's eyes lit up. The owners of the houses the Queen visited had often need of a singer of songs. 'Do we know where she's off to?'

'Walsingham would know. Are you still on speaking terms?'

'Yes, yes, quite friendly. We came to an agreement on that little matter.'

'Yes, well, Thomas, how often must I tell you? Sir Francis does not appreciate his people making free with his daughter. And her so recently a widow . . .'

Watson waved the poet to be quiet. 'Sshh, Kit, ssshh! It was a dalliance, nothing more.'

'I think that's what I mean,' Marlowe pointed out. 'However, the Progress has meant that all other matters are put to one side. Including mine.'

Watson looked hard at his friend. 'That doesn't sound like you,' he observed.

'No, it doesn't, I know. But I don't know how to go about the next step. It needs men, resources, time I just don't have.'

'I could help!' Watson looked brightly at Marlowe, like a puppy eager to please.

'Thank you, Tom, but I couldn't ask it of you. You will have songs to sing, women to dally with. A Progress wouldn't be the same without you. But,' Marlowe continued with a sigh, 'I feel I want to carry on with this. There is a woman dead, who did nothing to deserve it. And a man, who, if he had guilt on his conscience, had paid his dues many times over when his end came. I want to put things right, for them.'

'It does you credit, Kit,' Watson said.

'And,' Marlowe added with a laugh into his ale, 'Sir Francis Walsingham got under my skin. I want to show him what I'm made of.'

Watson laughed too. 'And that does you even more credit,' he said. 'But don't annoy him until I have all my Progress dates signed and sealed.'

'I won't. If I am lucky, he won't know what I'm doing until it's done. But, Tom, I am at a dead end with this problem. I roll the words around my head, day and night, and nothing comes together. The world. More than the world. Diamonds. Opals. Silver. Sir Francis Drake . . .'

'Well, there's a name to conjure with,' Watson said.

'Conjure. Conjure. Tom, I believe you have solved my conundrum as to who I go to for help.'

'Oh.' Watson was puzzled. 'I have? That's a good thing.'

'I could kiss you.'

Watson backed away. This marriage thing was being taken much too far, in his opinion.

'But I won't. I must be away. Don't wait up.'

191

And Marlowe was gone, his cloak flying, his eyes alight. He had dealt with Mercator and Joshua, albeit without resolution, during the day. But he must wait for another sunset before he could find the man he thought might hold the answer. The hunt was up and his quarry flew among the stars.

Twelve

It had not rained in London for weeks but that did not stop the river mist from creeping across the city in the early morning, wreathing its way over the Sufferance Wharves and up Billingsgate. It crawled westward, along Queenshithe, past Baynard's Castle and inland towards Ludgate.

Kit Marlowe had no time for the magic of the morning now. His poet's eye usually saw it all – the market stalls and the street criers, the alms-beggars, the crop-headed apprentices and the motherless children. They would all find their places in his plays, in his poems, in the smock-alleys of his mind. But now his mind was filled with something else. He had the clarity of a man who hadn't slept since the day before yesterday and unanswered questions chased each other through his brain like St Elmo's fire under the thunder. A man who surely had some answers was not far away, renting premises near the churchyard of Paul's on its high ground over Ludgate and the Cheap.

'He's not here,' a voice called from overhead.

Marlowe looked up at the first-floor window where a woman was shaking a rug into the air, dust flying in all directions.

'Who?' he asked. 'Who's not here?'

The woman stopped her work and frowned down at him. 'Is this some sort of riddle?' she asked, testily.

Were there other worlds? Like this one but alongside it? Marlowe had heard of such things. Perhaps he had found one now. 'I was looking for Master Mercator, the map-maker.'

'Aren't we all?' the woman said, suddenly attacking the mat with a cane beater. 'Foreign bastard owes me two weeks' rent.'

Marlowe was getting a crick in his neck. 'Do you know where he's gone?'

'Abroad,' she told him and leaned down to impart her nugget of wisdom. 'A bloody place.'

'May I come in?'

For almost the first time she looked down at her caller. He was a handsome rakebell, there was no doubt of that, well set up and wearing fine clothes. His shoulders were a little dusty, but she thought she might know the reason for that. No hat, though. She knew her Sumptuary laws – a man with no hat could never be considered a gentleman. 'Why would you want to do that?' she asked him.

'He may have left . . . a forwarding address,' Marlowe suggested. It didn't convince him either.

'If he'd left that I'd have sent my Jim round. To get my back rent. And to black his eyes.'

A grizzled head popped out alongside the woman's. His hair was cropped shorter than an apprentice's and a scar ran the length of his right cheek.

'Good morning, Jim,' Marlowe said and beamed. 'Thank you both for your help.'

He turned and made for the Cheap, cutting down Knightrider Street where the stalls were coming to life and awnings were being hauled into place

194

and creaking carts brought the fruit and vegetables from the country. If Michael Mercator had gone back to the Rhine there would be no finding him. Walsingham had men at various points along that river as he had along the Thames and they could help a fellow projectioner as he made his way in the Spymaster's twilit world. But there was somebody nearer to home who had answers too. And he lived in the Vintry.

Or rather, he didn't. Just as Mercator's premises were locked and barred, so were Joshua's. Only more so. A huge padlock hung from the doorcatch and the windows were boarded up with rough planks. The streets around were the usual hive of activity, heavy horses pulling drays of barrels, good hogsheads of ale and casks of wine. The air was heady already with the scent of the grape and the sun was not yet over the shattered spire of Paul's. Yet Joshua's home, his workshop and outbuildings seemed derelict, dead. Marlowe's knock had achieved nothing. He could hear it echoing faintly through the passageways beyond, but there was no reply, no rattle of bolts nor pad of scurrying feet.

He turned to go, frustrated twice already this morning, when he saw a movement in an upper storey window. A curtain twitched, he was sure of that. If the front was locked and barred, what about the back? There was someone in the Jew's house and Marlowe still needed answers. He hammered loudly on the neighbouring vintner's door. As it opened, he held up an old playbill of Tamburlaine he carried in his purse. 'Customs check,' he announced, batting aside the confused serving man who stood there.

'What d'you mean, customs check?' A younger, burlier man blocked his way.

'You are . . .?' Marlowe looked the man up and down. There is no more supercilious look than that to be found on a University wit, playwright of some repute and poet, when he wants to stare down the opposition. However, on this opposition, it appeared to be wasted.

'Asking you a question,' the man said, not giving an inch.

Marlowe looked at him closely, his dark eyes burning. 'Sirrah,' he said quietly. 'Are you familiar with the name Sir Walter Ralegh?'

'Of course,' the man said and blinked. 'Comptroller of Wines. Er . . . oh.'

'Walt . . . Sir Walter, was saying to me only the other day; "Kit," he said, "when you begin your new commission for me, don't forget to investigate the vintners by the Cranes." Now, you are . . .?'

'Oh, anxious to comply, sir, of course. My name is . . .'

'Fascinating.' Marlowe brushed him aside. 'This house links with next door?'

'Er . . . yes. The passage upstairs. But what relevance . . .?'

Marlowe stopped on the bottom stair. 'What relevance?' he frowned. 'Man, man, can you be serious? This hot summer has turned this great city of ours into a tinderbox. Sir Walter is concerned that all his properties are as secure as possible.'

'So . . . you're not here about the wine?'

Marlowe's stern face broke into a smile. Then

he chuckled, tapping the man's shoulder. 'Not this time . . . what did you say your name was?'

The vintner opened his mouth.

'Whatever.' Marlowe fluttered his hand and bounded up the stairs. 'Don't worry; I'll find my own way.'

He left the bewildered vintner with no name staring in confusion at his serving man and dashed along the passageway. There was a small door in one wall, set well into the brickwork and Marlowe knew instinctively that it led to the outside. He hauled it open and found himself on a narrow wooden bridge that crossed the space between the vintner's and Joshua's workshop. London was full of streets in the sky like this. He was in no mood to knock on the far door and he shoulder-barged it. As it crashed back he heard running feet inside the building. He found a stair-well and looked down. Somebody was hurrying towards the courtyard at the back.

Marlowe leapt the last four stairs and was out into the open air. A breathless lad faced him, a pair of metalworking tongs in his hand. The projectioner straightened. 'Ithamore, isn't it?' he asked. 'What are you going to do with those? Pinch me to death?'

The boy's mouth was hanging open. It was dry as the timbers around him and he was plainly terrified.

'Where is your master?' Marlowe asked. 'Where is Joshua?'

'I don't know, sir,' the lad managed. 'I haven't seen him since . . .'

'Since what, Ithamore?'

'Since you ransacked the place, sir.'

Marlowe was back in that Otherworld again. 'I ransacked the place?' he repeated.

Ithamore nodded dumbly, remembering only now to close his mouth. But he still held the tongs in front of him. This man was dangerous; you only had to look into his eyes. Marlowe smiled, those deadly eyes creasing as he did it. 'Did you see me, lad?' he asked. 'Did you see me ransack the place?'

'No, sir,' Ithamore had to admit.

'Then, how do you know I did?'

'Um . . .' Ithamore was a silversmith's apprentice and not a very good one at that. Nobody had ever asked him to *think*. 'The master said so, sir,' was the best he could do.

'The master,' Marlowe said, nodding. 'And did the master see me ransack the place?'

'No, sir.' The second confession of the morning.

'When did all this happen?'

'A couple of days ago, sir. Proper turned over it was. I put it all back.'

Marlowe laid a gentle hand on the tongs and lowered them, taking them easily from Ithamore's grasp. 'Was anything taken?' he asked. 'Did the master say?'

'No, sir. He couldn't find anything amiss. But he knowed it was you.' Ithamore could barely look Marlowe in the eye. The man was a gentleman, and gentlemen had money, with access to power and the law. More than that, gentlemen went armed. Ithamore couldn't see it, but he knew there was a dagger tucked in ready for action at Marlowe's back.

'Where is he now,' Marlowe asked, 'the master?'

'I don't rightly know, sir. He took all his books and his equipment and loaded it all on a cart. Well, to be precise, *I* loaded it on a cart. And he left town.'

'And you don't know which way he went?'

'No, sir. He told me to lock the place up and board up the windows. I hadn't quite finished when—'

'When I came back,' Marlowe said. 'No doubt to ransack the place a second time.' He slipped a hand into his purse and flipped out a coin. He took Ithamore's hand and pressed the silver into it. 'If the master comes back,' he said, 'tell me. You'll find me in Hog Lane, by the sign of the Grey Mare.'

He patted the boy's shoulder and dashed up the stairs the way he had come. On his way back through the vintners' he saw the two men still standing there, watching him anxiously as he came down to ground level.

'All well?' the vintner asked, wringing his hands just a little.

'It'll pass.' Marlowe was back in official mode again. 'By the way,' he said as he swept past the men, 'failing to give your name to an officer of Sir Walter Ralegh's Customs and Excise is a punishable offence. Remember that next time.'

And he saw himself out.

The rest of the day stretched before him. He had hardly achieved anything of what he had set out to do but that was not a unique situation for him. Muses' darling or no, sometimes the words just wouldn't come and today was one

199

of those days – people weren't where they should be; facts were not lining themselves up like ducks to be shot when the gypsies were in town with their games of chance, their dances and their singing. Usually when he was feeling like this, his feet led him to the Rose and today was no exception. But he didn't want to go in. So far, he had managed to avoid Philip Henslowe and his requests for just one more scene. Henslowe he could usually resist, but Tom Sledd also wanted his help and he and Tom went back a long time, back to the days when the road was long and straight and the whole world was at their feet. Even in their salad days, they knew there was evil abroad but then it had a face. Now he felt like a mariner on stormy seas and as soon as there was land in view, a squall caught his sails and tossed him in another direction. Terra incognita surrounded him on every side.

A nap, back in Hog Lane, might do it. He could hardly remember when he had slept last and suddenly his bed was calling. How easy it must be to be Thomas Watson – and he had after all taken his name in vain from time to time, when needs must – to be able to lie down in any bed and with any body and forget the world for a while. With a sigh, he turned from the welcoming arms of the Rose and let his feet take him to Hog Lane.

He was asleep before his head hit the pillow.

In the Rose, all was excitement. One of the bit players, always there from early morning till the last groundling had left, in case someone went down with something debilitating and he could snatch stardom from insignificance, had run in, grabbing Philip Henslowe by the sleeve and shaking his arm vigorously.

'He's here!' he shrieked. 'He's here!'

Henslowe shook the lad off and looked at his sleeve, which was crumpled and covered with something that looked worryingly like cheese. The boy, calming down, brushed off the remains of his breakfast and took a deep breath.

'Master Marlowe,' he said. 'I just saw him, walking up the lane to the side door.'

Henslowe brightened up. 'Marlowe? Here?' He started waving his arms and giving orders. 'You!' He pointed randomly into the pit and a voice called back.

'Yes, Master Henslowe?'

'Go out and ask Master Marlowe if he would like to come in and see me at his convenience. At his convenience, mind. Be civil.'

'Yes, Master Henslowe.' The dogsbody rushed off and the auditorium was briefly bathed in morning sunshine as the door opened and then swung to.

'Marlowe, eh?' Henslowe could see his troubles packing up their bits and traps and hightailing it out of the city by the nearest gate. He was pleased and relieved on another level too. He had sold his top money-spinner for a few coins and he had been worrying ever since. But here he was, hale and hearty, outside his very door. He turned to the bringer of the news.

'He wasn't . . . bleeding, or anything, was he?' he asked.

'Er . . . no, Master Henslowe. He looked a bit tired, but not bleeding.'

'Not limping, not injured in any way?'

The bit player shook his head. 'No, Master Henslowe. He looked as usual to me.'

Henslowe rubbed his hands together in anticipation and paced the stage.

Tom Sledd stayed well back in the shadows. If Henslowe knew that he and Alleyn had had Marlowe in their grasp only the previous day and had let him leave without so much as a word to show his passing through, then they would both be marked men. Lion of the theatre or not, Alleyn would be looking at ruin and Sledd was only as good as his last mechanical contrivance. Penury popped her head over the flimsy parapet beside him and stuck out her tongue in derision. Sledd closed his eyes. The day was young and had already gone to Hell in a handcart.

'What's going on?' The voice in his ear was so close it made his scalp tingle. He hoped it was Marlowe. He knew it was Alleyn.

'Marlowe's outside,' he murmured out of the corner of his mouth.

'No, he isn't,' Alleyn said, stepping out on to the stage. 'I just saw Marlowe going around the corner. He looked fit to drop.'

Henslowe spun round. 'What?'

'Tired. I would imagine he's going home for a nap. When I saw him . . .'

Sledd coughed a warning from the wings.

'. . . some time ago, he did say he had taken to staying up late and napping during the day.' As a recovery it had been seamless and Sledd sent him a silent round of applause. Alleyn laughed his most merry laugh, honed to perfection in his role as Muly Molocco. It hadn't been written as a comedy as such, but it was clear from the first Act it certainly couldn't be played in any other way. The playwright started drinking during the first performance and as far as anyone knew, had not stopped yet. 'Playwrights, eh?' he said, clapping Henslowe on the back in fellowship. 'This isn't getting the rehearsing done, is it?' He clapped his hands above his head. 'Beginners, please!' and he shooed Henslowe off the stage.

Sledd stepped forward. 'Good recovery, Ned,' he said. He reached out and grabbed the bit player by the ear. 'Listen to this lad, will you? I think he has the makings of a fine La Pucelle.'

The bit player almost swooned with joy, trying to look saintly, vicious and mad all at the same time as Sledd all but skipped off the stage. The day was beginning to look as though it might not be so bad after all.

Marlowe woke as night was falling. Hog Lane had been like the Seventh Circle of Hell all day, with fights, street cries and enough noise to wake the dead, and yet it had not woken him. He remembered lying down on the bed, fully clothed and so was rather surprised to find himself under the coverlet, in just his skin. Peering into the growing gloom of his room, he could see his clothes thrown in a heap in the corner and was relieved. This could only mean that Thomas had found him and put him to bed. Putting clothes away, according to Master Watson, was something that happened to other people and since it was usually the shedding of the clothes and getting down to the next stage of business that was normally the first thing on his mind, he had never really got the knack of folding. Marlowe slid from between the sheets and got dressed hurriedly. He was hungry now, too, and wanted to catch the pie seller who set up at the end of the road, come rain or shine. The man he was going to see was not ungenerous but, like Marlowe himself, he often forgot to eat if he was in the middle of something, so going there on a stomach that was growling like Marlowe's was now was never a good idea.

He clattered down the stairs and met Watson at the bottom.

'Thank you for putting me to bed, Tom,' he called, as he hared out of the door.

'You're welcome,' Watson replied, shrugging his shoulders. He leaned out into the passageway and called. 'Mary! A moment of your time, if you please.'

The maidservant appeared in the doorway at the end of the passage.

'Did you put Master Marlowe to bed?'

The maid bobbed a curtsy. 'Yes, sir. He was lying there in his clothes. It isn't seemly.'

'And is it seemly for you to strip him naked as a cuckoo and put him to bed?'

The girl giggled, a hand to her mouth. 'I've seen you to bed, sir, often as not,' she said, laughing.

Watson stepped out into the corridor. 'Oh, ho,

my girl,' he said, stepping high and slow towards her. 'What do bad girls get for cheeking their masters?'

'Ooh, sir!' the girl shrieked, cowering in the doorway but still laughing. 'I have no idea!'

'Then let me teach you,' Watson said, pouncing like a cat on a mouse. 'But tell me,' he said, kissing her and making her squirm. 'How is Master Marlowe made?'

'Oh, sir,' she said, smacking him lightly. 'You make me blush!'

'Is he . . .?' But the girl stopped him with her mouth on his and her hand inside his codpiece. There were some things that had to remain a secret between a maid and her master and this was one.

Marlowe stepped out into the street and stopped for a moment to breathe in the fresh evening air. The pieman was packing up and so he turned to catch him before he was gone. The squeals from inside the house stopped him briefly but then he remembered Tom Watson and a member of the opposite sex were both under his roof, so he ignored it. He had bigger fish to fry this evening and Tom Watson and his peccadilloes would have to wait until another day. Although if he carried on getting through maidservants like this, they may have to come to some other arrangement. 'Ho! Pieman!' he called and broke into a trot.

The pie lasted him until he was nearly at the corner of Godliman Street. He threw the casing to a mangy dog that lurked in the shadows and wiped his fingers on the inside of his cloak before rapping smartly on the door. He seemed doomed to knock at empty houses today; the knocking echoed and he could picture the room beyond the door: the stuffed cockatrice looking down with a jaundiced eye; the lump of amber propping open the door of a cabinet, inside which was kept a mermaid, small but perfect. There would be a ball of clearest crystal, lying on a velvet cushion and inside the ball, for those with eyes to see, would be another perfect world, like this one, but upside down. In front of the fire, which was not allowed to go out, would lie a deerhound that could smell out demons. By his side would be a black cat which could divine the future, if only its language could be determined. Marlowe smiled to think of all these things. He was a pragmatist, plain and simple. No God and so no Devil. No Heaven and so no Hell. No Angels; no Demons. Life should be simple in his non-believing world and yet somehow, it seemed, it was more difficult still. He stood in a reverie and was surprised therefore to realize that not only had the aged oak of the door disappeared, but someone was speaking from the level of his waist.

'Yes?' The voice sounded testy at best. He looked down and found him gazing into the steel grey eyes of the smallest woman he had ever seen. She couldn't have been more than a yard high, but was in perfect proportion. Looking down at her as he was made Marlowe almost giddy, as though he were standing on a height and she was very far away.

'I said, "Yes?"' She was far beyond testy now

and Marlowe noticed she was preparing to close the door.

'I beg your pardon, madam,' he said, sweeping a low bow. 'I was lost in thought.'

'State your business!' She didn't waste words, this one.

'I wish to see Doctor John Dee.'

'Well, that *is* a surprise,' she said, waspishly. 'Not many people ever come to this door and want to see Doctor Dee. They mostly come for the pleasure of my company.'

'And that is, of course, a very special addition to the pleasure of the visit,' Marlowe said. His well-renowned honeyed tongue wouldn't get him far here, he was sure, but it was still well worth a try. 'And perhaps when I have spoken to Doctor Dee you and I could spend some time, some sack and a sweet biscuit, our feet up on stools, chatting away like old friends. But for now, I really must see Doctor Dee.'

'Minima!' a voice called from a distant room. 'Minima! Is that someone at the door?'

The rancid tones turned to honey. 'No, Master. Just a pedlar.' She looked up at Marlowe. 'Now, you, just sling your hook, Master Whoever You Are, or it will be the worst for you.'

Marlowe blinked. The waves of animosity coming off this tiny creature were enough to curdle milk. 'I mean no harm,' he said, 'I just want to see Doctor Dee.'

She gritted her perfect little teeth. 'Are you deaf, lanky?' she hissed. 'Go away.'

'Minima?' The voice was nearer now. 'A pedlar at this time of night? We seem to get so many pedlars these days. Perhaps a charm of some kind . . . something to hang in the window . . .' The voice was getting nearer and the little woman darted across the room towards it.

Marlowe took his chance and stepped over the threshold. 'Doctor!' he called. 'It's Kit!'

'Kit!' The old man was suddenly in the doorway, his housekeeper batted aside like an annoying pet. 'Minima!' He turned on her. 'How could you mistake Kit for a pedlar? We must see if we can arrange something to help you see more clearly. Some tiny lenses, that's the thing.' He remained sunk in thought for a moment, then remembered his visitor. 'But . . . Kit, it is so wonderful to see you. Come, sit and tell me all your doings.' He dropped his voice, 'such as you can, of course.'

The little woman stamped her foot in annoyance and flounced out of the room. The two men watched her go.

'She's a fiery one,' Marlowe remarked as the door slammed behind her. 'Is she all you have looking after you? Wherever did you find her?'

Dee was also looking over his shoulder at the door, still quivering on its hinges. 'I won't be here long this time. It is a flying visit. She usually looks after the house without me in it – she means well. I . . . I am a little embarrassed to say this, but I bought her from a sailor. He had plans for her and . . . she didn't deserve that. She has set herself up as my guardian. The only way she can say thank you, or perhaps I should say, it is the only way that I can accept.' He turned round with eyes twinkling and smiled at Marlowe, pressing one hand between both of his own. 'Tell me what brings you here.'

'A problem, as always,' Marlowe said, ruefully.

Dee rubbed his hands together, with a sound like leaves rustling. 'A problem. Just what I like to hear. Does it concern conjuring of spirits at all? I ask because Minima is an expert at divination. What she can do with a pouch full of rabbit bones would astound you.'

Marlowe didn't doubt it.

'Or demons? I almost have that one off pat. Just a few slight adjustments and I believe I could have Beelzebub in my grasp.' The old magus raised a choppy finger in the air and Marlowe could almost feel the flames of Hell hot on his face.

'I am sorry, Doctor,' Marlowe said, 'but I don't think we will need demons to solve my little mystery. Perhaps another time.'

Dee looked crestfallen. 'That *is* a shame. But no matter – tell me your problem.'

'It concerns the world,' Marlowe said, by way of preamble.

Dee's eyes widened. 'My word! That is what I call a problem. What is the matter with it? Is it set to explode? Tumble from its axis and spin off into the vast realms of the Heavens.' His face shone with excitement. 'I think I should enjoy that; imagine what creatures we might encounter!'

Marlowe wished he was not in such a hurry. Just spending time with John Dee fired his imagination and his fingers itched for quill and parchment. But that would have to be put aside, for another time. 'No,' he said, stopping him in full flow. 'I mean this world.' He pulled out the silver Canterbury world from inside his doublet. 'This one has blood on it, insofar as a woman died protecting it. The other one –' and he pulled out the Morton jewel – 'similarly bears the lifeblood of a man, although how much he valued his life, I don't know. But life is sweet to all who live, or so I am told.'

Dee looked keenly at his friend, then at the worlds, displayed in the palms of his hands. 'I know these jewels, at least by reputation,' he said, picking up the one with the pinpricks of moonlight captured in its opal. 'Drake had them made, or have I got that wrong?'

Marlowe was unsurprised. Where there was a mystery, there was often Doctor Dee. 'There are eight,' he said. 'Two I have here, two are missing, stolen or inveigled from their owners. One other is here in London, but not in our hands . . .'

'*Our* hands?' Dee had spotted the salient word at once. 'This has Walsingham's hand in it, then?'

Marlowe acknowledged the truth of that with an inclination of his head. 'The other three,' he continued, 'we know nothing of as yet. Sir Francis has his men looking for them. Or, perhaps I should say, *had* his men looking for them. A Progress is afoot and he has called everyone back to protect the Queen.'

'The Progress, yes,' Dee said. 'That is why you find me here in London. Her Majesty wanted me to divine if the stars were propitious for her journey.'

'And are they?'

'No, not so you would notice,' Dee said with

a smile. 'In fact, the conjunction of Aries with Scorpio would seem to suggest that she would be better staying at home, but you know the Queen – once she has her mind set on something, all the demons in Hell could not dissuade her. But she likes to make it look as though she has taken advice. But between us, Kit, I think it really *would* be best if she did not venture too far afield.'

'Because of Aries and Scorpio?' Marlowe's voice was dripping with scepticism.

The magus laughed. 'No, not because of that. Because . . . it's silly, really. I just have a bad feeling about this Progress. I can't define it, try though I might.'

'By the pricking of your thumbs, something wicked this way comes.'

'Yes. That covers it very well. That sounds like a quotation, Kit – from one of your plays?'

'No, no – these lines just pop into my head sometimes. Then they are mostly forgotten.'

'The Muses can be fickle,' Dee said, 'even with you. But –' and he clapped his hands together – 'back to these little jewels of yours. I fear I don't know why Drake had them made. He isn't known for his generosity.'

'That's true. He isn't as mean as Frobisher, by all accounts, but he doesn't exactly shower his friends with gifts. And as far as we can tell, most of the recipients of these little things were not close to him.'

Dee fished out a lens from the recesses of his robe and peered at the diamond-studded world that had cost Jane Benchkyne her life. 'I can't quite understand why these worlds were made,' he said, half to himself. 'The workmanship is adequate, but nothing special. The gem is small and not particularly well cut.' He looked up at Marlowe. 'May I see the other?' Marlowe handed it over and again the magician bent over it with his lens. 'The opal on this one is full of fire, but very small. Opals are prized because they are rare – apparently.' He dropped the lens into his lap as he prepared to share his knowledge. 'Where they are found, in Abyssinia, a man can pick them up by the side of his path and they are as common as grains of sand in some parts. But bringing them back is hazardous, with pirates and others in the way. Some say they are the moon's tears. Others that they will confer invisibility.'

'Yes! Leonard Morton, the previous owner, said that too. He said it involved bay leaves and other ingredients.'

Dee perked up. 'Had he made the spell work?'

'I didn't get that impression.'

'Ah. Never mind. Invisibility is a hard trick to achieve and although I have had limited success myself, I find it tiring. However, my comments stand. These little jewels seem like trinkets with no value and yet you say people have died because of them.'

'So far, two that we know of. But two men have also left home and disappeared because of them, one woman has been disgraced and one man robbed. As for the others, until the news comes back, we don't know.'

Dee weighed the globes in his hand and held them side by side, peering at them closely. 'Do you know the other gems? Are they all different?'

Marlowe pulled out the list. 'Here they are,' he said. 'It is the silversmith's order, from Drake, by way of Mercator.'

'Mercator?' Dee took the paper from Marlowe. 'That explains the quality of the map, then. Let me see. Hmm . . .' He muttered to himself as he ran his eye down the list. 'With the exceptions of Walter Mildmay and Sir Oliver Starkey, I don't know any of these men.' He tapped the parchment. 'Someone in Canterbury, I see. Do you know the gentleman?'

'I'm not sure,' Marlowe said casually. 'It is a common enough name.'

'Yes, then,' Dee said, perspicacious as ever. 'What gems do we have? Hmm . . . they seem to be an odd collection. Could it be from a single piece, broken down?'

'Joshua the silversmith wondered the same,' Marlowe said. 'He was given the designs and the stones and told what to do with them.'

'Designs?' Dee looked at the trinkets again. 'I see what you mean,' he said at length. 'The opal and the diamond are not in quite the same place.'

'No,' Marlowe said. 'That is deliberate.'

'I wonder . . .' Dee muttered and, turning the globes to face each other, he turned them round clockwise and counter-clockwise. He scuttled off out of the room and Marlowe, knowing what a labyrinth the man lived in, set off in hot pursuit. To lose yourself in Doctor Dee's house might mean you would never be seen again. And that was without the added risk of encountering Minima around a dark corner.

Dee turned through several right angles and

anyone who had not been to one of his houses before would have expected to come out where they began, but time and space were no longer their usual selves and so they found themselves in a high-ceilinged triangular room, tucked in between here and there. A fire was burning in the narrow fireplace, which was hung with all manner of hooks and chains. Retorts with sullen liquids trembling faintly in the heat were ranged along a rack above the flames but although the fireback, etched with a coiling dragon, was red-hot, the room itself was, if anything, cooler than the night outside.

The magus was standing before a towering stack of bookshelves and was running his finger along the leather spines. Then, with a triumphant little cry, he pulled one out and opened it up on a nearby table. He beckoned to the poet to come and read with him. The words were in a crabbed hand, the ink sepia with age, but Marlowe could make out most of it, once he got his eye in.

'Read aloud, will you, Kit,' Dee demanded. 'Then I can look amongst my potions and see if I have what is needed.'

'Hmmm . . . *Quod conjugium gemmas*,' he read. 'The marriage of gemstones. Is that right?'

'Correct, as I would expect from you, Kit. Continue.'

'May I paraphrase?'

'Just don't miss out any ingredients or change the order of anything. That can have catastrophic effects. I once burned off all my hair by adding water and . . . well, a secret ingredient . . . in the wrong order.'

'But what are we doing?' Marlowe was running his eye down the page and could not for the life of him see how this was going to help.

'To cut a long book very short, the anonymous writer believes that certain gems, in conjunction, have properties that many can only dream of. You touched for example on the fact that Leonard Morton believed that opals could make a man invisible. Others have other properties such as the emerald, which can help to contain lust and also make a man more intelligent.' Dee paused for a moment. 'Those two attributes either go together like sack and sugar or make no sense, according to your point of view. But the theory of this book is that if you put two gemstones together in the right circumstances, their power is not simply added together but multiplied many times over.'

'So what you think Drake was trying to do was to multiply the effect of the gems delivered to Joshua. But why do that? Why not just use the gems and the spells without all of the work making the globes?' Marlowe was frowning down at the book, trying to make sense of it all.

'Yes.' Dee sounded uncertain. 'Perhaps he was trying to . . .' The magus rubbed his hands over his face. 'I don't know, Kit, to be truthful. Drake is so tricky, always one jump ahead of everyone. Let's face it, the man is a pirate, pure and simple. He will get on the wrong side of Her Majesty one of these days and then look out. I wonder if he was trying to simply keep the gems safe until he had perfected the spell. There's something not quite right about his circumnavigation, you know.'

'Really?' Marlowe didn't know. 'What?'

'Well, according to the reports I've read, he was at Antigua in the West Indies in June. The next thing we knew he was off Jamaica, except that by now it's February.'

'So?'

'So a sailor of Drake's ability could do it in two *days*. Eight months is a little . . . shall we say, leisurely?'

'So what do you conclude?'

Dee shrugged. 'That he either idled his time, soaking up the rays of the sun-kissed beaches or he went somewhere else and didn't want the rest of us to know about it. However,' he said and cleared his throat, 'I digress. The results are patchy at the moment, to say the least. Even the invisibility one, which most people consider the simplest, rarely works.'

Marlowe raised his most sardonic eyebrow but Dee was not to be stopped now he was in full flow.

'Some of the spells, further into the book, use esoteric gems that no man has ever seen.'

'Then . . .?' Marlowe was sure there was a way of couching the obvious question, but he couldn't think what it might be. He was fond of this old man and didn't want to belittle his craft, which he had seen with his own eyes could often achieve results nothing short of miraculous.

Dee flapped a hand at him. 'Yes, yes, Kit. I know. A theoretical gem is a hard concept to accept, but once you open your mind, the possibilities are literally endless.' He glanced up at the complex system of gears, cogs and dials that filled the chimney breast and exclaimed, 'Just look at the time! Minima will be in here soon to ready me for bed.' He caught the poet's eye and flushed. 'Minima is a great believer in routine. She says my humours are out of balance if I am too late going to bed.'

'Are there rewards for keeping to her rhythms?' Marlowe asked, with a poker straight face.

'I am an old man, Kit,' Dee said with a smile, 'which is not to say there are no rewards, but more in the way of telling you to mind your own business. However, I have a little time still so I will research more. Can you just tell me again the gems the worlds encompass and I will do more work on the morrow. Now, diamond and opal, I know.' He went to a chest of small drawers and, opening two, took out the gems in question. 'What else was there?'

'Lapis,' the poet said, working from memory. 'Amethyst. Ruby. Emerald. Umm . . .' He rummaged for his list.

'Don't worry,' the magus said and indeed they had to hurry as tiny, brisk footfalls could be heard approaching along the corridor. 'This has given me food for thought. I will let you know if anything pertinent turns up. Are you still alongside the Grey Mare? Norton Folgate?'

Marlowe nodded. He stepped away from the table and readied himself for Minima's entrance.

The door crashed back and she stood in the gap, bristling from head to toe and looking not unlike an angry bumble bee. 'Still here?' she snarled at Marlowe.

'Master Marlowe was just leaving,' Dee said mildly.

'Time for bed,' she crooned to Dee, taking his hand and leading him to the door.

'I think I will just see Kit to the front door, shall I?' Dee offered, hopefully.

'Master,' she said, softly, reaching up to stroke his arm, 'allow me. You can go and . . . start.' The emphasis on the word made Marlowe blush and he didn't even know what she meant by it. There was simply something in the tone that conveyed a wealth of meaning best left undetermined.

'I can see my own way out,' he said hurriedly. 'I will . . .' But before he could promise to be in touch with the old magus, the pocket-tornado had swept him up and through the door, to the land of pure delight.

Thirteen

Charles Angleton smiled down at the little ones in their cot. His darlings, the apples of his eye, lay side by side, their golden curls on their pillows, their fingers like starfish against the white of the linen. He bent lower and kissed each one on the forehead, smelling their soft skin as though for the first time and he blew out the candle. He licked his fingers and pinched the wick. You couldn't be too careful.

In the darkness, he heard the familiar call, whispered, half-asleep. 'Papa.'

Angleton chuckled. 'Hello, sweet stuff,' he said and lifted his eldest girl from her bed. He smoothed the long hair from her face and kissed her cheek. 'Can't sleep?'

'It's hot, Papa,' she said petulantly. 'I'm hot and grumpy.'

'I know, little one,' he said, smiling. 'I'll open the casement a little more. But you won't go near it, now will you?'

'No, Papa.' She shook her head with the exaggerated emphasis of a tired four-year-old.

'Because you know what's out there, don't you, if you pop your head out?'

She nodded. 'Demons,' she mouthed, afraid they would hear her.

'Astaroth, Beelzebub, Asmodeus,' he whispered their names. 'They're all out there, waiting to catch little girls like you.'

She stared at the window through which the city along the Thames looked black and evil. 'That's why,' he whispered as he kissed her again and snuggled her down in her bed, 'you must never go near the window.'

'Papa?' She was still whispering. You couldn't be too careful.

'Yes, precious?'

She was sitting up again, the coverlet thrown back as far as she dared. 'They won't get in, will they? Beelbub? They can't get in?'

'No, baby girl,' he assured her, his voice soft and gentle. 'Look. Look here.' He crossed the room and opened the window a notch. 'See this?'

'What?' She was peering hard.

'Exactly,' he said, straight-faced. '*You* can't see it. *I* can't see it, not properly. But *they* can, the demons of the night. It's a net, made of invisible thread, thread we can't see. And no demon in this or any other world can get through that. Keep away from the window, and you'll be safe. Understand?'

'Yes, Papa.' And she sank to her pillows again, grateful for the infinite wisdom of her papa and the infinite safety of the net. He kissed her on the forehead and closed the door softly on his way out.

At the bottom of the stairs, he passed a large manservant, wiping the sweat from his face with an old rag.

'Well, Bolo?' Angleton asked.

'Nothing yet, Master,' the man grunted. 'He's a tough one and no mistake.'

'What have you tried?'

220

'The knuckles. The straps. The boys and I have took out three fingernails.'

Angleton was surprised. He'd heard of Papists who refused to crack under torture. Puritans too. Both extremes were buoyed up by their God. But a business rival? This was a first. 'All right. Who's with him now?'

'Midge. And Alan.'

'Right. You wait here. And clean yourself up, man. Little Ellie's a bit fractious tonight and if she calls out, go to her. I don't want you dripping blood all over her.'

He swept on down the stairs to the ground level, pausing in the hall to wet his whistle from the ale flagon standing on the press. He wiped his mouth and opened the side door that led to the cellar, the little room next to his warehouse, the room he called his chapel of ease. The steps were stone here and he could smell the wafts from the river. It was particularly bad tonight, the stench of Old Father Thames. The tide was low and the mud lay slick and silver under the moon. Angleton hurried on down and turned left in the near-darkness at the bottom. He hauled open the door there and surveyed the scene.

Hugh Woodshaw was sitting upright in a chair, his hair clinging to his forehead with sweat. Tears had dried on his cheeks and his face was a mass of blood and bruises. His wrists were bound in iron to the arms of the chair and his legs shackled to the floor. His shirt was ripped, hanging off his bare shoulders that were scarred with the teeth of the cat, still swinging idly in Midge's hand.

'Good evening, Hugh, my boy,' Angleton said. 'How are you doing?'

Woodshaw tried to say something but he had lost too many teeth and his lips were swollen.

'Well, there we are.' Angleton nodded. 'Midge, put that thing away, will you? I think Hugh appreciates the ethos of the meeting by now and after all, we are not barbarians.'

Midge slid the whip with its nine thongs into his wide sleeve.

'Alan, get Master Woodshaw a drinky, would you? What would you like, Hugh? I have a cheeky little canary upstairs I think you'd appreciate. Ah, but you're an ale man, aren't you? Come to think of it, water's probably best for a man in your condition. Alan, fetch Master Woodshaw a flagon of well water. Not that river stuff; that can't be good for him.'

Alan clicked his knuckles back into position and went off to do his master's bidding.

Angleton pulled up a chair and placed it directly in front of Woodshaw. 'Do you like this?' He reached across the table to his left and unrolled a scroll. 'My new letterhead. I got the College of Heralds to design it. They'll do anything for a bung. See, here – my coat of arms. How did the cokes put it? "Gules, a plantain argent en soleil". Yes, I know, plantain is a little wide of the mark, isn't it? But I don't think the cokes had ever seen a tobacco plant, so that was the best he could do. Well,' Angleton continued as he rolled his eyes upwards, tutting, 'Rouge Dragon Pursuivant, he ain't. Still, I like it.'

Woodshaw tried to speak, but again, the pain and his wounds conspired against him.

'Why am I drawing this to your attention, I hear you croak.' Angleton smiled. 'Well, as you know, I am a fully paid up member of the Fishmongers' Company, hence the hall next door. But, as you know too, I've branched out recently into tobacco, the Heavenly weed. Trust me, fish are so yesterday. The real money's in pipes. Oh, but wait; that's your racket too, isn't it? Import/export? And –' he leaned back, frowning and cradling one raised knee in clasped hands – 'don't I remember something about that recently? Didn't you and I have an agreement, something about you keeping east of the Bridge and I'd keep to the west?'

He took up the clay pipe that lay on the table and lit his tobacco with the candle, blowing grey smoke into his rival's face. 'Now, I'm not one of those explorer cokes who understands compass points and maps and charts and so on. But I *do* know my east from my west. And you, Hughie boy, have been trespassing somewhat of late, haven't you? Creeping west like the bloody plague. And I seem to remember, there's something about a couple of missing consignments. A pair of cogs . . . er . . . that's it, *The Nimrod* and *The Elephant*. Oh, we found the ships all right – didn't we, Alan?'

'Yes, Charlie.'

'What we didn't find was the cargo. Several tons of tobacco all the way from the colonies. Which is why we're all here, having this little chat. But I'm sure Midge and Alan have explained

223

this already. Ah, Midge, the water. You're too kind.'

He was glad to leave the river behind and to duck up the fish alleys. It was as black as pitch here but at least the stink was less. The Swan stood locked and abandoned, its last topers having staggered home an hour ago. Charles Angleton's house, shop and warehouse stood by the Oystergate, larger and more impressive than its fellows crowded along the wharf. He padded past the steelyard, its gates locked and waited in the deep shadows as the Night Watch clattered past, their halberds gleaming under the moon. He followed the broad curve of the Ropery where sailors slept on the smooth stone, the flotsam of the sea who had been unable to find a bed for the night, washed up like gutted fish, drunk, broke and robbed blind. There would be Hell to pay by sun-up.

He crept past the black tower of All Hallows the Little and dodged back into the darkness. He heard drunken fumbling in the church's doorway and the laughter of a girl. He crossed the street silently and made for the spire of St Magnus Bridge that gave him his compass point. He had done some work on Charles Angleton. By day, the man was a pillar of London society, a member of the Fishmongers' Company. He had his own pew at St Magnus, one under the window that let the sun stream in to keep his young family warm. He gave generously to orphans and to widows and was on nodding terms with the Chancellor of the Exchequer. But it was the man by night that was of interest now. There were dark rumours about Charlie Angleton. He was a ruthless man of business and brooked no competition. Rivals had a knack of taking early retirement. A couple of them had left the country. One of them had fallen into the river. And wherever Angleton went, at least two heavies were always in attendance, armed to the teeth. Well, then, that was tonight's challenge.

He turned sharp left, then right and the house was in front of him. There was a shop window to the right of the front door, the room beyond it dark and empty. But it wasn't the front door that interested him. That would be solid, bolted, impenetrable without a battering ram. The window was easy, but shattering glass would wake the house and half the street. He had experience of places like this and he knew the pattern they followed. From Warwickshire to Kent, they were all the same. The strongroom, the most likely home of Charles Angleton's silver globe, would be in an upstairs room, towards the back. He squeezed himself between the walls and climbed. Friendly bricks and fancy buttresses aided his progress and he scampered up the side like a determined monkey, pressing himself to the stone as the Watch patrolled below him. He smiled to himself. Thank God the Lord Mayor appointed men who were deaf and blind to scour the streets.

He reached a window ledge on the first floor and peered in. The casement was open and he could make out three children sleeping peacefully in their beds. The next window along was ten or twelve feet away and slightly higher. That room could be empty, because the window was closed. There again, it could contain Mistress Angleton or any of the unknown army of servants who worked for her. On balance, he was safer with these children. It was the work of a moment to open the window wider and haul himself inside. He landed lightly and replaced the pane in its original position. The babies lay in a cot, fast asleep and he couldn't help but spend a moment looking down at them; he had always had a soft spot for twins. A little girl tossed fretfully in the bed nearest the door and he waited for her to settle again. When she had, he eased open the latch and crept out.

Now he had his dagger in his hand. Anybody he met now was likely to be an adult, like the old girl in Canterbury or that interfering busybody at Ness End Hall. He may have to use his blade again.

The voice came from below. 'Bolo –' he heard the scrape of a chair around the corner from where he stood – 'get your arse down here. Charlie wants a word.'

He heard someone rumble his clumsy way down the stairs and then the distant thud of a door.

The passageway stretched to right and left, but to the right lay the stairs and he could see the glimmer of light down there. Several people were still up, stirring. Was that voices he heard, coming from the bowels of the house? He turned left. There were two doors here, opposite each other, but only one had a padlock. *This* was his prize. Even so, he would take no chances. He eased the other door open with the point of his blade and peered round it. There was a tester in the far corner with the curtains pulled back and a naked woman lay on the coverlets, on her side with her thumb in her mouth. She looked as sweet as her children and he hoped he wouldn't have to slit that pretty throat. He closed the door again with a whisper of woodwork and turned to the other door.

There was little light here so he worked by feel, letting his expert fingers slide over the lock. When pushed for time, he would simply smash a lock like this, but noise like that would wake the entire house and he wasn't about to take on Angleton's private army. There was a click. Two. He held his breath. Then, he was inside.

In the bowels of the building, in his chapel of ease, Charles Angleton was taking delicate sips of the water that Midge had brought, wiping his lips each time with a napkin.

'Hughie, Hughie, where are my manners? Drink?' And he threw the ewer's contents all over the man. Woodshaw cried out, shocked and in pain as he already was, when the cold of the water hit him. He sat there, trembling and shuddering. Angleton leaned forward and moved the candle across so that the flame burned bright in front of Woodshaw's eyes. 'Did you read about that Francis Kett the other day? He's a madman who denies the Trinity or some such nonsense. Or should I say, he did. They burnt him at Norwich. Broad daylight, hot day, so he went fast. Well, fairly fast. In an hour or two.'

227

He moved the guttering flame nearer and Woodshaw flinched, sweat trickling with the blood from his hairline.

'Yes, everything around him was tinder-dry, apparently, as you'd expect in a hot summer like this one. But a man wringing wet . . . well, he'd take a lot longer to die, wouldn't he? Should someone apply a naked flame, say, to his bollocks? Yes, a *lot* longer.'

In the upstairs room, he was vaguely aware of a scream, but it seemed a long way off and he paused only briefly before clicking open the lock of the strong box. He smiled. A double lock, just like Mildmay's. Would they never learn, these people? His eyes focused on the chest's contents. Silver. Gold. Papers with seals and scrolls. But there. There it was. The silver globe of Francis Drake, with its hieroglyphics and its single stone of lapis lazuli. He grabbed it and turned back to the door. Just as he did so, a flame flashed before his eyes. Beyond the candle, the naked woman he had seen in bed stood there, blinking at him.

'Who are you?' she shrieked, too furious with the intruder to remember her own nakedness.

He pushed past her, throwing her aside. Woman and candle hit the floor simultaneously and the flame roared on to the rushes on the floorboards, flaring and spluttering as it reached the curtains trailing the floor by the window. Fed by years' worth of dropped wax and the tinder pith of the rushes, it sucked the air from the room and let go a mighty bellow as it took the wooden rafters that crossed the ceiling. He dashed across the

228

landing and into the children's room, stashing the jewel in his doublet and sheathing his dagger.

The little girl was kneeling up in bed, pointing at him and screaming, 'Beelbub! Beelbub!' Somehow the demon of her nightmares had got through the net. The noise from mother and children raised the whole house.

Down in the cellar, Angleton looked up. 'If you'll excuse me, Hugh,' he said politely to his guest. 'Domestic crisis by the sound of it.'

At worst, Charles Angleton suspected rats. They had bitten the babies before and there was always Hell to pay when they did. It was the price of living on the river and over the shop. As he reached the hall, however, he realized that it was not that simple. A fierce flaming light met his gaze as he looked up. The house was alight.

'Midge!' he roared. 'Alan! Water!'

'From the well, Master?' Midge called.

'Bugger the well, man. The bloody house is on fire. Shift yourself, you shit. What do I pay you for? Bolo, where the bloody Hell are you?'

Angleton reached the landing. He saw both doors open, his wife's and the strongroom's. Naturally, he turned right, but the chest was standing open and a dazed woman sat near it, nursing her head as the flames crackled around her.

'For God's sake, Isobel, get up!' He hauled her upright, looked into her blank face and realized that she had a concussion of the brain. He threw her over his shoulder and spun back to the landing. Midge was there already, a bucket of water in his hand. Angleton threw the woman to him and grabbed the bucket, hurling its contents at the flames. That had no effect at all, except to spit and hiss back at him and he threw the bucket down the stairs, narrowly missing the retreating Midge with Isobel dangling down his back like an undressed deer.

'And watch where you're putting your hands!' Angleton called after him.

He hurtled into his children's room. 'There, there, Phoebe,' he comforted the screaming girl. 'Papa's here.' He swept the hysterical child up and bent to lift the babies too. The flames had not reached this room yet, but the smoke had and all of them were coughing and crying as their papa carried them out. On the stairs, the maid-servants cowered terrified. They had hauled on their shifts or still stood in their nightshirts and they took the children from the master, scurrying down the stairs with them. He could hear Phoebe's cries of 'Beelbub!' fade as they reached the safety of the street. Beelbub indeed and woe betide him, demon or no demon, when Charlie Angleton got his hands on him.

Alan had reached the stairtop with another bucket and he threw it at the flames that roared and leapt now, crawling along the ceiling timbers and making the pitch spit and crack. The attack on his strongroom forgotten, Angleton took charge. 'Anyone who is not holding a child or a woman!' he shouted, 'fetch more water. I want a chain of people up these stairs now. And just remember – Mistress Angleton is due back tomorrow. We've got to sort all this before then!'

And he dodged aside as the roof timbers began to fall.

Marlowe took a boat below the Bridge and the ferryman rowed east, following the river's curves.

'Something's going up tonight, sir,' the man grunted as he bent his back to his oars. Marlowe turned. Beyond the guttering flame on the stern of the boat, there was a glow beyond the Bridge that threw the ramshackle buildings into stark silhouette. There were always fires in the city and in a summer like this it wouldn't be surprising if the whole lot went up. Marlowe turned back, facing the way the boat was going. To his right, the stews of Southwark lay dark and menacing, the Winchester geese going about their illicit business in the shadows.

'Captain Winter?' Marlowe popped his head around the cabin door.

'At your service, sir.' The man with the silver whistle around his neck sat at a table near the window.

'Formerly master of the *Elizabeth*?' It didn't hurt to double check.

'The *Elizabeth*?' The man belched. 'That was a long time ago. She's full fathom five now, I fear. Drinkie?'

He waved a crystal decanter and topped his cup up from it.

'It is a *little* early for me, Captain,' Marlowe said.

'Nonsense,' the man slurred. 'Sun's over the yardarm. And he filled a second cup, ushering

Marlowe to a chair. The bravely named *Wanderer* was wandering no more. Her sails had gone and her masts were sawn off at man's height above her decks. But this little barque had been John Winter's home for nearly five years, tucked away in a brackish backwater of the King's Yard at Deptford.

'Now, sir,' Winter said as he clinked his goblet with Marlowe's and sat back. 'Your business? As you can see, I'm a busy man.' On the table between them lay a new book, open at a page showing the world as it stood.

'Hakluyt?' Marlowe tapped the page.

Winter slammed the book shut. 'That depends who's asking,' he said, frowning at his visitor.

'Forgive me, captain,' Marlowe said, smiling at the man. 'My name is Kit Marlowe. Doctor Dee sent me.'

'John Dee?' The man's red-rimmed eyes lit up. 'Good God, I thought he was dead.'

'Many people do.' Marlowe nodded. 'But he is well and sends you his remembrance.'

'Well, well . . .' Winter was remembering with fondness some secret scene from his past, now half lost to time. 'But you didn't come all the way to Deptford to bring me John Dee's best wishes.'

'Indeed not,' Marlowe said. 'I wanted to know about Drake.'

'A bastard, that man, pure and simple.'

'But you served under him.'

Winter guffawed and quaffed his wine. 'As some men serve the Devil or so I'm told. Let's just say it was not a happy experience.'

'We're talking about the circumnavigation?' Marlowe checked they were on the same voyage down the years.

Winter nodded. 'What do you want?'

'The truth.'

'About Doughty?'

'About what you found.'

Winter took another swig and gritted his teeth as though every mouthful hurt him. He sighed and tapped Hakluyt's book. '*The Principal Navigations* my arse!' he spat. 'Have you read this?'

'I've dipped,' Marlowe lied.

'Well, I nearly vomited just reading his crawling epistle dedicatory, I can tell you. And to Francis Walsingham of all people. You know the Queen calls him her Moor, don't you?'

Marlowe knew. 'Really?' he said, wide-eyed.

'Walsingham invested in the circumnavigation,' Winter remembered. 'Appreciably less of course than any other investor. But all that –' the captain pointed to Hakluyt's book – 'rubbish. Pure invention.'

'But you were there,' Marlowe reminded the man. 'With Drake, I mean. You can tell me what you *really* found.'

Winter stood up, hauling his doublet down and smoothing back his greying hair. He crossed to the thick leaded panes that looked out over the shipyards and the grey, shifting river. Then he turned to Marlowe. 'How old are you, boy?' he asked.

'Twenty-five summers, sir,' the projectioner told him.

'Hmm,' Winter grunted. 'Your eyes look older, but you haven't even finished shitting yellow yet. All right; pin your ears back and prepare yourself to be amazed.'

He sat down again, his finger tracing imaginary coasts and inlets, bays and capes as he spoke. 'I have seen mermaids, Marlowe, beautiful women with the tail of a fish.'

'A fish?'

'Yes. Drives a sailor mad, you see, because you can't lie with them. No legs to open. I don't need to draw you a map.'

'Indeed not.'

'They climb into the trees at night and fight with the baboons and apes. Their cries . . .' He shook his head and swigged again, wiping wine and spittle from his beard. 'God, their cries. Terrifying. And that's not all.'

'It isn't?'

'The parrots there play chess.' He chuckled at a sudden memory. 'And they're not half bad at it either.'

'I'm sure not.' Marlowe was beginning to think that Dee had sent him to the wrong place. Bedlam lay in the other direction.

'I have seen women in those parts lay eggs as a chicken does and their babies are *huge*. The Scipodes have only one foot. Now, I know what you're thinking . . .'

'I doubt you do, Captain,' Marlowe said quietly. 'I wanted to know about the stones.'

'Stones?'

'Jewels,' Marlowe said. 'Set in a silver sea.'

'Zanzibar.' Winter nodded, topping up his cup

again. Marlowe held a hand over his. 'Emeralds, diamonds, rubies, sapphires. We filled two ships with gold, unicorns' horns and musk. And two adamant stones. Magnets, you see, that draw iron to them.'

Marlowe pulled Jane Benchkyne's globe from his purse and let it clatter on to the table in front of the *Wanderer*'s erstwhile captain.

'What's this?' Winter asked.

'I believe it is a map,' Marlowe said. 'Of Drake's voyage, to be exact.'

'Drake's voyage!' Winter spat contemptuously. The light of remembrance seemed to have gone and he looked tired, old, withdrawn. 'The *Elizabeth* was holed below the waterline,' he said. 'I had to put in for repairs. The *Benedict* did too.'

'The *Benedict*?'

'Harry Bellot's ship. Well, Tom Nowell's really, but Bellot was the pilot. Nowell didn't know his orlop from his rigol in my opinion. The *Benedict* was in such bad shape she had to be scrapped. By the time my carpenters had solved the *Elizabeth*'s problem, Drake was long gone. I came home with Bellot and the *Benedict*'s people.'

'This line –' Marlowe pointed to it, making Winter focus his rebellious pupils – 'what does it show?'

The captain peered closer. The light was not good and the drink didn't help. He nodded. 'Drake's route.' He turned the disc over. 'About here is where we parted company. The island of Antigua. Godforsaken place.'

'And the jewel?' Marlowe turned the disc back over. 'What does it signify?'

'They were just stories, Marlowe,' Winter said. He seemed suddenly sober. 'You can't believe a word of them.'

'Let me be the judge of that, captain,' the projectioner said.

'Very well.' Winter reached for his jug again but Marlowe touched his arm and he stopped. 'When they all got back, heroes they were. The Queen, God bless her, knighted Drake on the *Pelican*'s deck . . . just over there.' He waved his hand to his left. 'It didn't seem right. Or fair. Drake's was the only ship to come back. Harry Bellot was very bitter about it. When they all got back, there were stories, oh, whispered, of course, by men in their cups . . .'

Marlowe raised an eyebrow but the subtlety was lost on Winter.

The captain cleared his throat. 'If only half of it was to be true, no one would believe it. There were tales of treasure, of course, because what sailor would want to limp home from such a voyage without tales of treasure? But when it comes to stories of men wearing clothes made of gold and women eating sapphires to make their babies beautiful, well . . . some things just cannot be. The story goes that Drake burned down the houses where the Indians lived among such splendours and the gold ran in rivers and solidified to estuary banks more precious than any treasury in the world. But why do that? The *Pelican* could have brought at least some of it back. I know Drake well enough to know that he would rather load the decks with gems and leave his sailors behind to rot than leave so much as a groat's worth behind. Few enough came back as it was. Nowell's dead, that I do know. But Harry Bellot is still with us. I see him, sometimes, out and about. He comes from the east coast somewhere –' Winter waved a vague hand – 'but I believe he lives in Southwark these days. Leastways, that's where I bump into him, when I do. Which isn't often. I don't leave the old *Wanderer* more than I need to.' He shook the bottle hopefully and poured the last dregs into his cup. 'No. Nothing out there on dry land to interest me.'

Marlowe was beginning to feel that he had had enough of old sailors' tales for a lifetime. It was time to get this conversation back to the subject. 'So, was there *any* treasure on the *Pelican*?'

Winter thought for a while, trying to remember what they had been talking about. 'There was some, enough to please his investors. But all the riches of the whole world? No, even Drake, who has the luck of the Devil himself, even he did not find that.'

'So, this globe,' Marlowe said as he held the jewel out for Winter's perusal again, 'does not show where Drake hid his treasure?'

Winter spluttered a laugh. 'Life is not just about treasure, Master Marlowe, whatever men may say. I am happier here on my *Wanderer* than any man with a king's ransom in his treasure house. I have seen things, Master Marlowe, things to make your hair curl –' he glanced up – 'more.'

Marlowe could recognize when a tale was coming round again and stood up, pocketing the globes.

'Wait,' Winter called after him as he made for the stairs up to the deck and fresh air. 'Wait. I haven't told you about the Fanesii yet. I played at tables with them, you know. Their ears are long as cloaks covering their shoulders and arms. And the Apothani . . .'

But Kit Marlowe wasn't listening any more. He had places to be.

Fourteen

The summer was proving to be the hottest and longest that any man alive could remember. Katherine Marley lay back in the long, dry grass and fanned her face with her hand. Evening was coming but she just couldn't get cool and was relishing the privacy of the whispering blades so she could unloose her bodice just a little. It was a lifetime since she had run barefoot along the sands at the edge of the sea at Dover, skipping and squealing with her brothers and sisters, hopping over the froth of the white horses as they hit the beach at a gallop. It had been so long since she had felt the sharp sting of salty air on her bare skin and she wept for the loss of her life, shackled to a bully. For her children, both the dead and the living, dead to her in other ways. A tear trickled down from her closed eyes and ran warm into her ear and down her neck. She sniffed and made to dash it away, but Wim Grijs grabbed her wrist and instead, licked and kissed the tear away. The grass rustled as he turned over and put an arm across her waist.

'Don't cry, Kat,' he said. 'I didn't ask you to meet me so I could see you cry.'

'I know,' she whispered. 'But I don't know what you thought could be achieved by this. I have had years to get over you, Wim, and haven't been able to do it. And while you still visit, send notes, meet me here, there, wherever is private, I never will. Every time Kit looks at me with your eyes, my heart turns over. John Marley will see the likeness one day and then where will we be?'

Grijs smiled and tickled her under the nose with a blade of grass and made her sneeze. 'Don't be sad, Kat,' he said. 'We've had what we can, haven't we? And although I would like some more one day, that isn't why I asked you to come here today.'

She turned her head, setting her cap askew. 'Then, why?'

'I need to know – can I trust Kit?'

'With what?' Her heart gave a lurch.

Grijs drew a deep breath and seemed to hold it for ever before letting it go. 'He knows something which could harm the two of us, if it gets out. The problem I have is that he doesn't know it involves you – if he knew, then I know he would keep the secret to the grave. But . . . this is so hard, Kat.'

'Tell me,' she said, through lips as dry and stiff as bone.

'When you left me, to marry John Marley, I went to sea. I . . . made a lot of money.'

She sat up and just as suddenly lay down again. The grass was long but only concealed her when lying flat. 'You were a . . . pirate?' Her eyes were wide.

'It isn't how it sounds,' he said. 'The polite term is privateer. I sailed with many men who are famous now, who have left the taint of piracy behind. I won't go into it, I am not proud of it but that was then and I was angry. Angry at you, at Marley, at the world. Anyway, the fit passed but it left me with money in my pocket and a knowledge of the world so, when Drake was looking for investors in his voyage to circumnavigate the globe, I put some money in. It paid back, not handsomely but well enough, and as well as my dividend, I received a jewel from Sir Francis, with the instruction that I keep it safe, to look after it as I would my life.'

The woman beside him looked at the sky, not speaking, but a small muscle worked at the side of her jaw.

'Mistress Benchkyne, who you know went strange in the head in the last few years, saw it one day in my house and for some reason, had to have it. It seemed to exert some strange power over her, I don't know what. I wondered if that was why it was sent to me to keep safe; that it carried some spell or another, although in normal times I would not believe such things. She started selling off her things, coming to my house with bags of silver and gold, offering me all she had if she could own the jewel, but I always refused.'

'But you let her have it in the end?'

He reached out and stroked her cheek. 'Yes. Yes, I did.'

'Why? If you had been told to guard it? How did you know that it was not her you had to guard it against?' Katherine Marley had a simple view of life.

'I let her have it because she said if I didn't, she would tell John Marley about us.'

Even the grasshoppers and skylarks fell silent

241

as the woman took it in. She even thought she knew when Mistress Benchkyne had gained her knowledge. There had been a day, a day when she knew her husband to be away from home until the next morning, when Wim Grijs had come to the house, letting himself in at the back door and creeping up the stairs. Looking out into the back garden as he crept away with the dawn, she had thought she saw a figure over the hedge but had dismissed it as a trick of the light. But that was clearly not so.

Grijs was continuing his tale. 'She came round and offered me one last chance. She must have the globe or she would tell the whole town. She was so far gone in her madness by then that she said she would run through the streets, crying the news. Kat, I believed her. So . . . I let her have the globe.'

'What happened to her money? Folk say there was hardly a stick of furniture in the house when she was found.'

'She paid me.' He sounded disbelieving even as he spoke. 'She wouldn't have the globe for nothing. The threat of telling the town was just like the last payment, the one that makes the seller part with his goods. She was mad. But I had to protect you, Kat. And now, I hear, your Kit is going round looking for the other globes. I was a fool to think mine the only one. So in time, if he hasn't already, he will know that the one he has tucked in his doublet was once mine. And if he chooses to dig, he will find the body where we have kept it buried all this time.'

Talk of bodies made ice trickle down Kat

Marley's spine. 'It wasn't you who killed her, was it, Wim?' Even as she asked, she knew she didn't want to know the answer and she covered her ears with her hands, pressing the palms tight to the side of her head.

She could feel his breath hot on her face as he leaned in to make sure she heard. 'No, Kat. No, I didn't kill her. I wanted to; but someone got there first.'

The bats flitted in and out of the yews that guarded Walsingham's gates at Barn Elms. The night was a deep purple and as warm as day. Katherine Marley was not the only one feeling the heat. Women had gone into labour early. Grown men had collapsed crying in the fields, exhausted by the harvest. Children were tetchy and fretful. Babies would not shut up. And if lions didn't exactly whelp in the streets, well, it was only a matter of time . . .

Marlowe saw how low the water lay in the Spymaster's ponds. His carp would be flapping overland soon, looking for deeper water. But it wasn't the fish that held Marlowe's attention as he left the ferryman by the weir.

'Ho, Master Faunt!' he called.

Walsingham's left-hand man raised his hand to hold the ferryman. 'Kit, I must get back to Whitehall.'

'Is he in?' Marlowe asked.

'He is, but this is not a good time.'

'The Progress?'

'Or lack of it. It's been called off.'

Marlowe was surprised. It wasn't like the

Queen to change her mind once it was made up. 'Really?'

Faunt turned his back on the ferryman and walked with Marlowe a few yards into the trees. 'There was an attempt on the Queen's life today,' he said.

'There was?'

'You haven't heard? I would have thought the streets would be full of the news.'

'I've been to Deptford, talking to a madman.'

'Well, if it's madmen you're after, I suppose you went to as good a place as any.'

'What happened?'

'Master Topcliffe will no doubt tell us that come morning.'

Marlowe didn't doubt it. Richard Topcliffe was the Queen's enforcer, a man skilled in the art of pain. The screams from his victims, deep within the Tower, could be heard in Southwark.

'Personally,' Faunt continued, 'I think he's wasting his time. The fellow was duck hunting and his caliver went off. Could happen to any of us. Narrowly missed the Queen's barge, however.'

'You were there?'

'I was. So was Sir Francis. He's in bed.'

'Wounded?'

'Exhausted. It's this infernal heat, Kit. That and the cares of state. I've told him to slow down.'

'What did he say?'

Faunt laughed. 'Nothing I can repeat to a former choirboy like you. He's resting.'

'I'm going to have to wake him up,' Marlowe said.

'No.' Faunt was insistent. 'I'm serious, Kit. Leave him be.'

Marlowe shrugged. 'I shall tell you, then.'

Faunt turned and crossed the planking to the waiting boat, Marlowe in his wake. 'Ho, Ferryman. Are you deaf?' He held up a silver coin.

'Beg pardon, sir?' The man smiled a crooked smile and pulled an ear forward with his fingers. Faunt laughed and threw him the coin.

'All right, Kit.' Both men sat in the boat. 'What have you got?'

'I think Doctor Dee is away with his spirits again, Kit, from what you say. And Captain Winter is no better, though perhaps the spirits are different. Do you really think these globes are important?'

Marlowe looked his man in the eye, judging by the glabrous reflection of the moon, which was all he had to go by. The quiet 'thock' of the oars were all that broke the silence for a moment. 'Yes,' the playwright said at last. 'I know you will think that this is because I have been with John Dee and you know that can unhinge a man's thoughts somewhat, but it isn't that. I feel that they are heavy with menace. If they are ever put together, the world we know would end. Not with fire, war, pestilence, anything like that. Just –' he spread his arms wide in a flamboyant gesture that earned him a quiet 'Oi' from the oarsman – 'change. More change than we could bear.' He set his mouth in a rueful line. 'But it is just a feeling.'

Faunt sat back in the boat and didn't speak for a while.

'Jetty coming up, gents,' said the deaf ferryman. 'Hold on tight.' With a bump and a lurch, they had reached Whitehall Stair and the ferryman jumped ashore with the painter. Tying up expertly, he looked over his shoulder at Faunt. 'That's me for tonight, sir,' he said. 'Much later than my usual times, o' course.'

With a sigh, Faunt tossed him another coin. What with the usual fee and the extra to stop his ears, the man had done well tonight. The ferryman handed them up the slippery stairs and waited expectantly at the top, but Faunt had had enough and walked off towards Westminster without looking back. With no rancour, the ferryman shrugged his shoulders and set off home. It was no harm asking, even so.

'So,' Faunt continued seamlessly, 'you don't know what they are, why they are so important, they just are; John Dee is doing arcane things with diamonds and very small women and that is about the sum total.'

'As always, Master Faunt,' Marlowe said, bowing, 'you have your finger right upon it.'

'With the Progress off and Sir Francis in his bed . . .'

'You are worried about him, Master Faunt.' Marlowe had never been quite sure of the relationship between the two, but Faunt spoke more like a loving son than an employee, however senior. 'Will he be away from pulling his strings for long, do you think?'

'I can't get a straight answer from any of his medical men. It is a case of nervous prostration, as far as I can tell. It isn't like him but there is a lot to try him from the weather to the Queen and back again. He deserves a while away from the affairs of state. With him in bed, we are all at somewhat of a loose end. We don't have word yet of the other globes, although we should have news soon. But meanwhile, I have a plan.'

'I have plans, Master Faunt. I plan to be the greatest playwright the world has ever seen.'

'That didn't take you long,' Faunt laughed.

'You are too kind,' Marlowe said. 'I plan to spend a life of ease, writing my lines and reading my books, somewhere in a garden, heavy with the scent of honey from the flowers and the buzzing of the bees. And when winter comes to that garden, I will move off and find another where summer still rules. And after that another . . . and another . . .'

'You would tire of that soon enough,' Faunt told him.

'Perhaps. All I ask is a chance to find out.'

'But my plan is easier to carry out. We go to see Thomas Phelippes. If there is a cypher he can't crack, I have never met it.'

'Is this a cypher, though?' Marlowe was doubtful.

'Perhaps not a cypher as such. But a conundrum, certainly. We'll go to see him tomorrow, first thing. Don't go all the way back to Hog Lane now. Come back with me to my house. We can raise the kitchen, get some food, some drink. You can rest in my second best bed but before that I can tell you tales of Marie Starkey that will make your eyes pop.'

'Marie . . .? Oh, the emerald globe. I did wonder . . .'

'Oh, don't mistake me, Kit. I took nothing that was not freely given. In fact, she had had the globe wheedled out of her by a sweet talker only weeks before we began searching.'

'But no violence?'

'A little nibbling, but nothing out of the ordinary.'

'No.' Marlowe gave the projectioner a push. 'I mean, he didn't hurt anyone, hold up the household, rob them at knife point.'

'Oh, no,' Faunt said. 'Master Robin only needed one weapon with Marie. Well, perhaps two, but a sweet tongue in his head did the work, I don't doubt.'

Marlowe stopped in his tracks. 'Robin?'

'That's what she said. Of course, it doesn't have to be his real name.'

'No, indeed not. But I can guarantee the sweet tongue.'

'How so?'

'Because anyone who can get the better of my sister Anne must have at least a sweet tongue. And a whip and a good strong right arm if my father is to be believed.'

Faunt was quiet and the two men walked side by side for a while before either spoke.

'Have you seen her since . . .?'

'No. But I don't fear for her safety. If her dalliance with Robin had not gone well, the whole of Kent would have heard of it. And Robin is a common enough name. But still . . .'

'Indeed,' Faunt said. 'But still . . .'

248

They were at the gates of Faunt's house before he put a hand on Marlowe's sleeve. 'I know I don't have to say anything to you, Kit, but it goes without saying that Mistress Faunt knows nothing of this.'

'My lips are sealed, Master Faunt,' Marlowe assured him. 'Does she know what you do, by the way?'

'She knows I work for Sir Francis,' Faunt said. 'She thinks I am his secretary. Oh, thank you for reminding me.' He pulled out a small phial of ink from his pocket and daubed a small amount on to his thumb and forefinger, rubbing it well under the nail.

Marlowe nodded. 'That is a nice touch, Nicholas,' he said, admiringly. 'I'm not at all sure I would have thought of that.'

'Ah,' said Faunt with a sigh, pushing open the door. 'Married to Mistress Faunt one has to stay one step ahead of the game at all times. Sir Francis should employ her, not me.' Raising his voice, he called, 'Hello, the house. I'm home.'

That morning, Kit Marlowe set out for Thomas Phelippes' lodgings with a substantial breakfast under his belt. Mistress Faunt may be the nearest thing the domestic setting had to a Richard Topcliffe, but she kept a good dairy and kitchen and her cook had been tempted by a mix of fair words and threats away from the palace of Nonsuch itself. So he was in a very pleasant frame of mind when he woke the Phelippes' house with a rhythmical knocking on the front door.

The casement shot up but no outraged head

thrust itself out. Marlowe found he almost missed it. Instead, a voice called, 'Who is it?'

'Well, who are *you*?' Marlowe replied. 'You can see me, but I can't see you. You have the advantage of me.'

Now the head popped out of the window and there, in all his morning glory, was Master Thomas Phelippes, Master of the Queen's Cyphers. 'Kit? I heard you went back to Kent.'

'Your intelligence is out of date, Master Phelippes, as well as inaccurate. I went back to Kent, to see my . . . mother.' Marlowe would not say he went to see his parents, because his father was of no account.

'Is she well?' Phelippes asked politely. His head had disappeared now and there were signs which suggested he was struggling into his clothes.

'Thank you,' Marlowe said, with equal politeness. He could almost feel the paper burning the skin of his chest. Before he had spent half the night mulling over the problem with Nicholas Faunt, he had thought little of his list as a cypher. But now, the possibilities seemed endless. So many letters. So many permutations. It made the head spin. 'She is well. But I am here on business. A cypher.'

Phelippes' head shot out of the window again. 'Really? A new cypher? Oh, Kit, I have grown so bored with the simple posturing of spies these days. I am so glad . . . I'll be down directly.' The head disappeared again and Phelippes' progress through the little house could be heard clearly as he fell over shoes, the cat and anything else that had the lack of foresight not to move out of his

250

way, including several chairs. Finally, the door swung open and Phelippes, with no more pretence at politesse, thrust out his hand.

Marlowe sighed. He should have known that the man would not have learned any manners in the time since they had last met. He put his hand inside his doublet and pulled out the by now rather dog-eared piece of parchment.

Phelippes unfolded it with trembling fingers. He turned it to the light and peered with short-sighted, red-rimmed eyes. 'Fascinating,' he said, 'fascinating. Now, apart from the fact that the gems spell "El Dorado" what are you expecting to find?' He looked up, a friendly and expectant expression on his pale, scholar's face. 'Hmm?'

Marlowe looked at him closely for a long while, breathing slowly in through his nose and out through his mouth, a technique Michael Johns had taught him many years ago when he was a nervous boy at Corpus Christi, missing his mother and not doing very well with his Greek. Then, without another word, he plucked the parchment from Phelippes' fingers, turned on his heel and walked slowly down the street. 'E' for emerald, 'L' for lapis lazuli, two diamonds for the two 'D's, two opals, a ruby for the 'R' and a glittering purple amethyst for the 'A'. How, in the name of God and all His angels, could Kit Marlowe have missed that?

Phelippes, clutching his breeches closed around him, aware that in his hurry he had mislaced them to a ridiculous extent, leaned out of the door. 'Kit?' he called. 'Kit?' Finally, he realized that the poet was not going to come back and he

251

went inside, shutting the door. His total recall would be enough. Surely, the great wordsmith Marlowe wouldn't have missed that simple answer. There must be something more. He sat at the table, staring at nothing to all intents and purposes. But his inner eye was scanning and rescanning both sides of the parchment, the map, the names, the locations. Surely, something, *something* must be hidden there, if only he could see it. With a happy sigh, Thomas Phelippes settled down to cogitate. For Walsingham's Code Master, it was what kept the world turning.

It was between two and three of the clock when Kit Marlowe got back to Hog Lane. Tapsters were lounging outside the Grey Mare and the sun was a demon. He barely noticed the very large man leaning against the inn sign, whittling. Little shavings of wood flew from his blade and fluttered to the ground. But if Marlowe hadn't seen him, he had seen Marlowe. As the playwright reached for the latch of his front door, the big man lunged at him, his blade slicing deep into Marlowe's arm just below the elbow.

Marlowe staggered backwards. He tried to reach for his dagger but the pain in his arm was too much and he knew the knife had gone deep.

'What?' the big man growled, tossing the knife from one hand to the other. 'Is that it? I expected a bit more than that from the likes of you.'

'The likes of me?' Marlowe was retreating slowly, gripping his arm tight as the blood trickled over his fingers. 'Are you mistaking me for somebody else, sirrah?'

Men had scattered, overturning tables and chairs to get out of harm's way.

'Oh, no,' the big man said. 'There's only one Kit Marlowe. You're the bloody Muses' darling, aren't you, scribbler?'

'Nice of you to remember.' Marlowe still had the coolness to smile. 'Now, don't tell me; you're a bit of a writer yourself.'

'Me?' The big man laughed hoarsely. 'Oh, I know my limitations,' he said. 'This –' he threw the knife in the air and caught it again – 'is a present from Joshua, to thank you for turning over his workshop.'

He lunged again, but this time Marlowe was ready. He dodged aside and heard the bright blade bite into the timbers behind him. With one arm useless and the other one clawing for his dagger, he brought his boot up to hit his opponent in the kidneys. The man groaned and dropped to one knee. Then he saw Marlowe's dagger gleaming in his left hand and scuttled away to the shelter of the Mare's wall.

A crowd had gathered now, cheering and jeering.

'Take him, Will. He's half your size.'

'Kick his arse, Master Marlowe.'

'Before I kill you –' Marlowe was standing still now, watching his man – 'may I know your name?'

'They'll tell you in Hell when you get there,' the man said.

'He's Will Bradley, Master Marlowe,' somebody shouted. 'Son of the innkeeper.'

'Well, innkeeper's son,' Marlowe said, 'I don't

253

know what I've done to offend you. But if you'd care to die on the blade of a cobbler's son . . .' He beckoned him forward.

Bradley saw his chance and grabbed a sword from one of the crowd. It was a clumsy English weapon, heavy in the broad blade, but a killing device for all that. Now the man had a sword *and* a knife against Marlowe's dagger and here the projectioner was again outarmed in more ways than one.

'I'll take it, Kit.' A familiar voice called to Marlowe's right. It was Tom Watson, hurtling out of their house, with rapier and dagger in his hands. Valour was the better part of discretion today.

'What?' Bradley growled. 'You want some, do you? All right, lute player, that's fine by me. I'll deal with Marlowe later.'

'Tom,' Marlowe grunted, his right arm stiffening by the second, 'stay out of this. It's my problem.'

But Watson wasn't listening. He swung at Bradley with his sword and the clash of steel rang the length of Hog Lane. Women and children had joined the happy revellers from the Mare now and all of them were cheering on their chosen champion. Marlowe felt sick and dizzy, what with the heat, the sudden exertion and the loss of blood. He had never seen Tom Watson with a sword in his hand before and he was impressed by his skill. Once, twice, Watson's attack drove Bradley back so that the man had to use both his weapons just to stay alive. He half-stumbled and as he did, he grabbed a handful of dust from the road and threw it at Watson. The poet coughed and spluttered, his eyes in agony and his vision blurred. That was all the edge Bradley needed and he scythed with his sword, slicing a chunk out of Watson's sleeve. A second sweep and Watson's dagger had gone, knocked out of his grasp by the bigger man and clattering to the ground.

Marlowe broke away from the wall where he'd been resting but a hand held his good arm. It was Eliza, the companion of Watson's nights. 'Don't, Kit. He'll kill you both. You're in no fit state. Tom'll be all right.'

Marlowe doubted it. Bradley was fast for a big man and, for an innkeeper's son, he seemed to know all the moves of the Spanish school. His blade flashed in the afternoon sun, driving Watson back along the lane as the crowd moved with them. Money was changing hands already and odds were being shouted.

'Kill him, Will! Cut his pocky off!'

'Get him, Master Watson. Come on, you're walking.'

That wasn't exactly true. Tom Watson was stumbling and he knew he had the ditch behind him. If he fell there it would be all over and the fight that was not his fight would end with the death of Thomas Watson, generosus. He whirled right and left, desperately trying to keep away from Bradley's probing blade. Marlowe had had enough. Eliza's hand was still clinging to his sleeve but he brushed her aside and dashed forward. He was still jostling his way through the braying crowd, their blood up, when there was a roar and a scream. As Marlowe broke into the circle, Will Bradley was sinking to his knees, both blades clattering to the ground and crimson was spurting from his chest. He was coughing blood and Marlowe knew that Watson's thrust had penetrated the man's lung. Bradley's eyes rolled upwards and he crashed forward on his face.

There were boos and cheers in equal proportions and money changed hands for one last time.

'Tom.' Marlowe helped his friend up from his half-crouching position. 'Are you all right?'

Watson was panting heavily, his face running with sweat. 'Parry of sixte next time, I fancy,' he said and laughed as Eliza ran to him, covering his face with kisses. As the crowd scattered except the few stalwarts who always lingered around corpses, another commotion broke out and a constable came running. He wore the livery of the City and carried a stout staff.

'I am Stephen Wyld,' he announced, taking in the scene, 'and this is my patch.' He looked at Bradley lying face down, the blood still spreading over the Hog Lane dust. 'What's happened here?'

'A man's dead, constable,' someone in the crowd's remnants told him.

'You'll have to excuse him, Master Marlowe,' somebody else said. 'He's a tailor by trade. Not really cut out for the police job. Ha! Get it? Not cut out . . .' And the man's voice tailed away as Wyld's tipstaff jutted painfully under his chin.

'I'll do the jokes,' the constable said. He turned to Watson. 'Who are you?'

'Thomas Watson,' the poet told him. 'Generosus.'

Wyld had long ago stopped being impressed by gentlemen. So few of them actually were.

'You?' The constable turned to Marlowe, noting the blood still glistening on his sleeve.

'Christopher Marlowe,' he told him. And he winked at Watson. 'Yeoman.'

'Who's this?' Wyld knelt and turned the body over. 'Well, well.' He grinned. 'Will Bradley. Who killed him?'

'I did,' Watson and Marlowe chorused.

Wyld had already established that he was not a man who was humorously inclined. 'Well, whichever of you it was, you've done us all a favour. There aren't many shits as annoying as Will Bradley east of Cripplegate. Even so –' he stood up and assumed his official position – 'murder has been done. I shall have to ask you gentlemen to hand me your weapons and to accompany me to the Justice.'

Both men sighed. The Justice, if that term was not a complete misnomer, was Sir Owen Hopton, Lieutenant of the Tower.

'*Pro suspicione murdri,*' Hopton read the charge sheet in front of him. He sat in a high desk, his hair, white as snow, cascading over his ruff. He was not at the Tower today but at his home in Norton Folgate, the hall of which he had turned over for use by the Court. Clerks as ancient as he was scurried around, moving parchment, quills and inkwells from one table to another with all the panoply of the law. 'On suspicion of murder.' Hopton hardly needed to translate. Everybody in his hall spoke Latin like a native, but Hopton believed that the law should not only be fair but should be seen to be fair.

'The Limboes!' He bashed his own woodwork with the gavel. Marlowe and Watson were manhandled towards the door.

'Wait a minute!' Watson shouted. 'We demand to be heard.'

Hopton looked up, outraged. 'Did you kill this man . . . er . . . William Bradley?'

'Yes, but . . .'

'Disgraceful!' Hopton squeaked.

'In self-defence, sir,' Watson pointed out.

'In defence of me, in fact,' Marlowe added. He had lost all feeling in his arm now and the shock was sweeping through his body in juddering waves.

'If there's one thing I hate –' Hopton leaned over his desk, clutching its edge with bony fingers – 'it's conspiracies. We shall see what the Inquest brings. The Limboes.'

Kit Marlowe had been to Whittington's Palace before, but never as an invited guest. It lay under the shadow of Paul's and stood five floors tall. Not that Marlowe and Watson saw its sunlit storeys for long. The Limboes were the darkest reaches of the prison below street level. The dark was tangible, the stench unbelievable. Watson, the generosus, the poet, the gentle musician who had killed a man, found himself clutching Marlowe's sleeve convulsively as they were led ever deeper by the turnkey with the burning brand.

'This'll do,' the man grunted, and stood waiting.

258

There were no cells here, just a wild room, the stone walls of which ran with water. A solitary candle burned slowly on a black stone in the room's centre and Marlowe could make out shadowy figures in rags around the walls. He heard them moving, slithering their chains as they craned to see who had arrived.

'Don't let us keep you from your work, Sirrah.' Watson had found some bravado from somewhere.

'Iron pay, eh, Master Gaoler?' Marlowe looked at the man, greasy and unshaven in his leather jerkin.

'What?' Watson had entered a circle of Dante's Hell and he really didn't care for it.

'It's a quaint little custom they have here, Tom,' Marlowe told him. 'These poor fellows are paid so little they augment their wages however they can. They shackle your wrists and ankles with iron, for which they charge you. Then, when you cannot move because of the weight of the iron, they charge you to remove them, link by link. I'll wager this . . . gentleman . . . is richer than both of us.'

'You've got a smart mouth,' the turnkey snarled at him.

'It goes with the rest of me,' Marlowe said and beamed. The man swung at him, but, wounded arm or no, the projectioner was faster and he stepped aside, bringing his good arm down hard on the man's neck and forcing his face over the candle. There was a roar from the turnkey and delighted whoops and catcalls from the inmates who rattled their chains and clapped their approval.

'That's enough!' a voice shouted in the darkness. Marlowe jerked the gaoler away from the flame and everyone turned to see who had arrived.

'Master Faunt,' Marlowe half-bowed. 'This *is* a surprise.'

'Yes.' The Spymaster's left-hand man flicked his fingers at the gaoler. 'Put something on that burn before it festers.' He crossed to Marlowe and Watson and looked the musician up and down. 'Really Marlowe, I'm a little tired of getting you and yours out of the Stink.'

'Mine?' Marlowe frowned. 'Oh, Alice Snow. Yes, thank you for that. Has she settled in, with Walsingham, I mean?'

'My dear boy, the only reason I go into the kitchens is to help myself to a flagon if I'm thirsty or a hunk of bread if I'm peckish. I haven't heard to the contrary, so I expect she is doing well. Come on.'

'How did you know I was here?' Marlowe asked.

Faunt closed to him. 'I'd be a pretty useless projectioner if I didn't.' And he winked, slapping Marlowe on his good shoulder.

'What about me?' Watson asked.

Faunt looked at him again. 'What about you, sir?'

'I'm Tom Watson.'

Faunt turned to face him for the first time. 'I know who you are,' he said.

'Well, aren't you getting me out, too?'

'Master Watson,' Faunt said quietly. 'You killed a man. The law must take its course.'

Watson's jaw fell open before he found the

260

words. 'Wait. You mentioned . . . well, Marlowe mentioned Walsingham.'

'What of it?'

'Well, Sir Francis,' Watson said with a beaming smile, 'I know Tom Walsingham, his nephew.'

'I know you do,' Faunt acknowledged with a nod. 'You met him in Paris.'

'I . . .'

'In fact, Master Watson, I know rather a lot about you. Let's see; you were born in Bishopsgate and went to school in Winchester.'

'Oh, bad luck.' Marlowe shook his head, all concern.

'At thirteen, you went to Oxford . . .'

More commiserations from Marlowe.

'Then, of course,' Faunt became confidential, 'you attended the Catholic seminary at Douai . . .'

'The nest of scorpions.' Marlowe patted the side of his nose.

'More recently, you flitted around that group of poets calling themselves Areopagus – Philip Sidney et al. More importantly – and I'm quoting here from Sir Francis' little book on you – you are one of those "strangers who don't go to church."'

'Tom.' Marlowe frowned. 'I can't believe it of you. And to think I have you as a lodger.'

'Kit!' Watson felt the ground, bloody and shit-strewn as it was, sliding from under him.

'I have no instructions for you, Master Watson,' Faunt said and turned his back, leading Marlowe away.

'I'll get you out, Tom,' the more junior projec-tioner called. 'Keep your chin up.'

And neither of Walsingham's men heard a sly voice growl in the half-darkness, 'And a very pretty chin it is, too.'

'Keep away from me, Sirrah!' Watson ordered. 'I've just killed a man!'

It cost Francis Walsingham forty pounds to keep Kit Marlowe out of Newgate, something else that bit into his debts. At the inquest into the death of William Bradley, the innkeeper's son, at Finsbury the next day, Marlowe told Master Chalkhill, the coroner, and his twelve men and true what had happened in Hog Lane. He made no mention of Joshua the silversmith. The maid had cleaned his wound and an apothecary Marlowe couldn't really afford stitched it for him. Even so, it was damnably stiff and painful and he resorted to eating with his left hand.

'An inquest isn't a trial, Tom,' Marlowe explained in the Limboes later that day. 'You've studied the law.'

'Canon law, you silly bastard.' Tom Watson was in no mood to be humoured. 'Not criminal.'

'You'll be heard at the next Sessions. They'll have to acquit you. It was *se defendendo*, self-defence. You'll have to wait for the Queen's grace, of course.'

'Bugger the Queen's grace, Marlowe,' Watson snapped. He hadn't slept all night, keeping one eye on the rats that threatened to nibble his points and the other on the very friendly felon chained to his left who fancied his chin. All in all, it had not gone well.

'Careful, Tom,' Marlowe warned. 'We don't

want to add treason to the list of charges against you.'

He patted the man's cheek, a gesture of interest to the friendly felon watching them closely from his corner, and he left.

On his way out to the light and the fresh air of the parish of Paul, he passed a pretty girl on her way in. 'The turnkey will take you down, Eliza,' he said. 'He has his instructions. He'll be moving Tom to an upper room directly.' He looked down at the girl's bosom, almost bare under her cloaks and smiled. 'I think he'll be very pleased to see you. And so will Tom.'

Fifteen

Finally, Marlowe had the leisure to think over all he had learned since visiting John Dee. That the old magus would be happily rootling among his retorts and vials he had no doubt and he also was sure he would be happily engaged till Kingdom come, should that event be a viable option. Thomas Phelippes, also, was no doubt still mulling over the possibilities suggested by Joshua's list. What Joshua and Mercator were doing or even where they were, he had no idea. Captain Winter would, by this time of early afternoon, be slowly sliding off his stool on to the grimy deck of the *Wanderer*. And who knew what Nicholas Faunt was up to – that question would never have an answer.

Marlowe felt like chaff blowing in the breeze, leaving the grains behind on the granary floor. They had their purpose, but he was beyond them now. His brain was buzzing and he needed to settle his thoughts. As always, when he needed to feel calmer, he found his feet leading him towards the Rose. It was unlikely that he would be left alone by Henslowe once he was discovered, but if he could slip in at the back, at least he would be able to watch the last Act that was giving everyone so much trouble. He let the crowd go ahead of him as he reached the end of Rose Alley. Many were carrying bulky bags and he smiled for the first time that day. The ground-lings were beginning to organize and knocking Ned Alleyn out with a well-aimed vegetable would be a feather in anyone's cap. Soon, the crowd dispersed and the doors of the Rose clapped shut behind the last laggard. Marlowe leaned on the wall of the Bear Pit and waved a hello to Master Sackerson, Henslowe's bear, looking more moth-eaten than ever in the unre-lenting heat, flies buzzing around him and burrowing into his fur in search of dropped titbits.

'Is he really dangerous, do you suppose?' A voice behind him made the playwright turn.

'No,' he said. 'I doubt he has a tooth left in his head now. He can do some damage with his claws though . . . Excuse me, I normally have a good head for names. I know we have met, but I can't quite . . .'

'Poley,' the man said. 'Robert Poley.'

'Ah, yes, I remember. We met outside the Westgate in Canterbury.' It seemed a lifetime ago. He was now estranged from his family, another man's play had taken over his stage, his best friend was in gaol – but the social niceties must be gone through just the same. 'Marlowe.'

'I know you, Master Marlowe,' Poley said. 'Now as I did then. Your fame goes before you.'

'You are very kind,' Marlowe said. 'But hardly. Your business in Canterbury. Was it successful?'

Poley pulled a rueful face. 'In some respects, yes. In others, no. I found myself distracted by a most terrible murder. The constable told me all about it outside the scene of the very crime. But my business is often that way. I become distracted.

265

I win. I lose.' He smiled his charming smile. 'In the end, what does it matter as long as I end up on top of the heap?'

Marlowe looked at the man more closely. 'That is a hard-hearted way of looking at the world, Master Poley,' he remarked.

'Perhaps. But in my business, it doesn't pay a man to be too sensitive. Not every man can be as passionate as your shepherd.' A sly grin crept over his face. 'Although I have had my moments.'

Marlowe looked at the man and didn't doubt it. He was dressed as richly as Marlowe himself and turned a handsome calf. But his face tended to the weasly and his eyes were far too close together. Not a man to make long-standing friendships. 'You are here for the play?' he asked, still polite. 'The doors are closed.'

'I'm sure you can get me in, a man in your position.' The voice was harsher now, with an edge to it that put Marlowe on his guard. Even Master Sackerson, down in his Pit, sensed the change in the weather and, growling deep in his throat, began to pace to and fro, rearing up and punching the air at every turn. It wasn't the flies he was aiming at.

'I don't use my position, as you call it, to get people in free,' Marlowe said firmly. 'Every free seat is bread out of the actor's mouth.' As he quoted Philip Henslowe he had to suppress a smile; he had seen the coffers at the end of a run and knew that bread was not something to which the Henslowe family was often reduced.

'It needn't be free,' Poley said. 'I would pay my way.'

'It would be unfair to disturb the actors,' Marlowe said, standing up and turning away from the theatre. 'I have decided to go home for now. No one is there at the moment and the maid-servant worries.'

Poley gave an unpleasant laugh. Master Sackerson roared his distress. Marlowe thought that the bear was more sensitive than Master Poley and getting away from the man became an urgent need. 'Yes, I can see that with Master Watson in gaol, young Mary would be feeling at a loose end.' He made an obscene gesture with his fingers and Marlowe stepped back a pace.

'What do you know of that?' Marlowe said.

'What do I know of everything?' Poley said, nastily. 'I know you work for Sir Francis Walsingham. I know he recruited you from Cambridge – Corpus Christi, wasn't it?'

'You are well informed.' Marlowe's mistrust was growing.

'Men say you are Machiavel, that you deny the Godhead.'

'Do they?' Marlowe arched an eyebrow. 'They say a lot, don't they?'

'They say it,' Poley said with a smirk, 'but I *know* it. And most of all, Master Marlowe, I know that we can help each other become very rich. Richer than the richest man you know. Is that something that appeals to you, maybe? You could buy your mother somewhere to live where there was no room for her husband, somewhere pretty along the Stour, away from the stench of the tanneries. You could buy good husbands for your sisters.' Again, he made the obscene gesture, with

267

added gusto. 'My word, that Anne can give a man a run for his money. I thought she would wear me out, so demanding was she! Marie Starkey I could understand. The whole village was rife with rumours about her round heels. But Anne Marley!' He blew out his cheeks. 'Where did she *learn* those things?'

'Robyn!' Marlowe reached for the dagger at his back, but his arm was too stiff and he winced.

'The same.' Poley bowed but not so low that his eyes left Marlowe's face. 'Don't be angry with me. Your sister is a lovely girl and with those skills will make a man very happy one day. As long as he doesn't have to live with her, that is. My word, she had a tongue on her.' He paused. 'So to speak.'

Ignoring his painful arm, Marlowe lunged at Poley but there was no possibility that he could overpower him. Poley grabbed his left arm, immobilizing him, and started to walk him towards the theatre.

'I'll kill you,' Marlowe said, through gritted teeth.

'Possibly,' Poley conceded. 'One day. But for now, listen to me. Your little sister's honour is nothing in the scheme of things and I have a little proposition to make to you. One that you will like, I think. Although you appear to be on the side of right, justice, liberty and all the rest, I think you are just like me, Christopher Marlowe. In search of enough money to live a life of ease. Am I right?' He squeezed his arm. 'Well, am I?'

'Who doesn't like money?' Marlowe said, forcing a smile.

'That's right, Kit. May I call you Kit?'

'I would prefer it if you didn't.'

'Then Master Marlowe it is. I believe we each have something the other wants, Master Marlowe.'

'I doubt you have anything that I would want.' Marlowe was on his dignity but also playing for time. He couldn't beat this man alone, especially not with a stiff arm to contend with. And Poley wasn't stupid. He was squeezing his left arm so tightly that his fingers were beginning to tingle. Soon this one would be useless too.

They were at the side door of the theatre now and the shadows were deep. From inside came faint noises of declamatory speeches. Ned Alleyn in full flow could be heard a mile away, or so it was said. Poley put his face close to Marlowe's and hissed, 'The globes. You have two. I have three. That leaves me the clear winner, but I will be generous. If you give me yours, I will share the treasure with you, half for you, half for me.'

'That seems *very* generous, Master Poley,' Marlowe said. 'And that seems so unlike you, if I may say on such short acquaintance.'

'It will be worth it, Master Marlowe, make no mistake. There will be more than enough treasure to go round.'

A gaggle of Winchester geese came down the narrow alley, breasts barely balanced on the top of their bodices, skirts kirtled up, ready for action once the groundlings and gentlemen tumbled out of the play, their vegetables gone. One of them threw her arms around Poley.

'You look like a man who can give a girl a good time,' she shrieked and all her friends joined in the fun. 'Let's see what you've got down here, then . . .' And she rummaged about in the region of Poley's codpiece.

'Nah!' one of the girls screeched. 'Look at them. Holding hands, they are. They don't want the likes of us, dearie. They've got other things in mind. That's against God's law, that is.'

Poley's face worked in anger and he let go of Marlowe's arm. 'Don't you speak to me like that, you common slut!' he said, grabbing the girl painfully by her upper arm. 'I've had more like you than you've had . . .'

'Fools like you,' she finished for him, breaking away and running with her friends down the alley, breasts bouncing. One girl risked pausing at the end of the lane and, bending over, flung her skirts over her head, showing him her wares.

Poley watched them go in fury, then turned to see that Marlowe had gone. The theatre was the only place he could have hidden in so quickly and he too slipped inside the small door, where Ned Alleyn was wont to lurk for hours after a performance, waiting for the adoring crowds to appear. He had not been lucky thus far, but he was sure his day would come.

The narrow corridor was pitch dark and disorienting, even for someone coming in from the gloom of the alley. Poley looked back and forth but Marlowe was nowhere to be seen. From dead ahead there was the noise of Will Shaxsper's faltering attempt at a play, accompanied by hoots of derision from the groundlings.

Poley had lost his bearings a little, but could tell from the baying of the audience that the front of the stage was to his right. He turned to his left, therefore, and made his way, inch by careful inch, along the corridor, feeling his way along the wall. Suddenly, the wall disappeared and he was lost in space. He slid his feet forward carefully, one at a time, not sure what he might encounter. Soon, he knew. Marlowe's left arm came around his neck and squeezed.

'Master Poley,' he said quietly in his ear. 'If I can drag you away from the ladies for a moment, I believe we have something to discuss.'

Poley was a threat shorter than Marlowe and as the poet leaned backwards, his feet left the floor. His throat felt as though it were on fire and he scrabbled helplessly at the thick brocade that protected Marlowe's forearm. Marlowe shook him, using Poley's own weight against him and was gratified to hear a rattle coming from the man's chest. He could feel his dagger pressing into his midriff, so he knew that, for the moment at least, he was unarmed. He could finish it now, with no blood shed, and no one to say who the dead man in Southwark might be. But his basic curiosity was too much and he let the man fall.

Poley fell at his feet, choking and coughing. He clambered up on to all fours and Marlowe could hear his laboured breathing. Eventually, he could stand and leaned against the wall, panting. 'Pax,' he grated. 'We are on the same side, you and I.'

'Are we?' Marlowe asked. 'I doubt it.'

'My offer is good, Marlowe,' he said. 'Half each of all the riches of El Dorado. I have the jewel with the first point on it, you the jewel with

271

the last. With the ones we have in between, there is no need to collect the last three. Our five will lead us to it and we can bring back shiploads of gold and jewels, silver . . . you name it.'

'I don't believe it can be that simple,' Marlowe said.

'But I have you interested, Marlowe, don't I? The riches of the world today won't compare to what we will have tomorrow.'

Marlowe did not claim to be an economist; that discipline was not taught at Corpus Christi, but he could immediately see a flaw. He knew it would do no good, because the gold madness had Poley by the short hairs, but he had to tell him, all the same. 'If there is as much gold there as you say . . .'

'There is,' Poley said, 'there is!' and he broke off in a paroxysm of coughing.

'Will it not lose its value? If we bring back, shall we say, three times the amount already known . . .'

'Thirty times three and thirty times again,' Poley said, getting excited.

'As you say, many times the current known value, then, will gold not become as worthless as sand?'

Poley was silent. He was a cunning man, but not overly intelligent and big ideas took a while to percolate through his brain. 'How so?' But he sounded dubious.

Marlowe could hardly believe that he was standing here, in a pitch-dark corridor at the Rose, talking economics with a murderer, but needs must when the Devil drives and if he could keep him talking long enough, the play would end and they would be engulfed in actors streaming on to the stage to take their bows. Or collect the vegetables, depending on how the last scene had gone. 'Gold and silver, and jewels, if it comes to that, are valuable only because they are rare. If there were tons of gold in the world – as we know there are, of course, just not their location – it would no longer be rare and the value would fall accordingly. It would still be worth something, I suppose . . .' He stopped and thought for a moment of John Dee, endlessly searching for the Philosophers' Stone that would make all things gold. 'Just not much. So, all the death, all the privation that it would take to bring it back to England would all be for nothing.'

Poley was thinking hard, Marlowe could tell, even in the dark. 'But . . .' Poley had had the dream so long it was dying hard.

'He's right, you know,' a voice said from ahead of them up the corridor.

'Who's there?' Poley hissed and reached for his dagger.

A dim light was revealed and a figure walked towards them. He carried a rapier, held out straight in front of him and before anyone could do anything about it, had it pressed to Poley's throat. With his other hand, he raised his taper and all three men's faces swam in the wavering light.

'Benedict,' Poley whispered. 'What are you doing here?'

'I might ask the same of you, Shakespeare,'

the man said. 'And Master . . . Watson, is it? Or are you Marlowe today?'

A distant voice from above was heard to ask, 'Did someone just say Shakespeare?' It sounded like Philip Henslowe, prowling his theatre, sensing the mood of the crowd growing uglier.

'I am Marlowe today and all days,' the poet said. 'But this man isn't Will Shaxsper, Shakespeare, call him what you wish. His name is Robert Poley. May we assume your name is not Benedict?'

'You may. But I am disappointed in you, Master Poley. I thought we could trust each other more than that.'

Poley tried to step back, to relieve the pressure of the rapier's tip against his throat, but the man stepped forward too. Trying not to move his throat too much, Poley said, 'I used Shakespeare because my name is Poley. Do you see? Pole. Spear. I forgot about this idiot who tries to write plays.'

'Ah, a clever ruse, then. Funny, even.' But the man wasn't laughing at all. 'My name too is a joke, which I think Master Marlowe might understand.'

Marlowe looked into the man's eyes, bright in the tiny flame of the taper. 'I think,' he said, slowly, 'I think that you are Harry Bellot, pilot of the *Benedict*.'

Bellot's eyes widened and he smiled. 'Right on the money, Master Marlowe, and I mean that quite literally, as I am sure you agree. If you had been visiting the theatre with your usual regularity, you would have met me already. I am old Dick the Painter, always around the place, doing odd jobs. Ah, I see you thinking. If he is about to find the gold of El Dorado, why is he working at the Rose, at everyone's beck and call? And the answer is simple, Master Marlowe. When that popinjay Drake brought us all home, he gave us nothing. Some of us got some back pay but other than that, nothing. He got the Queen's rapier on his shoulder when he should have had mine through his filthy, thieving guts. And so I got myself a job. I didn't need much, just enough to put a roof over my head and be able to visit my old mother back in my home town now and again.'

'That would be Lowestoft, presumably?' Marlowe said.

'You know a lot, Marlowe,' Poley snarled but was brought up short with a prod of the rapier.

'We met,' Bellot said, 'though briefly.' And he quoted himself with his broad Suffolk vowels. 'They're a funny lot round here.'

'So,' Marlowe went on, half to himself. 'You heard of the globes, sent out by Francis Drake and you even saw the one that Leonard Morton had.'

'I did. I was an old friend of Master Morton's, back when we were young. A man in his time plays many parts, Master Marlowe. I have been a soldier, a sailor. I even survived the siege of Malta, for my sins.'

'You and Jack Barnet,' Marlowe remembered.

'But he didn't survive me,' Poley said with a grin. 'I left him with a slit throat.'

He winced as Bellot's blade tip slid sideways, drawing fresh blood and tearing Poley's collar.

275

'Barnet was a friend of mine, you bastard,' he hissed. 'But Morton was so innocent –' Bellot was choosing his moment to put Poley out of everyone's misery – 'he would show the globe to anyone he thought a friend. I couldn't work out what Drake was up to at first. He is known as a man who doesn't spend a penny that isn't to his own advantage. And then, I worked it out. The opal in Morton's globe was part of a treasure map. I started doing a little investigation, as far as I could while trying to earn a living. I found out where some of the other globes were – it cost me an angel or two, posing as a customer of the silversmith, for example, and getting friendly with his idiot boy, but in the end I had enough names to begin with. I had heard rumours, of course.'

'From the sailors on the trip home?' Marlowe checked. Poley was moving his eyes only, back and forth, finding out what the men knew. He had got out of tighter places than this. Even from this inauspicious position, all may be well.

'That's quite right, Master Marlowe,' Bellot said with a nod, like a schoolmaster praising a bright child. 'Some knew where the gold was found . . .'

Poley risked his life to lean forward. 'Along the Amazon's mouth,' he said. 'Everyone knows that.'

'But you see, Master Poley, as I suppose I must call you, that is not where the gold is *now*. The gold was loaded on to ships and moved to other locations. They are spread around the globe and the clue to those locations is in its turn hidden . . . elsewhere. This is what these globes will tell us.'

Poley's face fell. 'You lied to me!' he said.

'Of course I did, you little weasel,' Bellot said, easing the rapier a little. 'You would sell your own mother for an angel and a cup of wine. What price any secret you were told? Don't bother with an answer, I'll tell you. The price would be that of the highest bidder, that's what. And so I let you believe what you wanted to believe. As I remember it, I didn't tell you that the globes would lead to Drake's gold. I mentioned Drake. I mentioned gold. Your grubbing, grasping little mind did the rest.'

Poley was speechless. He didn't regret the deaths; men and women were ten a penny to one such as Robin Poley. It was the work he regretted. All that work and for a few paltry bags of coins. 'Why?' was all he could muster. 'Why?'

'Ah,' Bellot said, smiling. 'Why? That is the question. Perhaps *the* question, eh, Master Marlowe? Drake took the gold as any man might, for the greed of it. But then, as he journeyed, he realized what Master Marlowe here realized in a heartbeat. He might just as well take sand, or water, or God's fresh air back to England, for all the value it would have. He would have flooded the market and all that effort would be for nothing. And you know what *that's* like, don't you, Master Poley?' He pressed a fraction closer with the rapier so that Poley felt warm blood trickle down to soak into the linen at his neck.

Marlowe took up the tale. 'So, he hid the gold, and put the clues in the globes, where they would be safe. Because no one knew that others had the rest of the puzzle, he knew the treasures could not be found.'

'Quite so, Master Marlowe,' Bellot praised his star pupil again. 'But Drake, he always makes sure there is a plan beneath the plan, the skull beneath the skin, so to speak. He put the final clues in something he called the Money Pit and no one knows its exact location. But even if men find it and guess its purpose, they will find nothing there. Because the Money Pit contains no money. Just the way to find it, but elsewhere. Oh, he's a cunning one, is Drake. But I have beat him at his game.'

'Not really,' Marlowe said. 'We have two globes, you have three. But the other three are safe and beside which, Drake knows where the others are.'

'And there are plans,' Poley croaked. 'You told me Joshua the silversmith had plans.'

'Yes,' Bellot said. 'And you, incompetent fool, couldn't find them.'

Marlowe looked with added venom at Poley. 'So it was *you* who wrecked Joshua's workshop?'

'Yes.' Poley looked proud. 'I made sure he would make no more jewels, taking the work out of good Christian hands.'

Bellot looked at him aghast. 'You really *are* a weasel, Poley,' he said. 'I looked for the man for the job and sadly, I found you.' He turned to Marlowe. 'I understand that Joshua has caused you and your friend Watson a little trouble, Master Marlowe?'

278

Marlowe inclined his head. 'A little.' Everything was falling into place.

'I'm sorry for that. I began this enterprise to beat Drake at his own game. I would have had little pleasure from it. I will probably be dead and gone by the time he discovered that his plan was in ruins. But, if bones can hear or if souls in Heaven can see what happens here on earth, then my bones, my soul would sing to see him brought low.'

'What would you have done with the globes?' Marlowe asked.

Bellot's eyes were shining and Marlowe knew what was in his heart. It was just a shame for the dead that he had chosen Poley as his agent. It would have made no difference even had he shared his purpose. As soon as Poley and his ilk heard the word 'gold', all sense flew out of the window. 'I would have destroyed them, Master Marlowe. I would have taken them to the silversmith and asked him to melt them, beat them, whatever it might take to have them not exist any more.'

Marlowe nodded. It would take a strong man to do it, but if there was such a man present, then Bellot was that man.

Just then, a trumpet blast made them all jump and the corridor was full of rushing bodies. It says much for the magic of the stage, the smell of the crowd, that no one noticed that one of the men they brushed past so incontinently was Christopher Marlowe, a man so sought after by Philip Henslowe that just speaking to him could earn a man a groat. They didn't notice that old

279

Dick the Painter was standing with a rather weasly-looking man on the end of a rapier. It was time for the final Act of *Henry VI* and it was all hands on deck. There were vegetables to deflect and possible acting glory to win. As soon as they had appeared, they had disappeared and with them Robert Poley.

Marlowe knew the theatre like the back of his hand and there was only one place Poley could have gone, if not on to the stage and that was up into the flies. Marlowe dashed behind Tom Sledd's flats, almost knocking the royal palace on to the stage. Climbing the ladder was difficult with only one good arm, but he was determined that Poley shouldn't get away. He had slit the throat of Jack Barnet, who had only been trying to protect his master's belongings. He had smashed the skull and crushed the brains of poor, mad Jane Benchkyne. And there was vengeance in Kit Marlowe's heart.

He saw Poley hurrying ahead, balancing on the boards that gave Dick the Painter his platform when working at heights. Marlowe went for the man as the actors assembled on stage and another fanfare announced the arrival of Henry the Sixth, better known as the incomparable Ned Alleyn. The crowd's applause was less than ecstatic. They had seen Alleyn's Henry already and weren't exactly impressed. What they were after was a good solid death scene and apart from an off-stage burning there had been nothing yet. Some smoke wafted on from stage right and some falsetto screaming just didn't get the job done, theatrically speaking.

Poley glanced back. Marlowe was too close for comfort, a dagger at his back and there was no other way down. He took his life in his hands and lunged at the thick rope that hung there. He screamed as the rough hemp lacerated his hands, but he was on the ground, Marlowe after him, catching the wildly swinging rope and leaning into it so that he could ease the pain in his arm. The thud of them landing on the boards was followed by the hiss of steel as both men whipped free their daggers, facing each other.

Sixteen

The Earl of Suffolk was well into his stride by now. Jack Roland was used to nothing parts in nothing plays but he couldn't remember one as dull as this. It came to something when the Fiends that the Devil had sent to suckle the paps of La Pucelle, nonentities who had no lines at all, got a bigger clap than he did. But this was it. His big moment in Act V, Scene V and he was determined to milk it for all it was worth.

'A dower, my lords,' he shouted to everyone on stage. 'Disgrace not so your king . . .'

The groundlings all looked at Alleyn, the king of the same name, but he hadn't moved. For days now, he, Henslowe, Sledd and all of them had been trying to find a way to end this rubbish with a bang, but so far it had eluded them. So he just stood there while Jack Roland arranged his wedding for him.

'That he should be so abject, base and poor,' the man droned on, ignoring the fact that none of those words described Ned Alleyn at all. Oh, what a fall was this from Tamburlaine! 'To choose for wealth and not for perfect love. Henry is able to enrich his queen, And not to seek a queen to make him rich . . .'

'Get on with the play!' somebody in the gallery shouted, rigid with boredom. Nothing had happened since they burnt La Pucelle and that was done offstage, Philip Henslowe fearing for his tinder-dry theatre.

Roland misheard the direction of the shout and poured his scorn on to the groundlings who were milling below him like mutinous sheep. 'So worthless peasants,' he jabbed a finger at them, 'bargain for their wives . . .'

''Ere,' came the predictable cry. 'Who're you calling worthless?'

'As market-men for oxen, sheep or horse . . .'

'Animals!' somebody else shouted. 'He's calling us animals, now.'

There were boos and groans filling the theatre, almost drowning out Roland's words. He stood taller. He was the Earl of Suffolk today, by God, and people *would* listen. 'Marriage is a matter of more worth . . .'

'Tell me about it!' a henpecked husband had the nerve to shout back. His wife wasn't there.

'. . . Than to be dealt in by attorneyship . . .'

In the gallery, one bored lawyer turned to another. 'That's actionable, I would have thought.'

'Could be,' his companion yawned. 'I'll have my people look into it.'

'Not whom we will . . .' Roland was still struggling against the noise when a clash of steel silenced everybody. Enter two men, stage right. They fight. Tom Sledd blinked, looking at Alleyn who half-turned to him and shrugged. The prompter, already numb with the boredom of Will Shaxsper's lines, suddenly sat up and started riffling through his pages. Where was this bit? Why had no one told him about this bit?

In his hiding place in the gods, Philip Henslowe

blinked too. He didn't have a script but he knew this wasn't part of the play. They'd tinkered with it, tried it this way and that, but a duel? What the Hell was going on? And that . . . he peered closer . . . surely, yes, that was Kit Marlowe.

Poley was older than the Muses' darling, but not by much. He also had two good arms to Marlowe's one and the edge was telling. Neither man saw the others on stage, trying to get out of their way. All they saw was the face and the blade of the man bent on killing each of them. Roland gave up. He threw his chain of office to the ground, spun on his heel and left. Ned Alleyn, the famous rescuer of situations, worked desperately to make the audience think the whole thing was planned.

'What now?' He suddenly became far more imperious than he had been as the boy-king so far. 'A duel for us, an interlude to celebrate our forthcoming nuptials?' He was counting furiously in his head. No trace of iambic pentameter now, but he hoped no one would notice.

'Watch yourself, Ned,' Marlowe hissed as he circled Poley. 'This one knows his way around.'

That was too loud for Alleyn's liking. 'Fie, Sirrah.' He stayed in character. 'You forget yourself. I am "your grace" to sworders like yourself.'

The crowd had fallen silent now, the groundlings pressing forward to the stage. This was more like it. A bit of action at last.

'That's Kit Marlowe,' somebody shouted. 'I didn't know he could act.'

'Ah, but you can, can't you, Kit?' Poley darted

284

forward, his blade clashing on Marlowe's. 'Something else we have in common.'

'I've nothing in common with you, murderer,' the playwright said. Poley was retreating slowly, checking right and left to make good his escape. He didn't know this theatre, but he knew that Marlowe did.

Henslowe looked along the raked seats up in the gallery. Everybody was craning forward, rapt in the cut and thrust on stage. Now, if only he could turn this into a permanent feature. The word would spread after today. Good old Kit. If anybody could save Shaxsper's bacon, Marlowe was the man.

'Good sirs . . .' Alleyn was still trying to make it all work.

'Give it up, Ned, and get off the stage,' Marlowe muttered.

Alleyn had stopped being Henry the Sixth now and was himself, the greatest actor of his . . . of any . . . age. 'How dare you?' he shouted, 'Talk to me like that?'

'You tell him, Your Majesty!' a groundling shouted. After all, the man was king of England; it wasn't right.

An arm appeared behind the Arras at the back of the stage and yanked at Alleyn's sleeve. He struggled and in doing so the lad who had appeared as La Pucelle appeared centre stage. He still wore his petticoats, but because of the heat in the wings and the tiring room, he was naked from the waist up.

''Ere, you're dead!' a groundling shouted.

'Master Alleyn,' the lad hissed, ignoring the

285

things now flying from the pit. 'You must come away. It isn't safe. The Rose can't do without you.'

Alleyn dithered. Marlowe and Poley were prowling the wooden O, kicking furniture out of the way. He looked at the hero-worshipping lad and decided he was right. Kit Marlowe could look after himself.

'You're not only dead,' another groundling wit shouted at the retreating pair, 'but your tits have fallen off.' There were howls and hoots of merriment and Philip Henslowe in his high perch above the multitude, cringed. Was this what the theatre had come to? Daggers and tits? He shook his head. But now that the bit players had left the scene, the leading men held centre stage. No one was going to call the constable this time and there would be no Tom Watson to put his life on the line. Tom Sledd might have interceded, for old times' sake, but Ned Alleyn was blocking his view from the wings. The stage manager might take on whoever it was duelling with Marlowe, but Sledd wasn't up to tackling Alleyn too. He just watched from his vantage point behind everybody's favourite leading man, both of them dodging, ducking and diving with everybody's favourite playwright's every move.

A wild sweep from Poley's blade knocked Marlowe off balance and he fell off the stage into the welcoming arms of the crowd. A woman took his face in both hands and kissed him. She was the size of a kitchen press and grinned gappily at him. 'Ooh, wait 'til I tell 'em at the Mermaid who I've just kissed!' The crowd

286

extricated Marlowe from the woman's clutches but there was no way for him back on to the stage with Poley patrolling the apron. In the event, La Pucelle did what Tom Sledd had wanted to do – should have done – and hurtled across the stage, hitting Poley in the back with a broom and knocking him into the crowd.

'That's how we shovel shit at the Rose!' he squawked at the man he had just upended. The crowd erupted. Poley was on his feet in seconds, slashing the air with his blade. Once, twice, it caught on Marlowe's quillons and the playwright swung his man to the ground, driving his knee into Poley's face. He stumbled backwards, his nose pouring blood and his eyes a blur of tears. He hacked at the crowd who leapt out of his way and he scrabbled back on to the stage. Marlowe was after him, driving him back towards the wings, steel ringing on steel.

From his perch in the gods, Henslowe saw a movement in the flies, at his own level and above the open space of the groundlings. The sun was sharp here and the flies in shadow, but he could make him out nevertheless. Dick the Painter was edging his way forward, inching his body out on to the planks. He had a knife in his hand and was sawing away at a rope that held the counter weights that raised and lowered Tom Sledd's scenery masterpieces. Henslowe could see at once what he was trying to do. But it was risky. If Dick mistimed, even by a second, he'd hit Marlowe and no one was going to walk away from that.

'It's over, Poley.' Marlowe was panting. His

arm wound threatened to burst its stitches and he had knocked the wind from his lungs when he had fallen from the stage. The enormous woman had just completed what the fall had begun. Both men were tiring visibly now, their swings wilder, more erratic and the clashes as steel rang on steel were getting less. The crowd was still roaring them on and briefly Henslowe could have kicked himself. Money was changing hands among the groundlings. Why wasn't he down there, cashing in? After all, it *was* his theatre. The law would be on his side he felt sure – he'd ask the lawyers before they left. Then he checked himself, feeling something surge through his brain. It took him a moment to identify the sensation as guilt; not something Philip Henslowe had encountered that often.

'Look out, Kit!' Henslowe shouted. 'The flies!' All in all, it was an ill-considered warning, because it saved Robert Poley's life too. Both men looked up simultaneously as the huge weight came crashing down. They sprang apart as it hit the stage, shattering planks and sending splinters flying. It was followed by a scream and a thud as Dick the Painter followed it. He had lost his balance as he made the final cut and he hurtled through the dust-mote-swimming afternoon air to break his neck on the wooden O.

When Marlowe looked up, Poley had gone. He was about to give chase when the crowd roared, whistled and clapped. Henslowe was astonished. Even the languid lawyers were on their feet, shouting, 'Author! Author!' with all the others.

'Audience interaction,' he called to them, waving. 'It's the coming thing.'

Ned Alleyn knew how to work the crowd. He pushed La Pucelle on to the stage and Jack Roland and all the others. They passed around Kit Marlowe, still panting and reeling from the exertion of the fight and swept him centre stage, all of them stepping over the body of Dick the Painter. It's a harsh world, treading the boards.

'I thought I heard the name Shakespeare earlier.' Philip Henslowe was trying to make sense of the afternoon's performance while simultaneously counting his money. 'Where is he?'

'You did,' Marlowe told him. 'But it's not our Will.'

'He may be *your* Will, Marlowe,' Henslowe bridled, 'but he most assuredly isn't mine. Listen, I don't pretend to know what's going on here, but the crowd loved every minute. Can you write it up, do you think; you know, the mighty line?'

'The play isn't always the thing, Henslowe,' Marlowe told him. 'And it most assuredly isn't today.' He stopped the man from counting, putting aside a pile of silver. 'There's a dead man in the tiring room,' he said. 'You knew him as Dick the Painter, but his real name was Harry Bellot, sometime soldier, sailor. And, by his lights, a good man. See that he has a decent burial, will you?' He toppled the pile of coins that spilled out in a silver ribbon across the table. 'You can afford it, after all.'

'Of course, Kit, of course.' Philip Henslowe knew that look on Marlowe's face. Best not to cross him when he looked like that. 'Where will you be?' The theatre owner still had a play in tatters and these days the Rose was only as good as its last performance.

'Me?' Marlowe looked at him oddly. 'I've got to find Master Robyn Poley. There's a score to settle.'

Marlowe visited the dead man before leaving the Rose. Henslowe would give him a good send off and there was nothing actors liked better than a good funeral. It gave them the opportunity to hone their crying skills. Ned Alleyn was an expert at it and had graced many a committal, to the astonishment and usually delight of the bereaved. So he knew that Harry Bellot would not go to his grave alone. But there was one last thing that needed to be done and only Kit Marlowe, now, could do it.

The wardrobe department had done what they could in the way of tidying up Harry Bellot, but there was a limit to their skills and the man had after all fallen the whole height of the Rose, which was substantial. He had landed on his back, so his face was not too bad and if the cushion behind his head hid a multitude of sins, it wasn't obvious. They had left him in his own simple clothes, paint daubed and worn. Marlowe was grateful for that. He knew what happened to discarded things in the Rose – if they didn't go home with the understudy's understudy, they would be part of the costume for the next production before you could say knife. Carefully, he edged his hand inside the man's jerkin and fumbled for what he knew would be concealed there. He flinched as he felt the ribs give under his fingers but soon found what he was looking for. He drew out a little chamois leather bag and tipped it up so the contents fell into his hand. There were the missing globes. The emerald from Starkey Hall, Walter Mildmay's diamond and a lapis, which must have come from the London merchant's house. He turned them once, twice in his fingers then put them back in the bag and the bag in his breast. He put his hand lightly on one of Bellot's own and pressed it.

'I'll do what's right, Harry,' he said. 'You meant well. You just chose the wrong man for the job.' He smiled. Harry had become a man of the theatre, he would understand what he was going to say. 'Just like Henslowe when he let Master Shaxsper write a play. You should always pick your men with care. You didn't, and you died for it, as well as other people who deserved to live. Henslowe is just killing the art of theatre, but that's perhaps something for later. Don't worry. Your soul will be singing soon.'

And Marlowe turned and left the man alone, waiting for his God and his judgement.

Outside the theatre, a figure detached itself from the shade of Master Sackerson's wall. Marlowe tensed and reached for his dagger, back in its sheath as it was. The man held out his arms, hands empty and open.

'Kit!' It was Tom Sledd, a welcome sight at any time, but especially now. 'Where are you off to? Don't answer – I'm coming along, wherever you are going. I didn't do enough back there. Everything went by so fast and I didn't know what was going to happen next. Forgive me, but the theatre and the audience had to be my first concern.'

Marlowe quickened his pace to stand alongside the stage manager. 'Tom, it wasn't your fight. And you certainly are *not* coming along with me.'

'Unless you intend to stand here for the rest of your life,' Sledd said, 'I don't think you can stop me, because every step you take, I will take one too. And I don't think you want to wait; I know you well enough by now to know when you have something on your mind. On your heart, even.'

Marlowe gave Tom Sledd a long look and gave in. Tom had been by his side in many tight spots over the years and he had never let him down. He knew he wouldn't now. He was having to keep his right arm pressed to his side. The wound had bled again and the blood had dried, sticking the lawn sleeve to the skin. Every move pulled it free and it oozed some more. He just wanted to lie down and let kind hands soothe him, but that was for later. For now, he had a job to do and a murderer to watch out for. He knew that Poley would not give up this easily. Like all men with the glint of gold in his eye, the man had not taken in or believed Bellot's motive for wanting the globes. Poley could only see things from his point of view. He would still be chasing the globes and would not rest until he had them. Another pair of eyes to watch his back and another pair of hands to wield a blade would not come amiss. He nodded. 'Well, Tom, since you insist,' he said. 'But don't ask questions. The less you know the better; this may not be over, even now that Harry Bellot is dead.'

'Harry Bellot? I thought his name was Dick.'

'It's a long story. He had laid his plans for so long, including false names, that only a few people knew who he was any more. I wouldn't be surprised if most people thought he was dead. A drunken sailor down in Deptford told me about him, but I took no notice. In amongst stories of men with ears they could wear as cloaks and women eating precious stones, a name was easy to miss.'

'I don't want to know if you don't want to tell me.' Tom Sledd knew that in Kit Marlowe's world, the least said was probably the soonest mended. 'I'll just be your eyes and hands and then get back to the theatre. Where, by the way, we could do with you, if you don't mind.'

Marlowe allowed himself a chuckle. 'That play is very bad, isn't it?'

'No,' Sledd said, solemnly. 'It is very, very, *very* bad indeed.'

'How has Henslowe allowed Shaxsper to get away with such stuff? I'm surprised he hasn't had him rewriting it over and over.'

'That's the thing,' Sledd said. 'I was in the theatre the day that Shaxsper delivered the play. It was late – by about a month, I should say – and Henslowe was already getting testy. He had been filling in meanwhile with some bits and bobs that he had had in hand for years. He even

293

ended up putting on *Rafe Roister Doister.* Remember that?'

Marlowe laughed. 'How could I ever forget?' he said. Ned Sledd, actor manager par excellence had claimed the work as his own on many an occasion, although why anyone would want to do that Marlowe couldn't imagine. He might have known Henslowe would have a copy somewhere in his eyrie. 'How did that go?'

'Surprisingly well. He also trotted out *The Devil and Mistress Maguire* but the trapdoor didn't always work, so we only ran that a couple of times.'

'You are lucky that all your troupe are quick studies,' Marlowe said. He found writing words easy; learning someone else's had always given him rather more trouble.

'If only they were.' Sledd shook his head. 'It was a mercy on us all that all the pieces we put on were as old as the hills. In one or two scenes, the whole of the groundling pit were speaking in chorus. Quite an improvement, in fact.'

They had digressed as they walked and Marlowe brought the conversation to heel. 'So . . . Shakespeare delivered his play.'

'He did. He walked in, put it in my hands and walked out with hardly a word. And no one in London has seen him since.'

'Have you tried . . .?'

Sledd was ahead of the poet. 'Every woman who has ever so much as brushed past him in the street. He is with none of them.'

Marlowe didn't want to alarm the stage manager and erstwhile La Pucelle but he had worried ever since hearing that Poley had used the name Shakespeare with such freedom. Although not quite a byword where theatre-lovers gathered, Shakespeare had a tiny coterie of followers, those who had seen him on the stage and found him amusing. He had a way with him, Marlowe admitted. His domed forehead and neat little beard appealed to a certain type of woman and he had enjoyed a certain success in that direction. So, unless Poley was very provincial, and Marlowe doubted that very much, he had likely heard of the man. And Poley was not one to leave any thread dangling from any plan he wove. If Shakespeare was alive and well, Marlowe feared, it would be a minor miracle.

'Kit?'

Marlowe turned to see Sledd looking anxiously at him.

'Will is all right, isn't he? He's just with some lady somewhere, isn't he?'

'Yes,' Marlowe said, with more enthusiasm than he felt. 'You know Will. Like a bad penny. He'll be back when he's ready.'

They crossed the Bridge with its rotting heads and roaring tumult, jostling with the street sellers and the bawds, the Puritans who assured them that the end of the world was nigh and men hurrying into the public jakes, untying their codpieces just in time. After that, the two walked in silence for a while and their young legs ate up the distance until they turned into the Vintry by the Cranes to arrive outside Joshua's door. Marlowe was glad to have Sledd with him, if only to send into the vintner's as a fresh face should he need to enter Joshua's workshop by stealth. But no; the boards were down and men were working with lime and brush, painting the outside. Marlowe was not sure that this would be a good thing. Joshua had after all sent a man to kill him. That that man had ended up dead was not Marlowe's fault but he wasn't sure how much information he would be able to convey before he was run through by the furious silversmith. Motioning Sledd to stay back, he edged in through the door.

'Joshua?' he called. 'Ithamore?'

'Ithamore?' Sledd murmured behind him. 'What sort of name is that?'

'He has an inventive mother,' Marlowe told him over his shoulder. He raised his voice a notch. 'Joshua!'

The man was suddenly at his elbow. 'No need to shout, Master Marlowe,' he said, mildly. 'I only have one pair of legs.'

Marlowe flinched and the pain shot up his arm in red hot bolts. He went white and the silversmith noticed it.

'You're hurt. Of course, the fracas in Hog Lane. Do sit down until you feel better. Ithamore! A cup of water for Master Marlowe.'

Marlowe waved the help away. 'You seem very unconcerned, Master Joshua,' he said, 'bearing in mind it was your man who caused my injury.'

Joshua spread his arms. 'What can I do but apologize?' he asked. 'I thought you had wrecked my workshop.'

'You could have asked,' Marlowe pointed out.

'You were not here to ask.'

Marlowe could sense that this could go on for hours and so decided to agree to disagree. 'Let's put this behind us, Joshua, shall we? I have a boon to ask you and if you can do it for me, we will be even.'

The Jew looked at him from under his brows. 'What?' he said, suspiciously. 'I am not staying here, Master Marlowe. I am letting this workshop to the vintner next door. He needs to expand and it seems the ideal solution. Ithamore will become *his* problem, I mean, of course, apprentice, and will also be in charge of collecting the rent.'

Marlowe looked at the man and leaned closer. 'And be in charge of keeping the rent, too, if I know anything.'

The silversmith smiled. 'I have more than enough for my needs and he has nothing. So why not? I am going to live in Portugal; Lisbon, in fact. There are more of my people there, I will be among friends. I speak Portuguese of course . . .'

'Of course you do,' Marlowe said and smiled. 'If you can get through the ring of Francis Drake's siege.'

'What?'

'Nothing.'

Joshua swept on. 'So I will get along famously. But –' he rubbed his hands together – 'what is this boon?'

Marlowe looked behind him, checking to make sure that Sledd had his back, but the stage manager was standing in the doorway, arms folded, legs spread and although he may not be the biggest man in the Vintry at that moment, he certainly looked the most determined. Marlowe moved further into the workshop and, reaching into his doublet, drew out the two bags he had concealed there. Joshua looked on, intrigued, as he tipped out the five globes, which slid one from another until the worlds were aligned like planets in some impossible astrological prediction.

'So.' There seemed little else to say.

'So.' Marlowe folded his arms and looked down at the little gewgaws which had caused so much mayhem and misery.

'What do you want me to do?' Joshua picked up his favourite, the one with the lapis, the jewel an almost unimaginably deep blue, looking like a hole into another reality rather than a chip of rock.

'I want you to destroy them,' Marlowe said, simply.

'*Destroy* them?' The silversmith was aghast. 'But . . . you have spent so much time in finding them.'

'Before I knew what they were. But now that I do, I want them destroyed. By any means you like. As long as they are no longer recognizable.'

Ithamore was bouncing up and down in the doorway to the yard. His arms, always flailing to one degree or another, were positively wind-milling with excitement. Joshua tried not to catch his eye but in the end could do nothing other.

'Yes, Ithamore.'

'Can I, can I melt them down, sir, can I?' The boy's face shone.

'Master Marlowe and I have not yet decided

on whether they will even be destroyed,' the silversmith said solemnly.

'Master Marlowe has decided,' the playwright said. 'Whether they are destroyed here or elsewhere is the only thing in doubt.'

Tom Sledd was listening and smiling. When Kit Marlowe wanted something, that was what Kit Marlowe got.

'If you leave them with me . . .' Joshua began.

'No. I want to see them destroyed. Ithamore's furnace would be a perfect solution, as far as I can see. Prise off the jewels if you must, but beyond that, I want to see them become a puddle of molten silver before I leave this place.'

Joshua compressed his lips and his nostrils looked pinched with tension, then, he nodded to Ithamore. 'Blow up your fires, boy,' he said. 'This is your *very* last chance.' Then, to Marlowe: 'What shall we make from your silver, Master Marlowe?'

'It isn't my silver,' he protested.

'It is as much yours as anyone's. Will you leave it up to me, once you have seen your molten puddle, of course?'

Marlowe shrugged. 'Once I have seen it molten, you may do with it as you will.'

Ithamore was already outside, his bellows pumping like bees' wings. Joshua reached for his jeweller's pliers and, with a sigh, prised off the opal, lapis lazuli, diamonds and emerald from their settings, placing them with care on a white cloth. He looked up at Marlowe. 'This will take some time, Master Marlowe. Would you like to take a seat?'

'I'll stay, Kit.' Tom Sledd came into the work-shop. 'I've never seen molten silver before and I have a feeling I won't get a chance again. If you have other things to do, go and do them. I promise I won't leave here until the work is done.'

It would mean leaving Marlowe unprotected, but without the worry of the globes, he would be Poley's equal, injured arm or no. He nodded at Sledd. 'I will go, then, Tom, if you don't mind. I have a man I need to see about a weasel.'

As he slipped out through the door, he heard Joshua say, 'Is my English idiom letting me down, for once? Is the animal not usually a dog?'

Sledd laughed. 'If Kit says it is a weasel, you can be sure it is a weasel he means. He may be a poet, but when he is hunting down vermin, he doesn't mistake the breed.'

Seventeen

At first they were just shadows. Two of them, always at the edge of Marlowe's vision, mingling and blending with the crowd. When he could, he stopped, pretending to be uncertain of the way. Once he knelt on one knee to buckle his boot. And each time he did, he glanced at them. They were large, armed to the teeth and he didn't recognize either face. Poley had come looking for him before, outside the Rose. Had he sent his creatures instead, with instructions to finish his business with the Muses' darling, the over-reacher?

For a while he kept to the broad highway, sauntering along the Cheap moving east. He could see the spars of the galleons at the Queen's wharves and the solid, granite squareness of the Tower. He glanced down each alley he came to. They were all the same – dark and narrow and the perfect place for an assassin's knife to find a man's ribs, slipping between and slicing his life away. His arm was not his friend today and the two men clung to him like leeches. If he quickened his pace, so did they. If he sauntered, so they slowed. If he stopped, the pair would half turn and engage each other in the kind of earnest silent conversation that the bit players used at the Rose. Henslowe's stage directions said it all; spear-bearer shall speak unto spear-bearer.

Marlowe ran his options through his mind. He

could call a constable and claim that strange men were following him. The constable would take them all to the magistrate and it would soon be discovered that Kit Marlowe was out on bail with a possible murder charge hanging over him. He could hire a knot of apprentices, the crop-headed layabouts that loafed on street corners. All he had to do was cry 'Clubs' and pass a few coins among them and they would beat up the Queen if Marlowe asked them nicely. He could cut down the nearest alley, crouch behind a coster cart and stab them, one after the other, taking his chance with their greater strength, fitness and numbers. Or . . .

He turned sharply at the end of Leadenhall Street. 'May I help you, gentlemen?' he asked.

'Are you Christopher Marlowe?' one of them wanted to know.

The poet-projectioner had no time for quips now and was in no mood for clever answers. 'I am,' he said.

'Good,' said the other one. 'Sir Francis Walsingham would like a word.'

The Queen's Spymaster looked ashen and old. The once black beard and hair that had made Her Majesty call him her Moor was flecked with grey and his eyes watered in the early evening sun. Behind him, that same sun sparkled on the waters of the river that rushed and roared past Traitor's Gate. Walsingham liked the Tower least of all his many meeting places. And he longed to be in his bed at Barn Elms or at least dozing in his chair at Seething Lane.

Kit Marlowe had told him all he knew of the story of the killing stones, how drenched in blood they were and what Drake was up to. He knew that Walter Mildmay would not be surprised. Martin Frobisher would be delighted and many was the courtier, nobleman and seadog who would say something like 'I told you so' should the story ever come out.

'So now you're looking for Robert Poley?' Walsingham leaned back in his chair, his fingers clasped over his Privy Councillor's chain of office.

'I am,' Marlowe said. 'Harry Bellot didn't enquire closely enough into Poley's methods and for that he paid with his life. Poley is still at large.'

'Yes,' Walsingham said with a sigh. He pushed his chair back and got up, crossing to the window. 'And there he will remain.'

'What?' Marlowe sat upright. He must have misheard. Or perhaps the Spymaster was more ill than he thought and had not followed Marlowe's story after all.

'Robert Poley is one of us, Kit,' the man said softly. 'A Queen's messenger, a projectioner.'

'He's a murderer,' Marlowe countered.

'Which of us is not?' Walsingham asked. 'There is blood on your hands, Kit Marlowe, as there is on Nicholas Faunt's and Robert Poley's . . . and mine. We live in a naughty world and nobody's virtue is over-nice. I was in Paris when the streets ran with blood in the Massacre. Women, children, babies. Do you have babies, Marlowe?'

'You know I don't,' the playwright said.

303

'I do. Most of my people do. Is it for them that we knife our enemies in dark places? To keep them safe? Do we do it because the Queen commands? Because the Jezebel of England clicks her fingers?'

Silence answered him.

'I don't know,' Walsingham went on. 'But Poley is just doing what we all do.'

'No, Sir Francis, you're wrong,' Marlowe grated. 'Robyn Poley killed for gain, for greed. If Harry Bellot chose the wrong man for his particular job, then you, just as surely, have chosen the wrong one for yours.'

Walsingham spun to face his man. There was a time when Kit Marlowe might have died for an insult like that. But the years had intervened and the time was not right. There had been enough killing over the stones, the globes with their silver seas. He looked Marlowe full in the face. 'If I have chosen wrongly,' he said, 'then that is my burden to bear. I forbid you, Marlowe, to go anywhere near Robert Poley. For once in your life, let this thing go and do as you are told.'

Marlowe stood up. He had no words for the Spymaster, nothing he could find in his heart. Jane Benchkyne, Jack Barnet, Harry Bellot, all of them stood with Kit Marlowe, looking with contempt at the Queen's Moor, who had kept her and England safe for so long. Marlowe spun on his heel and was gone.

Walsingham reached down once the door was closed and rang a little bell. His long-suffering secretary scuttled in, the portable desk strapped to him, as always.

'Take a letter to Poley, Humphrey. Tell him he's to get himself to the Low Countries by the earliest ship. And to stay there until he hears from me.'

And Humphrey licked his quill-tip, dipped it into the ink and formed the words, 'Dear Robyn . . .'

Kit Marlowe was not a happy man and so his feet took him as if worked by automata towards the only place he truly felt at home in the whole world. He had a play to rescue, if nothing more. And another one was boiling in his brain; he just needed a few more threads to pull it all together, to make it live. 'After all,' he said to Master Sackerson as he stopped to drop off a bun coaxed from a stall holder at the bottom of Rose Alley for the purpose, 'all the world's a stage, and all the men and women merely players.'

'I like the sound of that.'

'Master Sackerson,' Marlowe said, severely, 'you must work on your diction. I scarcely saw your lips move.'

'Don't play the idiot, Marlowe,' the man behind him said. 'You know it's me. Turn around. I won't talk to the back of your head.'

'No.' The poet was adamant. 'I refuse to turn around. If I do, I will know whether you are a real, living man or a demon in human form. Before I turn around, I can pretend what I like. I can make you into the living man, which it may surprise you, I would very much prefer. If I turn around, you become a demon, with your face dripping from the bones of your skull, the very

305

worms that devour you peering from your eye sockets, your lips become . . . Oh, what am I talking about?' He spun round and took the newcomer by the shoulders. 'Welcome home, Will. Where in the name of all that's dramatic have you *been*?'

'Just back up to Stratford for a while. I like to see the children when I can.'

'And your wife.'

Shaxsper's eyes opened wide. 'Indeed, yes,' he added hurriedly. 'And of course my wife.' He smiled nervously. He always dreaded that his Anne would visit London one day and that everyone would discover that she was not the harridan he painted her but just a rather nice woman from Warwickshire, with more patience with her wandering husband than he had any right to expect. He rather liked her, if truth be told, but a man had dreams and sometimes people got left behind. 'Dear Anne,' he said.

Marlowe looked at him and saw the same cloud of homesickness hovering at the back of the man's eyes. But it was true what they said, you could never go back. Not really. But a man could always try. 'How are the children?'

Shaxsper's eyes lit up. 'Hamnet grows very strong and handsome. He has his mother's looks, for which I hope he will be grateful some day. The girls do well.' Marlowe knew that Shaxsper the father would have happily regaled him for hours, so he called upon Shakespeare the play-wright. He had no wish to sit here on Master Sackerson's wall all the day listening to nursery tales. 'They've been wondering where you were.'

'Who has?' Shaxsper looked puzzled.

Marlowe tossed his head in the direction of the Rose. 'In there. Tom, Ned Alleyn. Henslowe.' He dropped his voice dramatically on the final name. 'All your adoring fanatics.'

'Well, they knew where I was,' Shaxsper said, exasperated. Why was it that these theatre types always had to make such a drama about everything?

'They are not diviners, Will,' Marlowe pointed out. 'If someone seems to have disappeared off the face of the earth and they are not in their lodgings or those of . . . certain other people . . . then what can they think but the worst?'

'The *worst*?' Shaxsper's voice rose to a shriek. 'Do you mean they thought me dead?'

Marlowe reminded himself that it was not Shaxsper's fault that Robert Poley had decided to take his name in vain, but even so, most of his comment stood. A man should not just walk away, having delivered himself of a play, and not expect to be missed. 'It was the play, you see, Will . . .'

'Yes!' Shaxsper's face lit up. 'How has it been going? I know I can't expect any payments from Master Henslowe yet, it is early days and I know costs must be covered first but . . .' He grasped Marlowe's arm, unerringly squeezing just above the knife wound. He was so excited to be reminded of his play that he didn't notice how the man went pale. 'Kit, you have been in this position so often, that of the writer of a play that draws the crowds, makes grown men weep,

307

makes the earth shake, the seas boil.' He pulled himself up with a small and self-deprecating laugh. 'Well, perhaps not all of those. But grown men weep, I've seen that. How does it feel, Kit?'

Marlowe was perched on the curly poll of a quandary between the curving horns of a dilemma. Yes, he had been in the position of celebrated playwright, not once but several times. That Shaxsper believed himself to now be similarly placed, was something that could not be ignored – the man would discover his mistake very soon. The rotting vegetables were beginning to pile up in the gutters around the Rose. Even the most lowly of the staff were tired of picking them over for anything edible and they were simply swept into the street after each performance. He would discover that he, Marlowe, was on his way to the Rose to fulfil his promise to everyone there that he would do his best to rescue the debacle that was *Henry VI*.

Marlowe was used to difficult times. He preferred to think of them as interesting – that made them seem more manageable. But the last few days had taken it out of him. His arm still hurt a great deal, particularly when grasped by actors – or should that perhaps be playwright; only time would tell – and he still had the nagging unfinished business of Robert Poley to haunt him the rest of his days. He had promised Walsingham nothing; nor would he. There would be time for Poley; that much he knew. And now here was Shaxsper, heart on his sleeve, about to walk into the Rose, as innocent as the day, probably to be torn limb from limb in a four-way tussle between Tom Sledd, Ned Alleyn, Philip Henslowe and the Rest of the Cast. Could he let him? A thought occurred to him.

'Why were you surprised when I said we thought you were dead?'

'Well, I told young Ben – La Pucelle, you know – where I was going when I left the script with Tom Sledd. I asked him to pass the message on. It wasn't difficult. Even Ben could remember it, I should think. It went something like "I've gone up to Stratford for a while to see wife and children. Marlowe will help if you need any, but I think my words will stand without tinkering from a . . ."' Collecting himself just in time, Shaxsper ground to a halt. 'Words to that effect, anyway. So I can't for the life of me see why there has been all this drama.'

Marlowe's heart was hardened. He patted Shaxsper on the back. 'A misunderstanding, Will, I am almost sure. Perhaps I got it wrong myself. I have been a little distracted. If you take my advice, you will go in there now, straight up to Henslowe's office and ask for your payment. There must be something, wouldn't you say?'

Shaxsper nodded eagerly. His sojourn in Stratford had been more expensive than he had reckoned for.

'Straight up there, then, Will, and get your just desserts.'

'I will, Kit. Thank you.' Shaxsper turned for the stage door. 'Are you coming in?' He extended a hand as though welcoming Marlowe into his own solar.

'I'll stay out here, Will. Let you get your glory. You don't want me hanging on your doublet tails, do you?' Shaxsper shook his head. 'No, of course not. I'll see you later, I feel sure.'

Shaxsper broke into an excited little trot and disappeared through the side door. Marlowe could just hear cries of surprise and welcome but he wasn't interested in that. He moved round to the front, so as to be under Philip Henslowe's window. He waited for a moment or two before he got his reward.

'What?' Henslowe's voice roared. 'You're here for your *what*?'

And for the first time in a while, Christopher Marlowe, poet, playwright, University wit and spy threw back his head and laughed.

He was still wiping the tears from his cheeks and chuckling to himself when the auditorium door swung open and Tom Sledd appeared, looking around until he spotted Marlowe sitting on Master Sackerson's wall. He came over, walking purposefully.

'That was very unkind, Master Marlowe,' he said severely, then leant on the wall and went into paroxysms of silent mirth.

'Where is he now?' Marlowe asked. He didn't bear Shaxsper any malice; he wouldn't like to think of him twirling from a rope to consider his position or anything draconian such as that.

'Still in Henslowe's office. Henslowe has started that really low voice, the whispering. That can go on for hours.'

Marlowe nodded. 'Days, sometimes.'

'I've known that, yes. Oh –' Sledd rummaged

310

in his pocket – 'I have something here for you.'

Marlowe leaned forward.

'It's from Joshua.' The stage manager opened his hand and held it out to Marlowe. There, on the palm, was the most exquisite piece of jewellery that Marlowe had ever seen. Two hands were shown extended, the fingers lightly curled. In the palms was a world, round and polished as a pearl. The chips of diamond, emerald, lapis and opal marked the equator and the whole was set with a loop to attach it to a fine silver chain. 'It's the worlds.'

'I can see . . .'

'No, the worlds. Ithamore melted them down and then Joshua made this. They let me watch. It was wonderful. It must be so satisfying to be able to make something as lovely as this, with your bare hands.'

Marlowe turned the man gently around and extended his hand to show the Rose in all her pre-play glory. 'You make worlds every day, Tom,' he said. 'And a new one each time. This jewel is lovely, but your skill is no less. But . . . you have a wife. Give the jewel to her. I have no one.'

'You have a mother,' Tom said. 'Give it to her.'

'I can't. I said I would never go into my father's house again.'

'Is Canterbury a big place?' Sledd asked, innocently.

'Tolerably.'

'Then find another house. God in Heaven, Kit – you have a University education. Surely it doesn't take a ragamuffin like me to tell you

311

things like that. Take the jewel. See your mother. And this time, no murders, please.'

There was no murderous oaf standing outside the Grey Mare today, whittling. In fact, Hog Lane seemed extraordinarily quiet and Shoreditch was asleep in the noonday heat. Number sixteen was quiet too. There was no sign of Mary and Eliza visiting Tom Watson in the Stink. He was out of Marlowe's hands now – the wheels of justice in Elizabeth's England ground slow.

The poet-projectioner packed his valise, hauled on a clean shirt and flexed his arm to ease it in its bandage. His sword, with its curved quillons, he left behind, but his dagger . . . he slid it and its sheath out of the belt-loop at his back and buried it in the clothes in the valise. He opened the window and looked out on to the courtyard of the Grey Mare.

'Ho, Jackie!' he called.

'Master Marlowe?' A ragged urchin beamed up at him.

'Fetch my horse and see him saddled.' He tossed a coin through the air and the boy caught it with expert, practised hands. There was a play forming in Marlowe's head, a play about a Jew, from Malta, why not? What could he call him? Ithamore? No, too strange. What he needed was a name the groundlings could hiss and boo at. What about . . . Barabbas? Yes, that would work. Marlowe clattered down the stairs, the valise slung over his shoulder, plot and counterplot whirling in his brain. Barabbas would be a murderer – what else? Joshua the silversmith

312

could help, be a sort of technical adviser. He could go and stay with him in Lisbon, could sit and write in his bee-loud, honey-heavy garden. He sighed; that sounded good. And Ned Alleyn would jump at the chance to play the Jew of Malta. He had a bad play to live down, after all. And in the years ahead, if anyone asked him if he had ever played Henry VI, he would deny all knowledge of it.

Marlowe hauled open his front door and there stood his black, saddled and bridled. But it wasn't little Jackie holding his reins. It was Nicholas Faunt, the left-hand man of the Spymaster.

'Come to see me off, Master Faunt?'

'That depends where you're going, Master Marlowe,' the projectioner said.

Marlowe looked at him. 'Walsingham sent you, didn't he?'

'Perhaps.' There was no smile, no flicker of friendship. No face in England was more difficult to read than Nicholas Faunt's.

'Don't tell me.' Marlowe took the warm leather from Faunt's hands. 'He thinks I'm still looking for Robert Poley. Well, he might be right. But he won't know when and where I find him. And are you going to be at my elbow for the rest of my life?'

Now, Faunt *did* smile. 'God forbid it should come to that,' he said.

'I am going to Canterbury.' Marlowe tied the valise behind his saddle. 'I have a little present for my mother.' He swung on to the horse, taking up the reins as the animal shifted under his weight.

Faunt walked alongside him to the end of the alley, where the way broadened out into Hog Lane. 'Well, that's nice,' he said. He patted the black's rump and Marlowe trotted away. 'So, tell me, Kit,' he said, raising his voice above the sound of the echoing hoofs, 'will you be seeing your father this time?'